THE FIRES OF ALLAH

CODY'S WAR BOOK THREE

STEPHEN MERTZ

WOLFPACK
PUBLISHING
— EST 2013 —

WOLFPACK
PUBLISHING
— EST 2013 —

Paperback Edition

Copyright © 2019 Stephen Mertz

Published in the United States by Wolfpack Publishing, Las Vegas

Wolfpack Publishing
6032 Wheat Penny Avenue
Las Vegas, NV 89122

wolfpackpublishing.com

Paperback ISBN 978-1-64119-967-4
eBook ISBN 978-1-64119-865-3

Library of Congress Control Number: 2019952801

THE FIRES OF ALLAH

PROLOGUE

Kootenai County, Idaho

News flash: The more things change, the more they stay the same.

Jack Cody wasn't sure who'd said that first, thought maybe some old French philosopher, but it was true. Time altered some things; others, not so much.

Take Nazis for example. When they first got organized in Germany, roughly a hundred years ago, they'd come out of the closet wearing swastikas they stole from ancient Sanskrit, one a good luck symbol, blaming the Jews for all their troubles, preaching genocide against whoever didn't fit their profile of the "Master Race".

Today, same thing.

In spite of losing World War Two big-time, they'd managed to survive and burrow down worldwide, reviving from the Cold War era to the present in a thousand permutations, but remaining true to form. Still hating, ranting, raising hell whenever they could get their hands on guns, explosives, anthrax—pick your poison.

In the modern age, they mostly called themselves "white nationalists", blogging bullshit on the "alt-right" social media, still brandishing the same old symbols, peddling copies of *Mein Kampf* and pamphlets praising Adolf as the almost-saviour of their "pre-Adamic" race. Blushing, of all things, had become their trademark, claiming only true Teutonic "Aryans" were capable of showing "blood in the face".

Today, Cody wanted to let a few of them prove that.

Shaved heads or bushy beards, jackboots or tailored Brooks Brothers, five minutes with a Nazi and you couldn't miss the psycho, wild-eyed mien.

For some reason never explained, a lot of them had gravitated to the Pacific Northwest since the 1970s, calling it their "White Bastion" on a U.S. map redrawn to keep the races and religions strictly separated. Maybe they'd imagined its landscape was closer to Medieval Europe.

Cody didn't know and didn't care.

He'd come this far because one group had lapsed from spewing bile online to active, vicious acts of terrorism. They called themselves the RAHOWA Alliance—short for "racial holy war"—and their chosen *führer* was a lunatic whose parents named him Wendell Orville Walker.

Picture coming up through school when your initials spelled out "WOW".

Thanks, Mom and Dad.

He wasn't much to look at—five foot five, scrawny and balding—but when he addressed his "troops" or started pounding on his laptop's keyboard, he morphed into "Heinrich Kruger", superman, at war with "ZOG"—the mythical Zionist Occupation Government that ruled the world from Tel Aviv.

Sure, he was crazy, but that made him and his lackeys no less dangerous to so-called civilized society.

Of late, they'd started planting bombs at synagogues and Jewish schools, together with a mosque or two. Five dead and nineteen injured in Los Angeles, thirteen and twenty-one in New York City, six and fourteen in Miami Beach.

There was an irony to WOW and his crusaders hitting mosques, unknown to the dimwits who took their marching orders from the college dropout living in a bunker north of Coeur d'Alene. What Wendell/Heinrich didn't share was that some of his closest friends, behind the scenes, were Muslim terrorists who let RAHOWA take the heat for crimes they'd planned.

Tonight, that heat was coming home.

In spades.

Cody was dressed in midnight black, his face and hands shielded from errant moonlight by combat cosmetics. A veteran of Delta Force—the U.S. Army's Combat Applications Group or Task Force Green—he'd learned his killing craft from masters and applied it over time on battlefronts most people in America had never heard of, carrying the fight to hellholes where the toughest Navy SEALs and the Marine

Corps' Force Recon might hesitate to tread.

He'd managed to survive it all but couldn't say the same about his wife and three children, slaughtered at home by terrorists while he was off saving the world. That wasn't something Cody could forgive, much less forget, and he'd been chasing death with honor ever since, not strictly suicidal, but prepared—hell, *eager*—to check out while punishing his homeland's enemies.

To that end, he'd retired from military service more or less. The CIA came calling with an offer from the president himself: fight on alone, or with a team of hand-picked comrades Cody trusted. Live or die, but privately eradicate the foes who were beyond the reach of U.S. courts and desert-skimming drones.

Tonight, an unexpected holy war was moving toward RA-HOWA headquarters.

The FBI could probably have dealt with WOW and friends, but Langley had discovered Walker's covert link to militant Islamists whom he claimed to loathe, along with Jews, "mud people", and the rest of "God's mistakes". Unfortunately, no one had specifics on *which* Arab terrorists might be involved, or what else they were planning down the road.

Cody intended to find out or die trying.

In either case, he didn't plan on letting any Nazis walk away.

Cody had come prepared for anything. His lead weapon was a Steyr AUG assault rifle, a bullpup model chambered in 5.56mm, loading translucent 42-round magazines, fitted with an integral flash suppressor and launcher for NATO

STANAG 22mm rifle grenades without mounting an adapter or using blank cartridges. The rifle's Swarovski 1.5× telescopic sight, integrated with the Steyer's receiver casting, doubled as a carrying handle in emergencies, using a simple black ring reticle and basic rangefinder designed so that a man-sized target filled the scope at 300 meters, giving shooters an accurate range estimation.

Backing up the Steyr, Cody carried twin Glock 22 semi-automatics chambered for .40 Smith & Wesson ammunition, each with a fifteen-round mag, plus one more in its chamber. One pistol rode a high-rise holster on his right hip, the other nestled in a Galco Jackass rig beneath his left arm, two spare magazines under his right. The .40-cal rounds propelled 11-gram Federal FMJ slugs at 340 meters per second, striking with 468 foot-pounds of explosive energy.

On Cody's left hip, he wore a venerable Mark I trench knife that had served American warriors since the First World War. Its knobby, knuckle-duster grip was cast from bronze, with a conical steel nut that held its blade in place and served nicely for cracking skulls. Its seven-inch blade was razor-sharp and double-edged, blued with a black oxide finish, while the handle was likewise chemically blackened. For silent killing, it was hard to beat.

Attached to Cody's combat webbing, in addition to spare Steyr magazines, he carried M67 fragmentation grenades, plus AN-M14 TH3 nano-thermite canisters that burned through anything, in case cracking RAHOWA's bunker proved problematic.

The compound's sentries never saw or heard him coming. Cody was a shadow in the early-morning darkness, slipping up on each of them in turn, slitting their throats after he'd slugged them semi-conscious and relieved them of their automatic weapons, ditching magazines and stripping down the weapons' firing mechanisms so no other Hitler Youth could come along behind him and make use of them.

Six men, six silent kills, and warm blood on his knife hand that he wiped clean on his victims' brown shirts while they lay convulsing at his feet.

All good.

The bunker was mostly aboveground, roughly a hundred feet square. Spy satellites repurposed by the CIA and NSA had mapped the layout, but they couldn't penetrate the feroconcrete roof that featured rebar reinforcement, making it impervious to napalm and to normal field artillery. More to the point, they couldn't tell Cody how many underground levels there might be, of how far they extended.

How many fascists were inside? The FBI had slender dossiers on forty-seven members, counting cells in Brooklyn and Chicago, with a two-man storefront operation in New Orleans. Twenty-five or so had pulled up stakes to settle in the White Bastion over the past year and a half, six of them females.

Cody didn't like to think about the pairings that suggested, but whoever came at him with the intent to kill or maim, he wouldn't be discriminating on the basis of their chromosomes.

The butchers who had slain his wife and children gave no thought to sex or age, so why should he?

Come one, come all.

He was considering a point of entry to the bunker—only one door visible, surprisingly without surveillance cameras that Cody could discover—and wondering if he should start off with a thermite canister dropped down an air vent, when a guy in uniform who looked like something from the beer garden in *Cabaret* took all the guesswork out of it.

This one saw Cody and was trying to react but had his AKS-74U carbine slung over his shoulder and got tangled up with him somehow in the excitement of his final moments. Cody stroked the AUG's progressive trigger to release a three-round burst, the slugs stitching across his adversary's sunken chest and dropping him stone dead.

Not silently, of course. The sweet advantage of surprise was history.

Cody rushed at the door before it could swing shut, shouldered his way inside, scanning for other targets. Only Wendell Orville Walker mattered now, the only Nazi in their buried warren that he hoped to take alive for questioning.

The other rats were all disposable. Who'd miss them, anyway, beside the future victims they might traumatize?

Good riddance.

He had thirty-nine rounds left inside the AUG's first magazine, which added up to thirteen three-round bursts or would burn off in about three seconds of full-auto fire. Cody would have to take the targets as they came, husband his ammunition, watching for the one pale face he'd memorized from mug shots WOW had piled up since age seventeen.

Two Nazis—one a poster child for "Aryans", the other five foot five and porky—were the first responders to his gunfire on the bunker's threshold. Cody shot each of them once, then treated Fatty to a second round when he seemed hell-bent on remaining upright while he died. The shots echoed around inside the bunker, hellishly loud, but soft Uline ballistic earplugs kept them bearable.

Move on.

The bunker was an anthill, workers charging up from underground to help defend their nest and king, hidden away somewhere. Cody eliminated them as they appeared, fire discipline engaged, he figured WOW would be tucked up somewhere below, secured out of harm's way. With that in mind, he palmed a frag grenade, released the safety clip and pin, and lobbed it down the steep stairway in front of him; ducked back and down, raising his hands to help the Uline plugs.

The blast—four seconds later, more or less—filled the stairwell with smoke and screams, steel fragments from the lethal baseball's casing slicing flesh and chipping bone, some of it ricocheting off concrete. He waited for the last few shards to whisper overhead, then closed the gap and started down the stairs.

Bodies. No point in counting them, since Cody hadn't known the number of his enemies to start with, but he delivered mercy head-shots to a couple of survivors as they bucked and wriggled on the stairs. Not wasting rounds but making sure.

The only good Nazis were dead ones.

Cody descended through a pall of smoke and dust, some twenty feet, to reach the bunker's next level. Another "soldier" lurched out of a doorway to his left, waving a knock-off version of the classic Colt 1911 .45, but never got a chance to use it. Cody drilled a rifle bullet through his left eye socket and the youngster folded like a sack of dirty laundry.

Cody guessed that he was twenty, if that old, and felt no pity for the would-be ruler of an all-white world surmounted by the swastika.

Bad choices carried consequences, and the kid would never age another day.

Voices were audible inside the room he'd vacated. Cody peered through the open door and found three females ranged in age from late teens up to thirty-something. Two had bleached their stringy hair unearthly shades of blonde; the youngest had her scalp shaved from one temple to the other, circling around behind her head, sporting Moe Howard bangs, with long hair like Hasidic ringlets hanging down on each side of her face, and unkempt tresses tumbling from the lower hairline, down her back.

It might not be the weirdest thing Cody had ever seen—in fact, it absolutely wasn't—but it ranked among the stranger styles he'd ever found a person wearing voluntarily.

Two of the skinbyrds also huddled over baby bumps.

"One chance to leave under your own steam," he informed

them. "If you make a move on me, all bets are off."

Tearful and glaring, all three rose two of them wobbling, and started for the exit. After the expectant mothers passed and started up the body-littered stairs, he stopped the oldest one, with no baby on board.

"Point me toward Heinrich," he demanded. "Tell the truth as if your life depended on it, since it does."

She nodded past him, toward what Cody took to be the bunker's buried terminus. "Down there," she said. "The last door." Then, not quite defiantly, "He ain't alone, ya know?"

"He will be," Cody said. "Clear out, now. If you think of turning back to help, skip it. He's already bought and paid for."

"Man, I ain't no hero."

"Hey, who is?"

He watched her go, then started down the corridor, checking each silent room as he passed by. The last door had a pair of SS lightning bolts spray-painted on it by a none-too-steady hand.

If Hitler could have seen this dump, he would have blown a fuse.

Or maybe, when he'd capped himself and Eva Braun in 1945, the *Führerbunker* may have been just like this, Adolf raving in delirium, the Joseph Goebbels brood swallowing cyanide—their one-way ticket to Valhalla—and party's wiser officers racing for Argentina through ratlines they'd established in advance.

Reaching his goal, Cody surveyed the door. Steel solid core, no peephole, probably impervious to small arms fire. He didn't bother with the knob, presuming it was locked—or, if it wasn't, beckoning Cody into an ambush situation.

Screw that.

He backed off along the corridor, retreating to the stairs, and double-checked to verify the women had departed. There, kneeling, he palmed one of the STANAG 22mm rifle grenades and slipped it onto the Steyer's muzzle launcher.

Most rifles required a separate attachment for grenades, also demanding that the shooter load a special blank cartridge into the cylinder before he fired. The AUG improved on that with a three-position gas valve. The first setting, marked with a small dot, is used for normal operation. The second setting, illustrated with a large dot, indicates fouled conditions. The third, "GR" closed position launch STANAG grenades manufactured without bullet traps.

Bracing the rifle's stock against his shoulder, Cody peered through the Swarovski scope and sent the grenade sizzling down range toward impact. When it blew, the steel door buckled inward, sagging half-off its hinges. Coughing and cursing echoed from the room beyond.

Cody rose, switched his rifle's gas valve back to normal operation, and advanced. A sharp kick helped the door collapse and cleared his way into WOW's inner sanctum.

What a dump it was.

The place might have been tidier before Cody sent hellfire rapping on its door, but from the fast-food bags and wrappers, crumpled beer cans, and disordered paperwork, he doubted that.

Why wouldn't rats live in a rat's nest, after all?

Walker was crouched behind his army surplus desk, eyes and receding hairline barely visible above it, looking like he'd seen the future and he didn't like it one damned bit.

Smart little punk.

His bodyguards, all three of them, were reeling with the blast's concussion, one on hands and knees, puking, the other two fumbling for weapons that they'd dropped when the explosion hit. They meant nothing to Cody, so he shot them, one-two-three, and left them leaking on the concrete floor.

Coming as close as he could get to Tommy James—a wash at imitating Tiffany—he sang to WOW across the smoky room, "I think we're alone now."

"You can't waltz in here and pull this shit!" his target whined. "Don't you know who I am, asshole?"

"Why do you think I'm here?" Cody replied.

"Jesus! Did ZOG send you? I *knew* they'd do something like this. You don't look Jewish, but with plastic surgery these days—"

Cody squeezed off a shot into the far wall, passing maybe half an inch from Walker's ear.

"You need to shut up, 'Heinrich.' Don't open your mouth again, except to answer questions. Can you manage that?"

The pallid Nazi bobbed his balding head.

"Good," Cody replied. "Let's see how badly you want to survive, shall we?"

As if the weasel had a hope in hell of getting out alive.

CHAPTER 1

St Louis, Missouri

"And you believe him, Jack?"

Cody considered it and answered, "Somewhere close to 95 percent. Why would he lie?"

"Torture," replied Sara Durell, his contact with the CIA. "We learned from nine-eleven what we should have known already, that it almost always gets results, but not the right ones, necessarily."

"It wasn't torture," Cody said. "I offered him a chance to live. Well, anyway, to die with dignity he hadn't earned."

"Still."

They'd agreed to meet midway between Langley and Idaho, strolling along the west bank of the Mississippi River, near the soaring Gateway Arch. Tourists ignored them, which was part and parcel of the plan.

"Okay, then," Cody said. "You told me he was dealing with

Islamists, and he copped to it with details. If you'd rather not believe it now..."

"When you say 'details'," she broke in, "you don't mean names, locations, anything like that?"

"Not yet," he granted. "That's still left to come."

"Assuming we have time."

Sara wasn't a classic beauty—no one Cody would have noticed when his wife was still alive—but Cody recognized her as the kind of woman who had been described as 'handsome' in another era. She was hot enough to be familiar with the Old Boy's Club that ran the Company and would have made it tough on her, advancing up the ladder of command, earning the Distinguished Intelligence Cross for her work in Iraq, and the Intelligence Star for Afghanistan, awarded for "voluntary acts of courage performed under hazardous conditions or for outstanding achievements or services rendered with distinction under conditions of grave risk".

That was the kind of thing you didn't ask about and likely wouldn't get an answer if you did.

She'd gotten bloody in the sand on that tour, around Ghazni, Kandahar, and Taloqan. 'Nuff said.

"You have new information for me?" he inquired, watching a couple with a baby stroller pass them, headed in the opposite direction, smiling as if all was safe and normal in their world.

Dream on.

"A bit, but not enough," Sara replied. "A rumble about good-sized dirty nukes."

"Sounds pretty standard," Cody said.

"Agreed. But there's a ... let's say *urgency* about the talk this time. It feels like more than blowing off some steam around the mosque after *Yawm al-Jum'ah*. Our analysts believe there's actually something going on this time."

Yawm al-Jum'ah. The standard Friday prayer.

"And they believe that...why?"

"We're getting help from the inside."

Cody perked up at that. "Inside which group? Al-Qaeda? ISIS? Al-Shabab? Boko Haram?"

"It's none of the above, unfortunately. But we have an *imam* at a mosque out west who claims he's on our side."

"Oh, yeah?"

"You'll have to size him up yourself, of course. He wouldn't be the first walk-in who lied his ass off, hoping to become a mole and feed the other side intel."

That didn't call for any back-and-forth discussion. Cody knew the score on double agents and had taken out a few of them himself, since he'd retired from Delta Force to chart another path with even fewer rules.

The main ones being: Get it done, and don't get caught.

The bulk of John and Jane Q. Public were entirely in the dark about the perils that surrounded them. They all woke up when something massive struck stateside—like 9/11 or the Oklahoma City bombing—but soon enough, when suspects were incarcerated and the herd got bored when Homeland Security's Advisory System dipped back to orange or yellow, seemingly stuck there in perpetuity.

Few civilians could exist long-term on high alert. The

military lived with it and mostly followed orders, keeping one eye on the welcome budget overruns that came along with crises on the grapevine. If an act of terrorism never came to pass, it proved joint chiefs of staff were running up to speed. If something grisly happened…well, like Daffy Duck singing his Christmas song, they wanted more, more, more.

It didn't worry Cody when the Pentagon reported "losing track" of money tabulated in hundreds of millions, as the folks in charge had grudgingly confessed in February of 2018. He knew a lot of that had vanished into various "black budgets"— funding projects a majority of people knew nothing about, and Congress barely recognized. Another chunk was built into defense contracts, the grease that kept wheels turning more or less on time.

And some of it kept Jack Cody employed, doing the dirty jobs never imagined by the Founding Fathers when they wrote the Constitution.

Great on paper, but it didn't last long on the battlefield.

"Who is this guy?" Jack asked.

"Fahim Rafa ibn Kaldun. We've run his background, naturally. No red flags."

"There wouldn't be," Cody replied, "if someone groomed him going in."

"Agreed. But since he first made contact he's been under round-the-clock surveillance, taps and bugs, shadows, the whole nine yards."

"They'd be expecting all of that."

"Which is exactly why I said you'll need to take a reading

on him for yourself."

"Somewhere out west, you said?"

"Vegas."

There were two in the United States, one in Nevada, and the other in New Mexico.

"The famous one," Sara replied.

"They've got a mosque in Vegas. I've just heard of quickie wedding chapels."

"Oh, ye heathen. They had five hundred churches at last count, still outnumbered three-to-one by gambling joints, but it's a funky point of pride with praying folks. You'd have to check the phone book for denominations, if you care."

"I don't," Cody replied. "But I'm surprised they've got a mosque there."

"Not just one," Sara corrected him. "Kaldun's Masjid An-Nur is one of seven, if you can believe it."

"Wonders never cease."

"They've got it all. Buddhists, Hindus, Serbian Orthodox."

"Okay. Tell me he doesn't know I'm coming."

"Jack, would I do that to you?"

"I hope not."

"And I aim to please. An asset in Clark County told him *someone* will be coming to debrief him, no description and no ETA. Surprise him. See if he gets shaken up."

"I know the drill."

"Of course. I have to say this, anyway. If he gives off a hinky vibe, please disengage, report back, and I'll handle it from there. Try not to kill him, if you don't mind."

"Hey." He took a stab at sounding wounded, missed it by a country mile. "I don't kill everyone I meet."

"Lucky for me," she quipped.

"Discretion is my middle name."

She let that pass and said, "This is important to the president."

"I guessed that when you set the meeting."

"No one likes a smartass, Jack."

"I wouldn't go that far."

"Okay, then. No one in authority. How's that?"

"Better. When do I leave?"

"As soon as you can pack and book a flight out of Saint Louis Lambert International."

Cody subconsciously collected trivia. He knew, for instance, that Missouri's busiest airport was named for Albert Bond Lambert, an Olympic medalist in golf and famed St. Louis aviator, dead since 1946, three weeks shy of his seventy-first birthday. Same way he knew McCarran International in Vegas bore the name of an Irish-American senator who'd bent over backwards and then some, promoting the cause of legalized gambling.

Fun facts known by few and cared about by fewer still.

"Good thing I never bother to unpack," he said.

"Smart thinking. Go bags at the ready."

"Always. Except for flying naked."

Sara didn't ask if he was cracking wise. She knew that he meant traveling unarmed and was concerned about remaining that way after touchdown.

"You'll be met. Someone discreet, so there's no rental contract for your ride. Junk in the trunk. If you have any specs, text me an hour out from landing."

More trivia he'd memorized: the trip spanned 1,371 miles between airports. With impossible precision, the two nonstop commercial carriers—Frontier and Southwest—

"estimated" travel time at three hours and twenty-two minutes, including ten minutes' taxi time for departure, five minutes for landing.

Cody could have given her the hardware list right then, trusting that she'd remember it, but it would feel like he was being hasty. Not the best impression, overall.

"Will do," he said, and let it go.

She handed a photograph, resembling something taken for a passport. "Meet the storyteller," Sara said.

Bland face, bearded of course, under a *taqiyah* cap stitched with artful scrollwork.

"I wouldn't peg him for a radical," Jack said. "But then, who knows, these days?"

"Exactly. If our analysts are right, so much the better. If they're not, I'll think about how to proceed, once you've reported back."

He knew what that meant. Had no feelings on it, pro or con. If Kaldun proved to be a "good guy", even within self-imposed limits, Cody would try to work with him. If not...

People were dying every day. He knew that 2017 had been Clark County, Nevada's worst year for murders since 1990, up 23.5 percent over 2016, with 264 victims and 51 cases remaining unsolved. The stats weren't in for 2019 yet—slow bean counters—but homicide was clearly on an upward trend, solutions just so-so.

"Whichever way it goes, you know I have to speak the magic words."

" 'No comebacks on the Company'," he said, as if by rote. "Total deniability."

"Sorry. It's in the contract," Sara said, not sounding all that broken up about it."

"You do it well," Cody replied. He handed back the photo of Fahim Rafa ibn Kaldun and said, "I'd better get a move on, then."

"Good luck."

They separated, Cody moving toward his rental car in a nearby parking lot, while Sara ducked into the greenery of Gateway Arch Park and vanished. Something else that she was good at: disappearing when she figured there was nothing left to say.

Now, all he had to do was text a shopping list, same way he usually did, most recently two hours prior to touchdown at Boise International Airport. Cody hadn't flown directly into Coeur d'Alene's regional airport, a county-owned facility too close for comfort to the site of his intended strike.

No comebacks. Words to live or die by in the cut-throat world Cody inhabited.

The drive from Gateway Arch to St. Louis Lambert International was thirteen miles northwest on Interstate 70, rolling through late morning traffic for seventeen minutes or so. He dropped the rental where he'd picked it up two hours

earlier, at Avis, then wandered down the concourse, brows-
ing. The first flight out was on Southwestern, departing at
4:47 p.m. and reaching McCarran at 6:37. Jack ponied up $267,
using the Company's plastic, then considered how to spend
the next four hours and change.

His stomach grumbled, reminding Cody that he'd eaten
nothing since a turkey sandwich on the flight eastward from
Boise, so he followed signs that led him to the food court.
There was no end of possibilities, but he went with old habits
and ducked into Chili's, adjacent to Gate C15.

Jack knew their menu, and it hadn't let him down so far.
Bearing in mind that this could be his last meal until he had
wrapped things up in Vegas, he went with a favorite stand-by:
the chicken fried steak, mashed potatoes with white sausage
gravy, roasted corn on the cob, and two fluffy dinner rolls, all
piping hot on arrival. He balanced that out with Corona, two
frosty long-necks, and went away happy, leaving the waitress
a tip large enough to earn him a smile, not so big that she'd
talk it up after her shift.

Still two hours and ninety minutes left to kill before liftoff.

Cody breezed through security, his hands washed half a
dozen times since Kootenai County, his night suit discarded,
nothing to excite the TSA's FIDO Explosives Detector hardware from ICx Technologies, using a system developed at
MIT called amplifying fluorescent polymer. It was a useful
tool, but Cody had his doubts about detecting certain IEDs,
like those implanted surgically inside a would-be martyr's
body.

Approaching his departure gate, Jack stopped at one of the airport's several Hudson Bookseller's shops—"The Travelers' Best Friend"—and bought the latest paperbacks from Lincoln Child and Gregg Hurwitz. Some folks might call that a busman's holiday, but what the hell? Excellent writing sold the tale, whether romance or blood and thunder.

By the time a disembodied robot voice called boarding for his flight, Cody was seven chapters into one of his new acquisitions and could easily have sat there, on into the evening, but duty called.

Again.

Las Vegas, Nevada

"Are we certain?" asked Achmed Adil Fatah.

Abdul Karim Qadir turned steely eyes onto his second in command. "You mean, am *I* mistaken?"

"No, sir! But I wondered if—"

"The sheikh made some mistake? If he has lost his mind, perhaps?"

"I beg your pardon, sir. Forgive me, please. I didn't mean—"

"What *did* you mean, Achmed? What should I do to put your troubled mind at ease? Shall I disturb him now, to ask if he has made a different decision in the past ten minutes? If he has new orders for us canceling his other plan?"

"No, sir! I simply thought..." Achmed Adil Fatah's words trailed away to nothing, as if he had swallowed them.

"Enlighten me, Achmed. In Allah's holy name, what *did* you think? What are you thinking now, but too afraid to say aloud?"

"That it is dangerous. The plan, sir."

"I agree. An element of risk is always present in such things. It's why committed warriors such as we are trusted to perform the task."

"No, sir. Abdul, I speak of danger to our whole community. If we do this—"

"Remove a traitor from our midst?" Qadir cut in. "How else do you remove the cancer from a healthy body, but to cut it out?"

"With all respect, others may not perceive it thus. This city has received Muslims into itself, with only minor protests from the Christian fringe."

"There is no 'fringe', Achmed," Qadir corrected him. "The whole Crusader's faith is Islam's mortal enemy and has been through the centuries. Are you forgetting that?"

"No, but—"

"This nation we inhabit is the Great Satan, Achmed. This place—'Sin City', as they boast of it in advertising—represents the worst sink of perdition outside Washington, DC."

"But will not converts question us? Our motives?"

"Some may, certainly. Let them identify themselves on television and in whining letters to the filthy newspapers. When they have been exposed as traitors to the One True Faith, we may excise them, in their turn, and purify the land."

Achmed Adil Fatah fell silent, lowering his eyes.

Qadir immediately challenged him. "You disagree? You doubt the course of our *jihad*?"

"No, sir!"

"And if we hesitate at this first step, if we admit defeat, what happens next? Who will ignite the fires of Allah in their turn?"

"I understand the error of my thinking, sir. The plan shall move ahead, exactly as you say."

"I say nothing, Obasi. Our leader speaks for Allah the Almighty. Only from his lips are we enlightened."

"*Allāhu akbar! As-salaam-alaikum.*"

"*Wa-alaikum-salaam,*" Qadir responded, not quite smiling. "Now, confirm the preparations for me, if you'd be so kind."

"Of course, sir."

"First, which soldiers have you chosen?"

"All our members volunteered. I chose the most four best suited."

"And they are, in your opinion…?"

"Nasrallah Anisur Rahman," Fatah replied.

"The Eagle Eye, I think they call him?"

"Yes, sir. Next, Ziaur Rida Abdolreza."

"Blooded in Syria," Qadir said, nodding his approval. "Not a sniper, but he shows no fear."

"Third, Sharifullah Abdur Raqib," Achmed pressed on.

"Known to his fellows as The Reaper, if I'm not mistaken."

"You are not, sir."

"And the last?"

"A relatively new recruit: Gurid Abdus Salam."

Qadir allowed himself the smallest frown at that, then turned it upside down, into a narrow smile. "Why not? If young men never gain experience, how will they learn?"

"Yes, sir."

"Be certain that he acts in a subordinate position to the rest. And you make five?"

"Just as you say, Achmed."

"On to equipment, then."

"AK-74s," Fatah replied. "The carbines, with their folding stocks and shortened barrels."

"There is no need to describe the rifles, Achmed," said Qadir. "I am familiar with them, likely more so than yourself."

He couldn't tell if Achmed blushed. With Arabs, it was often hard to know.

"Of course, sir. I apologize."

"And backup weapons?"

"Pistols from the stockpile. Two Beretta M9s, one Glock 17, and for Gurid, a Browning Hi-power."

"And you? Still the .357 you adore?"

Perhaps a hint of blush, just then. "Yes, sir. Unless you think—"

Qadir waved off the rest of it. "No matter. If the mission comes down to your pistol, all is lost."

"Yes, sir."

"And I shall take a Glock, as well, along with the Kalashnikov."

"You, sir?"

"And why not?" Qadir challenged him. "Should I sit back

and merely watch, when so much planning is invested in this first step of the master plan?"

"No, sir. I only meant—"

"For Allah's sake, Achmed, don't start that all over again. I'm coming with you. That's the end of it. We'll need a vehicle to comfortably seat the six of us, disposable when we are finished."

"All arranged, sir. While I only counted five, it is a Lincoln Aviator SUV, taken last night from the airport's long-term parking lot, now wearing license plates from out of state. Coincidentally, it has three rows of seats for seven passengers."

"So, one to spare, then," said Qadir.

"Yes, sir."

"No need to ask if you have checked the fuel, the tires, the engine." Though, of course, by saying that, Qadir *was* asking, none too subtly.

"As you say, sir. All in readiness."

"Now, if we confirm the timing and a definite location for the target..."

"Done, sir."

"Minimizing unintended casualties?"

"Yes, although we must allow for unintended circumstances. Tourists, passers-by, some visitors we cannot be aware of in advance."

"Yes, yes. The usual," Qadir, bland-faced, showed no uneasiness. "We cannot concern ourselves with collateral damage, Achmed. In fact, a few more bodies might help drive the lesson home."

"The lesson, sir?"

"Of course. Consider it a teaching moment for our enemies and straying brethren, eh? Associating with a traitor may result in certain...consequences. Even inadvertently, you see? The point of terror, Achmed, is to *terrorize*. Teach everyone to shun even coincidental contact with a traitor to the One True Faith. Require them to assess all their acquaintances and strictly separate the sheep from goats."

"Yes, sir."

"Compose yourself, Achmed. Find calm and fortitude within."

"I am composed, sir."

"I hope so. This challenge is a relatively minor one. Are you prepared to make the final sacrifice in Allah's holy name, upon command?"

"Yes, sir!"

"Tonight, we prove ourselves. Summon the troops."

CHAPTER 2

McCarran International Airport

Las Vegas never makes you wait. Instant gratification of any desire is its *raison d'être*.

Come to gamble, like most tourists? Have your cash in hand as soon as you deplane. No rush to hail a taxi or pick up your waiting rental car. McCarran's concourse has bright, noisy banks of slot machines on standby, to relieve you of your spare change or life savings before you reach open, desert air.

The airport started life in 1920, as Anderson Field, growing over time into a mini-city of its own: four busy runways and two terminals, welcoming thirty-eight airlines and no end of private planes owned by high-rollers, dubbed "whales". Some 50 million passengers arrived in 2018, last year with conclusive stats available. A few of them progressed no further, lost amid the slots and restaurants until their allocated time and cash ran out.

The city's called "Lost Wages" for a reason. Most of what happens in Vegas and stays there proves to be your hard-earned money—and the college fund you've saved up for your kids, if you turn out to be what the casino bosses call a "degenerate gambler".

Never let it hurt your feelings. Just pay up and take the beating you expected.

Cody hadn't wasted Langley's money on a round-trip flight. He knew that one-way tickets were an early-warning flag for terrorists, but with the Company behind him, picking up his tab and backstopping his cover, he could let that worry slide.

He didn't patronize the slots in transit from Arrivals, on his way to Baggage Claims. If he had felt like throwing change away, he would have dropped it into a Salvation Army bucket, or just ducked into the men's room, literally flushed it down the drain to see what that felt like.

He claimed one bag, conscious of uniformed security and CCTV cameras observing him, not worried about either. If technicians in an upstairs office tried their facial recognition software on him, they'd be disappointed.

Jack Cody was strictly off the books since leaving Delta Force. The little man who wasn't there—until he suddenly came up behind you, and then *you* weren't there, ever again.

Trusting Sara Durell—who'd never let him down so far—he passed the auto rental kiosks: Alamo and Avis, Hertz and Enterprise, a line of others where young men and women smiled professionally, stamping contracts, noting driver's license numbers, peddling crash insurance. None of them were snaring him tonight.

Outside, beyond the reach of air-conditioning, Cody stepped into heat from the departing day, scented with smog. A line of taxis waited; shuttle busses hissed upon arrival, then groaned off toward various "resort" hotels; nonstop flow of circling private cars slowed down on each pass-by, congesting traffic, drivers squinting into neon for a glimpse of a familiar face.

And in the middle of it all, two cars were parked against a red curb, one generic white guy standing next to each, oblivious to anything around him but the stream of fresh meat spilling out onto the sidewalk. Cops from the Clark County Sheriff's Office didn't hassle them—some kind of violation in itself, Jack thought—pretending both the autos and their stoic attendants were invisible.

Cody knew Company employees when he saw them stateside, usually dressed in suits that rose in price from Wholesale Linked online to off-the-rack at J.C. Penney, Brooks Brothers, and on to tailored wear from L.A., New York City, Hong Kong or London, as buyer's climbed the intelligence ladder toward Langley's "Mahogany Row".

Jack usually passed on that, unless a costume were required, preferring casual attire that let him move at need, whether camped in a stakeout vehicle or fighting hand-to-hand.

He stepped up to the closest of the waiting assets—neither one holding a sign, of course, and spoke the magic words: "Is

Vegas always dry like this?"

And got the answer back: "Until it pours."

"I'll drive," he told the guy, accepted the key to a new, white Honda Accord, and slid behind its wheel. His helpful weatherman sat in the shotgun seat as Jack nosed into traffic, followed closely by the second midsize car, a black Audi Q5.

Cody preferred the white Honda. It wasn't flashy, but at night its paintjob would reflect the city's endless, ever-changing light show and leave witnesses confused when talking to authorities. The "Fremont Street Experience"—still known to locals as Sin City's downtown "Glitter Gulch"—supposedly had 3.5 million LED lights all its own, inflaming five canopied blocks. Good luck to any fool who wanted to count lightbulbs on the Vegas Strip.

"We've got a service area ahead," Jack's passenger advised, and Cody nosed into a gas station mysteriously standing dark and idle. Maybe by design?

He switched off the Accord's K24V engine—what headquarters in Tokyo had tagged the "Earth Dreams" model—and walked back into the glare of headlights, as the Q5 parked behind his borrowed ride.

Before he popped the trunk, Jack asked his poker-faced companions, "Any problems with the shopping?"

"Easy peasy."

Jack waited for him to tack on "lemon squeezy," and was thankful when he skipped it.

Youth. Christ, had he ever been like that?

Inside the trunk, headlights revealed two duffel bags in

basic black. He opened both before inspecting either one's contents, then sorted through the hardware Sara had arranged for him. They seemed right at first glance, but he leaned in to make a hands-on survey, just in case.

Suspecting that the local office might not have a Steyr AUG on tap, despite the city's glut of gun stores, Jack had opted for an M4 carbine version of the M16A2 assault rifle. Shorter than its parent by ten inches, with a telescoping stock and a 14.5-inch barrel (down from 20), it still weighed the same 7.5 pounds with a loaded 30-round mag of 5.56mm cartridges, with the same cyclic auto-fire rate of 700 to 900 rounds per minute.

Cody guessed the weight discrepancy derived from the addition of an M68 Close Combat Optic device in place of the M16's carrying handle, mounted on a Picatinny rail. Also known as CompM2, the device is a battery-powered, non-magnifying red dot type of reflex sight for firearms, manufactured by Aimpoint AB in Sweden.

The M4 came with two dozen spare magazines, all loaded.

In the second duffel bag he found a pair of his favorite Glock 22s with holsters to fit. The lightweight windbreaker included with them was Jack's perfect size, of course, and would be welcome shortly when the desert's temperature started dropping toward its nighttime average of 59 degrees Fahrenheit.

At least, no casual observers would detect his hidden hardware at first glance, or think he was a lunatic for putting on a jacket during springtime.

If you want to see fashion *faux pas*, hang out around the penny slots at any joint in town—but bear in mind, before you play, that "penny" slots demand accumulating buy-ins, averaging forty to fifty minimum bet on all lines, while max bets cost up to a five spot.

Vegas. It will find a way to get you, every time.

Jack hadn't ordered up a trench knife or grenades this time but settled for a Benchmade Pagan automatic knife—switchblade, that is—with a four-inch chisel-ground, double-edge spear-point blade, now legal anywhere statewide, except on schoolgrounds.

Have to keep the kiddies safe until a loony random shooter came to visit for the day.

When he was satisfied, Jack pocketed the knife, strapped on the Glocks, and moved the other hardware to the Honda's footwell on the shotgun side. "Where should I leave it, if I have a choice?" he asked his taciturn escort.

"Wherever. It's LoJacked."

A faint alarm sounded in Cody's head. "But I'm still flying solo, right?"

"Yes, sir. Orders."

No further chitchat as he drove away and headed for his destination, two blocks off West Sahara Boulevard, near Rainbow Park, to see a guy about a guy.

"We're almost there," Achmed Adil Fatah announced, to no one in particular.

"We all know the address," Abdul Karim Qadir informed him.

"Yes, sir. I apologize."

"Of course, you do."

And what in *Jahannam* was that supposed to mean? Another insult, clearly, coupled with Qadir's assessment of Fatah's performance as his second in command?

For all his loyalty to the cause and their supreme leader, Fatah thought it would not have hurt Qadir to offer modest words of praise, as well, even if only at the close of Ramadan.

No matter. Achmed Fatah had a job to do, despite misgivings he'd been forced to swallow, and he meant to spare no effort toward completion of that task.

"Can you speed up a little?" Sharifullah Raqib called out to him from the middle row of seats.

Fatah scowled at his critic's dark reflection in the Lincoln's rearview mirror, both men knowing he'd been ordered to drive safely and thereby avoid a traffic stop, until Qadir chimed in, "Yes. Faster now."

Fatah sped up as ordered, musing over how a motorcycle officer would act if he approached the Aviator, sizing up its occupants, with all their military hardware on display. Would he immediately soil himself, or try to draw his pistol first? Maybe keying the standard shoulder-mounted microphone during the split-second of life remaining to him.

"Here," Qadir said, pointing past Fatah's face. "To the left."

"Yes, sir. I see it."

Pulling in, he parked the SUV and waited for instructions

that were sure to follow, with Qadir repeating everything they had rehearsed no less than half a dozen times already.

But their leader did not speak immediately. Rather, he was looking up down the street, examining the target building's stucco eastern side: an access door padlocked from the outside, no windows visible from where Fatah and his companions sat.

"Examine weapons," Qadir ordered, as he went about that task with his own AKS-74U carbine, then drew back his Glock's slide far enough to verify a live round in the chamber and returned it to his belt holster.

Fatah confirmed that his short rifle's safety was "off", then drew his Colt Python with four-inch barrel, swinging out its cylinder to see once more the six .357 Magnum rims and primers gleaming back at him before he shut the cylinder again.

He left the Python's hammer down. The weapon would not fire unless he squeezed its double-action trigger or thumbed back its hammer for a single-action shot. And when he did, a jacketed hollow point slug weighing eight grams would hurtle toward impact at 1,450 feet per second, killing anything except, perhaps, a fully-grown rhinoceros or outsized crocodile.

No living man could stand before the Magnum, which would also crack a car's cylinder block and bring it limping, wheezing to a halt.

Fatah was on the verge of asking how much longer they must wait, risking another reprimand from his commander, when Nasrallah Rahman beat him to it.

"Can we get this done and leave, sir?" Rahman asked their boss.

"On my command, and not before," Qadir replied, not even bothering to turn around and face his critic.

"But the police, sir—"

"What part of 'on my command' confuses you, Nasrallah?" asked Qadir.

"I'm sorry, sir."

Qadir let that apology go by without a snide remark, eyeing their target through the Lincoln Aviator's tinted windshield. Nothing moved around the building till a tabby street cat flitted past and vanished down a dark alley.

"All right, let's go," Qadir ordered, as if the furtive feline were an omen of success.

Fatah had still seen no one on the premises, and without any windows showing light, he couldn't even say if the building was occupied.

"*Allāhu akbar!*" said Qadir. Five voices answered him in unison.

Achmed Adil Fatah agreed that God was great, indeed. But would He smile on them tonight and see them through the trial ahead?

Finding the Masjid An-Nur mosque wasn't much of a challenge, since Cody had memorized the relevant parts of a Vegas street map. Traffic slowed him down a little, even when he'd turned south from the Strip, on West Sahara, but he took that as a given for a town that never slept.

Casinos ran 24/7, with no pesky wall clocks to distract the players, and if one of them desired a time-out with some sexy company, that could be easily arranged.

Nevada legislators, in their infinite wisdom, had outlawed prostitution in the Silver State's most populous county—ironically Clark surrounding Las Vegas—while fifteen other counties had the choice of voting "yea" or "nay". Five more had banned it over time, which left ten open to commercial sex, supporting twenty-one "resorts" and "ranches" at last count. The nearest whorehouse to Las Vegas, situated sixty miles across the desert and beyond the Spring Mountains.

Of course, as usual, no statute penned by man would stop pursuit of pleasure in Sin City. Vegas had streetwalkers, hauled in and fined occasionally, so the cops could say that they were "doing something about vice," but there were also scores of licensed "escort agencies" that offered male or female "dates" upon request, for a wide range of tastes and fees—all strictly on the up-and-up, of course.

Sometimes, police mounted sting operations to make sure. Some escorts were detained and blacklisted, with mandatory tests for HIV; more rarely, their employers might pay piddling fines. And sometimes, Jack surmised, the deputies got laid, then promptly lost the evidence. Defective video recorders were their blessing and their bane.

It was a tough town for an honest clergyman to handle, without feeling beaten down and shamed. Some just rolled over, like the cops, officiating in the chapels set aside by gambling houses or performing quickie marriages—in costume, if requested; Elvis was a holy hit long after dropping dead—and a few pastors praised "suspected" mobsters for their bountiful philanthropy.

Jack didn't have a clue regarding *imam* Fahim Rafa ibn Kaldun's honesty or motives prior to facing him. He only knew that Kaldun had approached an FBI man at the Foley Federal Building on South Las Vegas Boulevard, offering information on a terrorist conspiracy in progress. Acting against type, the G-man had notified Homeland Security instead of headquarters, earning a pat on the back from a Company asset, along with a brisk reprimand from his own special agent in charge.

As in J. Edgar's bygone day, embarrassing the Bureau still ranked No. 1 on its short list of cardinal offenses. Rumor had it that the thoughtful G-man had been shipped to Anchorage, watching for Chicom submarines gliding around the Bering Sea.

Another Vegas loser, gone and soon forgotten.

Approaching Kaldun's mosque, Jack boxed the block and found an open parking space a short block to the south, along Laredo Street. Brief hesitation. Should he leave the duffel bags up front, or stash them in the trunk again?

Trusting in luck, he left them where they were and made damned sure that he locked the Accord.

Full night had fallen over Vegas as he started walking back, but it was never really dark. From dusk to dawn, all those garish lights combined to wipe the sky of stars, the Milky Way replaced by the orange glow of high technology touting an ancient sybaritic fantasy.

Cody wasn't a praying man, himself, and never had been, raised by free-thinking agnostic parents who'd set him at liberty to make his own choices, as long as no one else took any shit from him because they saw the world another way.

And that had worked.

Cody had never harmed a soul for cleaving to a given faith or creed. But when they used religion as a weapon, to impose their will on others as tyrants and terrorists, he offered them a first-class, one-way ticket to the hellfire of their choice, with all expenses paid by Uncle Sam.

Jack came around the backside of the Masjid An-Nur mosque, moving along an alleyway of garbage cans and dumpsters waiting for next morning's pickup, till he found the mosque's backdoor, blazoned with a painted star and crescent.

Having done his homework, Cody knew that Kaldun and his Vegas clock were Sunni Muslims, part of the religion's largest faction. Next in line, at No. 2, were Shia Muslims, followed by the third-place Sufis, each group broken into sub-divisions that perpetually quarreled on subjects ranging from Muhammad's rightful heir back in 632 C.E., to arcane trivia involving dietary rules and jurisprudence.

Way too much for Jack to wrap his head around, assuming he had cared to try.

His task tonight was twofold. First, assess Kaldun and figure if he had a solid tale to tell, or if he was a double agent, possibly a mercenary bullshit artist looking for a handout. And if Kaldun passed muster, there was still his story to be weighed and judged.

What were the details of his story?

Was there anything supporting them as factual?

Had someone else fed Kaldun lies that *he* believed were true, passing them on with good intentions, but to no result?

Finally, was the man himself a liar? And if so, for what motive?

Somebody could have put the *imam* on a polygraph, and while law enforcement agencies still made extensive use of "lie detectors"—screening criminal suspects, witnesses, and prospective government employees—Cody didn't trust them much. Persuasive studies indicated that the polygraph's reliability rate waffled somewhere between 50 and 70 percent in skillful hands. When the examiners were biased or just stupid, it fell off a cliff.

Cody had been examined twice so far, while working for the Company; as part of the recruiting process, and a second time after he'd lost a valuable asset in the field through no fault of his own. Each time, certain results had been inaccurate. The guy in charge of testing new Langley employees claimed Cody had lied about using recreational drugs. A series of tox screens had proved the jerk wrong—but as far as Jack knew, he was still on the job, still serving as a roadblock to desirable recruits.

So, Kaldun was an unknown quantity, and Jack would be the human lie detector in his case. Bad luck for the *imam* if Cody sized him up as traitorous, in which case his life span would hit a screeching halt.

Jack tried the backdoor's knob. Wasn't surprised to find it locked. Two minutes with a Dyno Lock tool beat it, both the knob's lock and a deadbolt, whereupon he eased his way inside. He trailed low-volume music—"Despacito", not at all what Jack expected—to an open office door. Inside, Fahim Rafa ibn Kaldun sat at a desk, perusing paperwork.

Cody stood in the doorway, one hand on a Glock, and said, "I think you've been expecting me."

The startled cleric nearly jumped out of his chair, maybe out of his skin. He wore a different *taqiyah* cap than in the photo Cody had examined in St. Louis, bland face registering shock, his eyes furtive and flicking all around the office, as if looking for an exit that the builders had forgotten to install.

"Expecting you?" Kaldun managed, after some twenty silent seconds. "Who *are* you?"

Jack answered with a question of his own, "What's in a name?"

"Identity?"

" 'John Doe' should do, for now."

"And you have broken in because...?"

"No doorbell in the alley," Cody said. "And since you asked for me in secret, I assumed you wouldn't want me out front, where I could be seen by any Tom or hairy Dick."

"*I* sent...Wait! You are from the US government?"

"That's close enough."

"You have credentials, I assume?"

"Damn! Must have left them in my other pants."

"Excuse me, but without some proof of what you say—"

"That's my line, man. You dropped some hints about a storm coming, and I've been sent to check it out. Let's find out if you pass, shall we?"

"But...without proof that you are who you claim to be...I mean...you could be anyone."

"And so could you. Working for anyone, in fact."

"You think *I* am a terrorist?"

"I'm not judging your beard or your religion, pal. You claimed to have proof of a mass-destruction plot impending, right? Now, if you're putting some conditions on explaining that—you have to meet the first daughter, or something—I can tell you here and now it isn't happening."

"I have demanded nothing!"

"And you've said nothing that's actionable yet. Feel free to go all silent now. The Constitution guarantees the right to shut your pie hole. I'll just toddle back the way I came and tell my boss this was a wash-out, yeah? Somebody may want to review your green card, but that's got nothing to do with me. I'm not with ICE."

As Cody turned away, the *imam* cried out, "No! Wait! Please!"

"Five minutes to convince me that it's worth another five," Jack said, crossing the small room to be seated in a chair planted in front of Kaldun's desk. "Tick, tock."

"Yes, well...are you familiar with the Flame of Allah?"

"Maybe rings a distant bell. Go on."

"It is a militant jihadist group. Hard-core and merciless."

"So far, those sound like synonyms to me," Jack said.

"They have been orchestrating terrorist events from the Arabian Peninsula to the United States. Explosions in Los Angeles, New York, and in Florida."

Cody was skilled at purging all emotion from his face and body language. He gave no hint that Kaldun's words were pointing to the late RAHOWA Alliance and Wendell Orville Walker's claim of hooking up with fellow anti-Semites in the Middle East.

"Okay," Jack simply said. "Go on."

"Sadly, I don't have names of those responsible, or dates of the coming events," Kaldun went on.

"Sad's right," Cody agreed. "Without one or the other, what am I supposed to do? Look for referrals on the bathroom wall at Taco Bell?"

"But I believe—I'm nearly certain of it—that I can obtain more information, given time."

"How much time?"

"Well..."

"See, that's the rub," Jack interjected. "If we've got some kind of major blowup coming down the pike, you won't make any friends by fiddling while Rome burns."

"Perhaps a few more days?"

"You're asking me? Mister, I don't know who or where your information's coming from. There's no point asking my advice on how long it should take."

"I can't afford to rush my source and bring suspicion back

upon myself."

"So, it's a standoff, then," Jack said, rising out of his chair. "Under the circumstances—"

"No! Give me a day, at least!"

"Thing is," Cody replied, "the time's not mine to give. If nothing's really happening, and this is all hot air, feel free to take a year. Hell, make it a decade, okay? But if you could've headed off a serious attack, and it goes down because you got cold feet, expect a quick transition to hot water."

Kaldun slumped backward in his swivel chair. "Tell me," he said at last, "what should I do?"

"You're asking my advice?"

"I am, sir."

"My choice would be getting out of here right now. I can install you in a safe house, make arrangements for communications out of there, and see what you can turn up overnight."

"Leave? But my congregation—"

"Will survive without you, till you're on the other side of this. That may not be the case if you stay here, and hostiles show up looking for you."

Jack couldn't tell if Kaldun was about to faint or hyperventilate just then. Somehow, he found his nerve and bolted to his face. "All right. Let's go."

"You need to pack something?" asked Cody.

"What? I don't know where we're going, or how long I'll be away."

"Good point," Jack said. "No point hanging around here any longer than we have to."

"Do you have a vehicle?"

"I do, a couple blocks away. Let's hit the bricks."

"Bricks?"

"Skip it. Follow me."

"Yes, yes. I'm coming."

Kaldun glanced around the office for a second, shrugged at last, and followed Jack to the backdoor. Cody slipped through, the *imam* on his heels, pausing to shut the door behind them.

Jogging off to reach the Honda, Jack kept sweeping shadows with his sharp eyes, watching out for any opposition, spotting none. The car was waiting where he'd left it, undisturbed. Keying the locks from thirty feet away, he got to the Accord ahead of his flustered companion, shifting heavy duffel bags from the front footwell to the backseat.

"Get in there and buckle up," he told Kaldun. "We—"

Splat!

The hit came first, before the gunshot's echo, and Kaldun's head burst on impact, like a ripe melon. Its warm, wet contents spattered Cody's face, the guy already gone before he dropped, and Cody hit a crouch beside him, whipping out the Glock from his hip holster.

"Mother—"

Two more shots came at him, rapid fire, one taking out the Honda's right-rear window with a crash, the next one plunking through its backdoor, inches from his blood-streaked face.

Cursing a blue streak, Cody rolled and crawled around the vehicle, but no more rounds pursued him. He heard squealing tires, a revving engine, and looked up in time to see a jet-black, full-sized SUV peel out.

Abandoning nearly-headless Kaldun, no good to anybody now, Jack threw himself into the driver's seat and roared off in pursuit.

CHAPTER 3

Vegas streets are laid out for efficiency, not speed. The city's action is intended to occur indoors, or else in swimming pools, on golf courses—the usual. Its thoroughfares were planned to funnel nonstop streams of traffic: tourists, locals, funeral and wedding parties, service vehicles. Aside from fender-benders, occasional disruptions of routine—like the public assassination of Tupac Shakur in 1996—they weren't designed for drama.

Enter wild card Jack Cody, hot after a stylish Lincoln Aviator filled with terrorists who'd scrubbed his mission but were dumb enough to let him live.

First thing, after he gunned the Honda in pursuit of his assailants, Cody reached around and brought his duffel bags of hardware back up front. He couldn't reach the M4 carbine yet, without losing control of the Accord, but close was always better than beyond his reach.

First thing: the Honda's 2.0-liter "Earth Dreams" engine

had been dropped into the middle of a high-speed nightmare, its ten-speed continuously variable transmission trying to keep up with the Lincoln's 4.6-liter overhead camshaft V8. Call it 192 horsepower, chasing 302 hp, but that didn't make it hopeless.

Depending on accessories, the SUV weighed close to three tons, not counting its payload of shooters and weapons. The Honda's curb weight was roughly one-third of that, plus Jack's 200 pounds, and he might still catch up to his intended prey—unless one of a hundred things went wrong.

Screw red lights and stop signs. He still had to watch out for cops, drunken drivers, and those who assumed that a green light gave them right-of-way to proceed. At top speed, any random motorist who didn't hit his brake in time could be as deadly as the automatic weapons in the SUV ahead of Jack.

Worse, maybe, since the mass and impact of another auto crashing into the Accord would stop him dead, where bullets stood a decent chance of missing Cody and the Honda's engine block.

As for police—who could be lurking anywhere, down any alleyway or side street—if and when they joined the chase, all bets were off. Cody was under standing orders to avoid contact whenever feasible, but that still left a world of situations where it couldn't be avoided.

Killing cops—at least, the honest ones—was frowned upon at Langley, but he knew the Company and predecessor agencies, had done worse in the past, starting with "Operation Underworld", back in the years of World War Two, through the Iran-Contra cocaine-running fiasco and beyond.

Sara Durell reminded Jack from time to time that cloak-and-dagger people couldn't always work with nice folks in the field, and some of those his government saw fit to tolerate for purposes of national security were assholes, on a par with their committed enemies.

Duvaliers, Somozas, the Saudi royals. Hell, even Saddam Hussein had been a pal when he was killing off Iranians—until, one day, he wasn't anymore.

Same thing with cops, who ran the gamut from heroes to willing servants of the Mafia and drug cartels.

And sometimes they were just roadblocks, requiring swift removal without thinking twice.

Jack hoped it wouldn't come to that tonight. But if it did, he had one job to do and nobody was standing in his way.

"Who is this madman?" asked Achmed Adil Fatah, behind the Lincoln Aviator's steering wheel.

Abdul Karim Qadir glanced at his wing mirror and saw the smaller vehicle still following, closing on them now. "It makes no difference," he said. "The FBI, Homeland Security, local police. In Allah's holy name, will someone *please* get rid of him?"

They hadn't fired upon the chase car yet, hoping the Aviator could outrun the smaller vehicle, but that no longer seemed to be an option on the city's straight, broad streets. The time had clearly come for drastic and decisive action.

Behind Qadir, his soldiers were reacting, recognizing that his question—although phrased politely—was an order. Only two of them, Ziaur Abdolreza and Nasrallah Rahman, had joined in slaying their intended target, but they'd failed to drop his escort at the same time.

Call that glitch a serious mistake.

All four of the commandos ranged behind Qadir were eager to unload on their pursuer now, but simple physics limited the number who could actually fire. Granted, all four could lean from their respective windows, carbines primed, but if they all cut loose together, those hunched in the Aviator's middle row of seats would likely wound or kill the backseat shooters.

Abdul Qadir made his picks. "Sharifullah, Gurid. Dispose of him!"

"Yes, sir," they snapped in unison, and powered down their tinted windows, letting in a rush of warm night air. Gurid Salam leaned out his driver's side window, twisting around to face his left, while Sharifullah Raqib squeezed into a mirror-image firing posture on his side.

That handicapped Raqib, since both men were right-handed, but he was compelled to fire his AKS-74U with his left hand, his dominant eye closed to help him aim. On top of that, the guns ejected spent shells to the right, meaning that Salam's spilled out into the street, Raqib's would leap into his face and fall around him, on the Lincoln's seat and floor.

Bad form, but unavoidable, the very reason why all recruits serving the Flame of Allah members were required to strive for ambidexterity in weapons training. Right arms could be wounded, broken, even blown away—but while a spark of life remained, the Lord's guerrillas were expected to fight on.

The AKs opened up, short bursts, spiking Qadir's eardrums. He clutched his own piece to his chest, wishing that he could join the firefight. Snapped at Fatah, "Faster! Take evasive action."

"Yes, sir. But these streets—"

"No damned excuses! Do as you are told, Achmed!"

Fatah made no reply to that, but bore down on the SUV's accelerator, then whipped through a left-hand turn, eliciting curses from Salim and Raqib as he spoiled their aim.

At this rate, Qadir knew they'd soon attract police, their sirens wailing, blue-and-white lights strobing, calling in for reinforcements: helicopters, SWAT, whatever was on standby.

And he also knew the chase must end before it reached that point, or none of them would live to see another desert sunrise.

Every man inside the Lincoln was prepared to die, freely acknowledged when he joined the ranks of Allah's Flame, but this was not the end Abdul Karim Qadir had pictured for himself.

He still had work to do, and seas of blood to spill.

Jack Cody kept the hammer down, ducked lower in his seat as 5.45×39mm slugs cracked the Honda's windshield, others whipping past and going to either side. The Lincoln's wheelman spared him from that fusillade a moment later, when he veered off to the left and hurtled down a side street, where the halogens were spread farther apart.

Jack followed, checking out his dashboard warning lights. No indication yet that any of the hostile rounds had found their way into the Honda's radiator or beneath its hood.

His Accord, smaller and lighter, cornered somewhat better than the fleeing SUV, but being second in the race meant that his adversaries were already firing once again as Cody revved into the side street.

Their new route was two lanes versus four, a residential street, with other vehicles parked at the curb, aside from those in driveways. At that hour, lights still shone in most houses along the street, no more than one in every six or seven dark, and Cody could imagine startled tenants dialing 911, reporting drive-by gunfire in their upscale neighborhood.

How long before squad responded to those calls?

The nearest precinct house was Metro P.D.'s Spring Valley Command Substation, situated on Eldora Avenue, a long block south of West Sahara, say a mile from where the rolling firefight was in progress. Cody and his enemies were northbound now, pulling away from there, but with prowl cars and motorcycles circulating through the district, cops could show up anytime, from anywhere.

Choppers would take a little longer, even if already on patrol, receiving their directions from headquarters, downtown at 400 South Martin Luther King, Jr. Boulevard, but they could make up any lag time in the air, avoiding ground traffic below.

So many kinds of trouble rushing toward him now, and Cody knew he couldn't fight the whole damned force, along with one carload of terrorists.

No matter how he sliced it, somebody was bound to die within the next few minutes—and Jack didn't want it to be him.

He had too many things to do at once, but none of them could wait.

Steering with his left hand, ducking as far below the dash as he could manage without going blind, Jack drew the larger duffel bag into his lap and pinned it with his left elbow while his right hand opened the zipper. Thankfully, it didn't stick before he splayed the bag, grappled the M4 carbine free at last, and placed it on the shotgun seat beside him, dropping its duffel on the Honda's floorboard.

He couldn't try the M4 yet, but maybe with one of his Glocks...

Drawing the pistol from his right-hip holster, Cody thrust it out the open driver's window, aiming instinctively, unable in that moment to align the fixed polymer combat-type sighting arrangement: a rectangular notch at the rear, ramped front sight with a white dot at the killing end. Its integrated trigger safety meant no switch to be released, only a steady 5.6-pound pressure to send death whistling down range.

And no time like the present.

Cody spent one .40 S&W round to test his aim, then cranked off four in rapid fire.

Achmed Fatah twitched at the Aviator's steering wheel, re-acting to the implosion of the SUV's rear window in a hail of pebbled safety glass. Behind him, all four soldiers ducked for cover, down below their adversary's line of sight, Gurid Salam and Sharifullah Raqib no longer unloading on their enemy.

"Keep firing!" Abdul Qadir shouted at them. "Do your job!"

As if in answer to his words, a bullet passed between Fatah and their commander, shearing off the Lincoln's rearview mirror, dropping it one of the center console's cup holders. This time, it was Qadir's turn to recoil, and Fatah almost smiled at that.

Almost.

"*Ibn al kalb! Kol khara!*" Qadir spat the bitter curses, turning in his seat and triggering a long burst from his AKS carbine through what remained of the rear window. Showing pan-icked eyes, all four gunmen in the rear seats ducked lower to keep from being killed by not-so-friendly fire.

Too late, Abdul appeared to realize that he had kept the rest from firing at their would-be slayer, but he didn't seem to care. "I gave an order!" he reminded them, enraged. "Obey it!"

With no window at the Aviator's rear to block them any longer, Raqib and Salam began firing across the SUV's tail-gate, while Ziaur Abdolreza and Nasrallah Rahman craned from their open windows, joining in the fight. Achmed Fatah drew his Colt Python, placed it in his lap, but had no chance to use it without crashing the Lincoln.

Suddenly, he heard a siren closing in. A moment later, a

Metro Police cruiser appeared in front of them, lights flashing from its roof and grill, turning out of another side street, rushing to meet them head-on.

"*Kess ommak!*" Qadir blurted a vile obscenity, then shouted at Fatah, "Watch out!"

Fatah was well ahead of him for once, swerving the Aviator, scooping up his Python as they raced toward the patrol car, passing within inches of the solitary driver's side. He saw the middle-aged, mustachioed officer with his mouth agape in shock, and fired a Magnum round into that suntanned face before it passed them by.

Fatah's wing mirror showed him when the squad car veered off to the dead or dying driver's right and leaped the curb, churning across a manicured lawn and crashing into a ludicrous pickup truck jacked up on bulbous off-road tires.

"Well done, Achmed," Qadir said, but Fatah felt vaguely ill despite the unaccustomed praise.

It wasn't killing an American lawman, which would have been ridiculous, even pathetic, but his stomach churned as if—

Before he could complete the thought, a bullet ripped into his shoulder from behind and exited below his collar bone, spraying dark blood across the steering wheel and dashboard. Paralyzed by agony, Fatah slumped over and released the wheel. Before Abdul Qadir could lunge across and take control, Fatah's weight on the gas pedal propelled them toward explosive impact with a Kia minivan parked at the right-hand curb.

Jack saw the lone patrolman die and put it out of mind. Tough luck came with the badge. He'd cranked two more Glock rounds into the Lincoln SUV and knew he'd hit somebody when the Aviator swerved and crashed into a van at curbside, stopping dead amidst a rising cloud of radiator steam.

Step one toward evening the score for Fahim Kaldun, lying dead a mile or more behind Jack's present battle site.

How many steps to go?

He saw five bodies spill out of the Aviator, two guys on the street side, three going the other way. A resident opened the nearest home's front door, likely cursing the damage to his minivan pinned in his driveway, then retreated in a rush as one of the gunmen squeezed off an AK burst in his direction.

By that time, Cody was out and crouched behind the Honda's open driver's door, scanning the street through his M4's Close Combat Optic sight. Off to the Lincoln's left, two swarthy guys—one six or seven inches taller than his sidekick—had their SKS carbines leveled from the hip and spitting death his way, but Cody didn't flinch away from it.

Instead, he triggered two bursts—three rounds each, determined by weapons fire selector setting—and he dropped them twitching to the pavement, one half-dead man triggering a final skyward spray before he shivered out and finally lay still.

Two dozen 5.56×45mm NATO remaining in his carbine's magazine, before he had to switch it out.

He scanned across the steaming SUV, noting that no one had emerged yet from the driver's seat. A hit there on the fly, whether the wheelman had been killed or just debilitated, would explain the Lincoln's crash after its occupants picked off the hard luck cop. Cody would have to keep an eye out for the driver when he moved on the remaining three, but for the moment, they comprised the greater threat.

And one of them was breaking toward the house, lurching along as if the crash had thrown him out of joint somehow. Instead of pondering the point, he chased the runner with a three-round burst that brought him down, full metal jacket rounds ripping into his pelvis at 3,100 feet per second, crushing bone and wreaking bloody havoc with his bowels.

Which left two standing in the middle of the yard, one swapping out an empty AK magazine, the other aiming his last rounds at Cody's vehicle. Jack heard the Honda taking hits but didn't worry about where, just then.

Should worse come down to worst, LoJack would bring a team of Company adjustors with a tow truck, possibly a hearse for Cody, and some half-assed explanation that the local yokels would reluctantly accept if they knew what was good for them.

And if not, they'd be duly overruled by someone higher up the food chain, whether by the governor in Carson City, by the DHS in Washington, or by The Man himself.

It was a variation on the motto mouthed by narcotraffickers south of the Rio Grande: *doblar o romper.* In English, that was "bend or break".

Wise words to live or die by, if you were disposed toward giving up your pride.

If not, the only question left was who lay broken, dying, when the smoke cleared.

Abdul Karim Qadir had never felt such pain before and reckoned that he never would again. Successive jolts of agony shot through his lower body, worsened by the swelling of internal bleeding and revolting filth leaking from perforated bowels. His slacks were soaked with blood that managed to escape, their waistline strained by rapid bloating from within.

His legs, by contrast, were entirely numb and paralyzed, presumably from damage to his lower spine. A blessing in disguise, perhaps.

Qadir had lost his carbine when the bullets brought him down. He couldn't see it anywhere, despite a yellow porchlight burning only yards away, casting a jaundiced pall over the yard and crumpled vehicles. He smelled fuel leaking from the Lincoln, from the minivan, or maybe both, and welcomed its intoxicating tang in preference to the rank odors emanating from himself.

A glance back toward the street showed him his killer hurrying to reach him. Qadir rook an eon rolling slightly to one side, teeth clenched against fresh pain, and managed to unholster his Glock 17. He kept it cocked at all times ready at a touch to meet his countless enemies with sudden death.

If only he could manage that tonight.

Before he had a chance to aim, the gunman who had massacred his Vegas team veered off-course, toward the Lincoln SUV, and peered at Achmed Fatah through the driver's window. May have spoken to him, Qadir couldn't say, but obviously got no satisfactory response. He raised a short rifle and fired a single round into Fatah's left temple, punching the final survivor of Qadir's troop over to his right, across the Aviator's console.

Only I remain, Qadir thought, wondering if he should try to kill his enemy, risk falling into law enforcement hands alive, or shove the Glock into his mouth and end it all.

Vengeance carried the tug-of-war.

He rightly guessed that if he failed to slay his murder, the rifleman would finish him. Conversely, if he should succeed, Qadir would still have time and sixteen more 9mm rounds to end his own life before officers surrounded him.

It struck him as what the Americans would call a win-win situation.

Or, looked at another way, he had already lost, but had at least fulfilled his final mission by eliminating Fahim Rafa ibn Kaldun, traitor to the will of God, embodied in the principles of Allah's Flame.

Behind him, near the SUV, his enemy called out, "You feel like talking, Pal? Or should we just cut to the chase?"

The gut-shot terrorist rolled over with a pistol showing in his hand. Cody could see and hear how much toe movement cost him, from the grimace on his sweaty face, a stifled cry of pain. He smelled it, too. No point in calling for an ER diagnosis to decide the guy was dying from a combination of blood loss, encroaching shock, and septicemia waiting around the corner, for a triple whammy.

Jack supposed an airlift to a first-class trauma center *might* have saved him, but it wasn't in his stars. The prick had rolled snake eyes and crapped out—literally, in this case. For all intents and purposes, he was already dead and likely knew it.

But that didn't render him innocuous, by any means.

A dying viper can inject a lethal dose of venom into any fool who makes a grab for it, and maybe drift off smiling to Snake Heaven. This two-legged serpent held a Glock in his right hand, not steadily, but if he started cranking rounds in rapid fire, he might get lucky with a slug or two.

Best not to take the chance.

"Okay," Jack said, "if that's your choice." And fired a 5.56mm round into his chest from twenty feet.

It didn't kill him outright, missed his heart on purpose, but ripped through a lung and left him blowing crimson bubbles that ran down his chin and cheeks after they burst. Cody stepped in and kicked his Glock away, then crouched beside him, knowing he had only moments left before the Grim Reaper and Metro P.D. turned up on the scene.

"You want to help me out?" he asked, not hopefully. "Tell me your end game and the name of who's pulling your strings."

The dying shooter muttered something wet, incomprehensible, despite the fact that Cody spoke passable Arabic.

"Right, then," he said, and started going through the shooter's pockets while the light of life faded from dark, expressive eyes. He came up with a billfold on his second try, opened it, pocketing the cash—because, why not?—and found a Texas driver's license in the name Habib ur Manaf, with a Houston address and phone number.

Leaving the mess to Metro dicks, he jogged back to the Honda, found it drivable, and put some ground between himself and ground zero. Two miles away, he pulled into a shopping mall's vast parking lot and left the motor running while he removed an Iridium GO!⃟ roam phone from a pocket of his windbreaker and dialed his current contact number for Sara Durell.

The call was sensitive, but safe. Iridium furnished the first-ever reliable worldwide connection for direct conversations and texting, funded by a flat monthly fee with now erratic, exorbitant roaming charges. Better yet, it was untraceable, each call he placed routed through multiple accounts in fourteen countries on four continents. A built-in scrambler meshed with Sara's when she picked up on the second ring, providing more assurance of security.

"Tell me," she said, without preamble.

Jack wasted no time on niceties, spared her the euphemisms. "I got to Kaldun ahead of anybody else," he said, but shooters jumped us on our way to stash him in a safe house. First shot took him out. The guys who wasted him are all done, now. Nothing to say before the end, but I retrieved a Lone Star driver's license, out of Houston."

"Info," she directed him.

Cody gave her the dead guy's name, assuming it to be an

alias, along with his address, no way of telling from Las Vegas whether it was solid or a vacant lot in some grim barrio. He didn't know if Sara memorized the information, or was jotting it down as he spoke, and didn't care.

"I'll check it out and call you back," she told him.

"Roger that. I'll drop the car in long-term parking at Mc-Carran."

Jack severed the link, their call too brief to trace, even if that had been an option with his round-the-world leapfrog defense in place. Cody hadn't unpacked his go bag since arriving in Las Vegas, and a walkaround assured him that the Honda's battle scars weren't obvious enough to raise a flag immediately, when he rolled into the airport sometime in the next half-hour.

As to fingerprints and other CSI-related clues, forget about it. Cody's record had been wiped clean when he said good-bye to Delta Force and shifted over to the Company. The data mining tools at Langley were extremely thorough, scrubbing out his former military records (classified and otherwise), along with any law enforcement run-ins (nothing but some parking fines that dated back more than a decade).

Once he was erased, it was as if Jack Cody never had existed. From his birth record, medical files scattered around the country and the world, civilian driver's license and employment records, even the Social Security number he'd secured for his first summer job in junior high school: all vanished in the fog of covert war.

It was as if he'd never lived at all.

Some of his enemies, if they'd been breathing now, would doubtless wish he never had.

And more still waited for him, fifteen hundred miles to the southwest, beside the Gulf of Mexico. Whatever they were planning for America and for the world at large, a storm was bearing down upon them.

And they didn't even know it yet.

CHAPTER 4

McCarran International Airport

It seemed like Jack had barely left the airport since arriving—and in human terms, he had. Five lives had ended on his Vegas visit, bodies in the county morgue by now or on their way.

He wondered for a second, give or take, if any of the newly dead had found their way to vestal virgin Paradise. Decided that he didn't care and dropped his Honda in a fairly full aisle of McCarran's long-term parking lot. Stood waiting for a shuttle that made circuits every fifteen minutes and rode back to the Departures terminal.

No time for comparison shopping tonight. Jack charged a $99 one-way ticket to Houston via Spirit Airlines—a new one for Cody—and got in under the wire for their equivalent of the Vegas red-eye express, predicting two hours and fifty-seven minutes in the air, nonstop.

On check-in, Cody used a different I.D. than he'd employed on takeoff from St. Louis. It was probably unnecessary, but why not? His plastic from the Company was "corporate", and hadn't raised an eyebrow yet, no matter where on Earth he slapped it down.

Hungry despite himself, Jack found McCarran's food court and tried something called Baja Fresh Express to get him in the Tex-Mex mood. A sign touted its meals as "BIG, FRESH, and DELICIOUS!", which in fact turned out to be exactly right. With time to spare before takeoff, Jack ordered two "Dos Manos" burritos, one chicken, one pork carnitas, and enjoyed them both thoroughly, beans on the side, all washed down with Corona.

He reached Spirit's departure lounge with thirty minutes left to spare and left the paperbacks he'd purchased in Missouri zipped inside his carry-on. Jack planned on sleeping through the flight, no worries about dozing off, in spite of what he'd just been through or what—if anything—was waiting for him at the other end.

Houston could be a washout or a blowout, either way. The dead assassin's "Habib ur Manaf" I.D. was almost certainly bogus, and even if the name proved accurate, Jack put no faith in the listed address. He'd check it out, though, as he felt obliged to for the mission's sake, and if it left him flat, he would rely on Sara to uncover something he could use.

And failing that, like 60-odd percent of tourists who spent any length of time in Vegas, he would be shit out of luck.

While he was thinking of it, waiting for his boarding call, Jack texted Sara with his Houston wish list, trusting her to pass the word along, have decent wheels and hardware waiting for him when he landed.

Although he'd never visited the premises, Jack knew the Company's office was located on Allen Parkway, in a building called the America Tower—not "American", mind you—its forty-two floors rising 590 feet above street level, making in the city's nineteenth-tallest structure. The tower, in turn, was part of the American General Center complex, situated in a part of west-central Houston that locals called "Neartown".

Near what? Already bored with the geography, Jack thought instead about the hubbub that his text to Sara would create.

As soon as she reached out to Allen Parkway, men and women Jack had never met would be in motion, lining up a "cold" car and supply of "colder" weapons to at least approximate Cody's requests. The office would be busier than the Las Vegas outpost on a normal day, adjacent to the Port of Houston—America's busiest port in terms of foreign tonnage, second-busiest in overall tonnage, the sixteenth-busiest on Earth—with its staff and assets on constant alert for internal and external threats.

And if that all turned out to be a mere coincidence...then, what?

Then, squat.

Jack was the sharp end of a dedicated covert lance. Without solid intel, he'd have no target, and the whole trip would be a colossal waste of time.

The only way for him to check that out was on the ground.

Baitul Al-Sadiq mosque, Houston

"Wiped out?" Talal Wahid ibn Ataullah was unable to conceal his shock. "How is that possible? The FBI? Police?"

"Not local law enforcement," Abbas Abdul al-Rasheed Maarku replied to his lieutenant. "They are now involved, of course, together with a host of federals: the ATF and FBI, Homeland Security."

"Who sends this word, sir?"

"Ah. The cell was not annihilated altogether," Maarku said. "Abdul Qadir led five of our men to eliminate the spy and traitor to Allah, Fahim Kaldun. Those six are dead, but two men from the cell were left behind, both presently at liberty. One of them called me from Las Vegas with the news."

"Are they returning here, sir?"

Maarku nodded. "If they aren't arrested first. I've ordered them to travel separately, one through Phoenix, and the other via Albuquerque."

"Is there no suggestion how they were discovered?"

"The survivor couldn't say. He only knows that Qadir and the rest seemed confident, but now they're in the morgue, awaiting autopsies."

"Disgraceful!" Talal fairly spat the word.

Islam discouraged autopsies, preferring a swift burial whenever possible, except in cases of suspicious death, where the proximate cause is deemed equivocal.

"Our laws do not protect us here," Maarku reminded his

subordinate. "We have no contacts on the Metropolitan Police Department there, but it appears there is confusion about who attacked our men."

"And all of them were shot?" Ataullah asked.

"Apparently. Perhaps, if there were any true believers at the medical examiner's department...but approaching someone there presents too great a risk. We must be vigilant, guard against subversion of our plans in progress."

"I will see to it myself," Ataullah said.

"I would expect no less," Maarku replied, stating the obvious.

"If there is interference..."

"We shall be prepared for anything, as usual, Talal, with nothing left to chance."

"Just as you say."

"Our lives mean nothing, beyond service to the cause. Destruction of our enemies."

"*Allāhu akba!*" Ataullah replied.

"Indeed. From this point forward, make sure all our warriors are prepared for action at a moment's notice."

"As you say, sir."

"They must be discreet, of course, without drawing attention to themselves in any way, until swift action is required."

"I understand," Talal affirmed.

"Upon the day, nothing must be allowed to halt Allah's ferocious stroke against our enemies."

"And nothing will, sir."

"See that it does not." Maarku waved for his second-in-command to leave the office, waiting silently until the door closed and sealed him into solitude.

It would not do for his subordinates to recognize Abbas Maarku's level of personal concern at the Nevada massacre. He did not grieve the dead, assuming that they must have been responsible, at least to some extent, by letting down their guard when it was most important to remain alert.

But if their sloth had jeopardized The Day...

Seething with rage and apprehension, Maarku made a silent, solemn vow that he would not allow the master plan to fail.

George Bush Intercontinental Airport, Houston

It's easy to get lost at George Bush Intercontinental, sprawling across ten thousand acres, twenty-three miles north of Downtown Houston. The facility includes five domestic terminals plus an international arrivals building, all connected by a Skyway transit system, processing 44 million passengers in 2018. Five runways host thirty-three scheduled airlines and a nonstop flow of private charter flights.

Jack Cody counted on the crowd to cover his arrival.

Many travelers supposed the airport had been named for George W. Bush, forty-sixth governor of Texas and forty-third U.S. president, but they were wrong. In fact, the name was lifted from his late dad, George H. W. Bush, eleventh Director of Central Intelligence and forty-first president, whose name also graced CIA headquarters at Langley, Virginia.

Those Bushes got around, although Junior's international travels were somewhat restricted. In May 2012 the Kuala Lumpur War Crimes Commission convicted him and seven key administration members in absentia, for illegally invading Iraq nine years earlier and triggering war without end. Fellow defendants included Vice President Dick Cheney, ex-Secretary of Defense Donald Rumsfeld, and their legal advisers: Attorney General Alberto Gonzales (who deemed the Geneva Convention "quaint", David Addington, William Haynes, Jay Bybee and John Yoo.

The panel recommended extradition to Europe, but that went nowhere.

Funny old world. At least the eight were wise enough to steer clear of Malaysia.

Cody's flight touched down five minutes late, due to headwinds, and was among the last deplaning passengers, merging at an amble with the human horde that offered fair cover.

Airport security was split between the feds and Harris County. The TSA screened passengers, their baggage, and maintained surveillance over aircraft, while the rest fell to the Metropolitan Transit Authority's police department, its 190 sworn officers thin on the ground, covering all METRO facilities supported by a general sales and use tax, spanning 1,285 square miles.

As at McCarran, Jack bypassed the standard rental agencies and made his way outside, walking into a replay of the vehicle handoff in Vegas. This time out, the greeter was a blonde woman, say early thirties. Her companion, standing by the second car, was male and fortyish, crewcut, who looked like he chewed broken glass instead of gum.

Greetings exchanged, sans any names, Jack looked over the car reserved for him this time. It was a black Subaru Legacy, the mid-size, four-door 2.5i Premium model. Its hood concealed a 2.5-liter flat-four FB25 engine, generating 113 horsepower, for a top speed of 137 miles per hour. A continuously variable transmission (CTV) took the worries out of shifting if Jack was confronted with another chase.

Beyond its basics, the Legacy was a minor automotive miracle of sorts, including an 11.6-inch touchscreen controlling all trims, plus a facial-recognition system using cameras to warn a driver if the system detected distraction, fatigue, or disabling injury. To that, add Subaru's side monitoring system, incorporating Blind Spot Alert, Lane Change Assist, and Cross-Traffic Alert functions.

Say what?

That meant an amber light located in the respective sideview mirror burned steadily if another vehicle was detected in the blind spot or was approaching fast enough to interfere with a lane change. The same light flashed, with an audible alert, if the driver indicated a lane change or backed out of a parking space with any object approaching.

But that wasn't the end of the Legacy's techno-magic. It also came equipped with Subaru's EyeSight system, using twin windshield-mounted CCD cameras—charge-coupled devices—to simulate stereoscopic vision and monitor roadways, reacting to driving conditions and helping avert collisions. The Adaptive Cruise Control function senses the speed and pace of vehicles ahead, automatically adjusting the Legacy's speed to maintain one of four user-selectable gaps in traffic.

Meanwhile, Pre-Collision Braking used the same two cameras to monitor activity of vehicles ahead, alerting the Legacy's driver visually and audibly. If the driver failed to react, more alerts sounded, and the car would actively brake itself.

Presto!

Beyond the safety features, once they found some privacy, Cody went trunk-diving and tallied the aggressive hardware. This time out, the Company had found a Steyr AUG for him, with loaded mags and the usual 22mm rifle grenades. Add a matched pair of Glock 22s, one's muzzle extended and thread-ed to accept an Osprey sound suppressor, seven inches long, rectangular and flattened on the side rather than tubular, constructed from aluminum and stainless steel, boosting the loaded pistol's weight from 34.38 ounces to 45.18.

Contrary to Hollywood's FX fantasies, suppressors are not "silencers", and they don't work at all on revolvers, where sound and gas particles escape on all sides of the cylinder. Sound registers in decibels, with your average vacuum clean-er generating 70 decibels and a garbage disposal about 180. Eardrum pain begins around 125 dB, with potential damage impending beyond 140.

A standard .40 S&W round produces 156.5 dB, reduced by the Osprey suppressor to 130 —but silent? No freaking way.

At best, the tool reduced sound, further muffled if a shot was fired indoors or with accompanying background noise.

Still, it was better than nothing. And Cody would take all the edge he could get.

"Know where you're going?" asked the blonde.

"All set," Jack said. "It's LoJacked, I presume?"

"No worries there. Good luck."

And that was it. He climbed behind the Legend's steering wheel and went hunting.

George Bush Center for Intelligence; Langley, Virginia

"Still nothing?" asked Denham Boyd, White House liaison to the Company project whose files were buried deeper than a shipwreck in the Mariana Trench.

Sara Durell replied, "Only what Jack picked up in Vegas."

"So, a phony name and address."

"We don't know about the address yet."

Boyd nearly smirked at that. "You think a hitman for the Flame of Allah—maybe a cell leader—would be honest with the Texas DMV."

"I gave up reading minds, Denham."

"Which means you don't know what your boy is thinking."

"Our boy. Or has that slipped *your* mind?"

"Nope. He's good. We both know that. But I still haven't seen him work a miracle."

"I have," Sara replied. "He does it every day, just waking up alive after the shit we put him through."

"No need to make it personal, Sara."

"I haven't," she told Boyd. "Cody's a weapon in a war. That's all."

Not strictly true, of course. She liked to think that they were friends, at least, within the limits of their two respective jobs and marching orders. Sara was Jack's superior inside the Company, his handler, and a decorated warrior in her own right, prior to signing on with Langley.

Still...

They'd definitely had "a moment" some time back, during their first mission together. She'd still been on top—logistically and, briefly, physically, when she had *really* handled him—but personal attachments could be hazardous in covert life.

A kiss sometimes turned out to be a kiss of death, in fact.

"Excuse me?" Boyd's voice cut into her fleeting private thoughts. "I asked you—"

"What he plans to do in Houston," Sara cut off his complaint. "I heard you. Do you want a thoughtful answer, or should I just blow some smoke?"

"Best guess, at least."

"It's not a guess. Soon as he lands, he'll go to check the address from this driver's license for this stiff who called himself Habib ur Manaf."

"No such name in any of our data banks," Boyd interjected.

"And that's no surprise. You know as well as I do, the jihadists like to use 'war names' once they're inducted. Some groups make it mandatory. Osama's people called him 'Prince.' 'Emir,' 'Sheik al-Mujahid,' sometimes the 'Lion Sheik'—the list goes on and on. Inside his family some called him 'Abū 'Abdāllāh,' which means—"

"The father of Abdāllāh. Yeah, we both took the same classes, but I'm talking here and now, Sara."

"Which should be *there* and *soon*. Jack's flight should land in Houston sometime in the next—" she checked the government wall clock and finished up—"thirteen to fifteen minutes."

"And you've got people waiting for him," Boyd said. Not a question.

"Bringing him supplies. Not tailing him."

"In this case, maybe we should—"

"What?" she challenged him. "Tell them to tag along with Jack and slow him down, or maybe get him killed through inexperience. If you want *them* dead, put the contract out yourself, and leave Jack out of it. If you want *him* dead—"

"No one's saying that, for Christ's sake!"

"Then, you can't be second-guessing him from the West Wing. Nobody over there can do what he does. That's why Jack exists. That's why I'm here and listening to you, instead of checking with the field."

"Nobody's irreplaceable, Sara."

She met Boyd's eyes and said, "The voters prove that, every four to eight years. Which tells me you're on borrowed time."

He sighed and said, "Sounds like my cue to get out of your hair."

"It's not the worst idea you ever had."

"But stay in touch, dammit!"

"When have I ever not?"

Boyd left her wondering if their exchange would mean a curt notation in her dossier, even a formal reprimand for insubordination, then Sara decided that she didn't care. If she wore out her welcome with the Company, experience assured her there were far worse things than being canned.

Losing some jobs, in fact, might come as a relief.

She had her military pension, partial disability, although no one could ever guess that just from watching her at work. The scars she carried as reminders of her service to America were hidden under fabric.

Still, if she *were* fired and frozen out, Sara knew what she'd miss the most.

That would be touching base with Cody, guiding his pursuit of mortal danger in benighted hellholes all around the world.

And worse: if Sara gave up that official contact, she would never know if Jack was still alive or had been killed in Africa or Eastern Europe, Asia or Latin America—wherever bodies dropped and were forgotten, even as they hit the ground.

Houston

The drive from George Bush Intercontinental to the Braeburn neighborhood, in Southwest Houston, was approximately thirty-four miles over surface streets, with travel time severely underestimated at a wishful-thinking forty minutes if you checked online. Whoever made that guesstimate must have been thinking of deserted, post-apocalyptic streets like those depicted in *The Walking Dead*.

It took Jack closer to an hour in his Subaru, giving him ample time to test the Legacy's various automatic safety features against other cars driven by numskulls talking on their cell phones—even texting, if you could believe it—touching up mascara in their rearview mirrors, and in one case, getting head from a young not-so-hottie who popped into view beside her porky boyfriend when her work was done.

People. Sometimes, Cody wondered why he bothered saving them at all, but then he'd run across a happy, loving family or some kid with a long, bright future still ahead of him/her, and he didn't have to ask.

On other days, he thought that soldiering had always been his destiny.

Braeburn was situated on the north bank of Brays Bayou and immediately east of Interstate 69, aka the Southwest Freeway. Its only claim to fame, as far as Jack could tell, was the discovery of a fossilized giant armadillo, found on the bayou and now on display at the Houston Museum of Natural Science.

Frozen in stone for hundreds of millennia, it likely still moved faster than some of the shoppers he'd been stuck behind at Walmart on weekends.

The house he sought—if it existed—was supposed to be on

Reamer Street, within a subdivision called Braes Timbers. The homes he passed weren't mansions, nowhere that an oilman would kick off his hand-tooled boots and hang up his ten-gallon hat—but they seemed decent from the curb, starting around a quarter-million dollars if you planned on moving in.

Jack rolled along the street, eastbound and checking numbers, fitting with the neighborhood behind the wheel of his Subaru Legacy. He was a bit surprised to find the address he was looking for, but that proved nothing. Someone could have picked it from a street map or the telephone directory and scrawled it on a driver's license at the DMV when they had never even glimpsed the place.

Jack slowed on the drive-by, checking it out. Dark windows, nothing in the driveway leading to a double-car garage. No rolled-up newspapers scattered around the lawn, no backed-up mail protruding from the brass post box wall-mounted to the left of the front door.

Vacant? Or had its occupant(s) gone off to Vegas for a while?

If it was long-term empty, Jack would have expected a "FOR SALE" sign in the yard, with an attachment reading "SOLD" if someone took the bait.

No sign told Cody it was occupied or had been until recently. Beyond that supposition, there was nothing he could find out from his seat inside the Subaru.

He drove on past the empty driveway. Parking there would only spur some nosy neighbor to report him, speed-dialing

Houston P.D. Instead, he drove around the block, parked in an alley lined with garbage cans, and went in through the back, scaling a redwood fence after he'd peered over the top and whistled softly for watchdogs, arousing none.

Five seconds later, he was in the backyard, with his muzzle-heavy, muffled Glock in hand.

CHAPTER 5

Cody was right: no dogs. The backdoor wasn't any kind of challenge, either, once he'd checked around it for alarms. It opened on a kitchen smelling of falafel, curry, and lokma—deep-fried balls of dough sweetened with cinnamon and honey for dessert. Jack checked the dishwasher. Found plates, glasses and silverware still waiting to be cleaned from days ago.

Because the tenants were in Vegas, busy being killed?

Leaving the kitchen, he proceeded to a dining room, six straight-backed chairs around its table, nothing in the way of decoration on its walls except the kind of nudie calendar you might expect to find in a commercial garage somewhere, so out of place it made Jack do a doubletake. The women on display plainly weren't vestal virgins, but perhaps their ample charms inspired jihadists while they waited for their one-way ticket to *Jannah*.

There was a sideboard, but its drawers and lower cabinets

were empty, not so much as a stray spoon or saucer to suggest that it was ever put to any use. Cody moved on, creeping the house, using a penlight and avoiding windows as he went. No point in rousing curiosity among the empty home's neighbors, prompting them to phone the cops.

His search had three main focal points. First, anything that might confirm Habib ur Manaf as the Vegas corpse's name, or offer up a viable alternative I.D. Second, find out if "Manaf" had resided here alone, or if any other members of his cell had been his roommates. Finally, seek anything, however tenuous, that might enlighten Cody to their plans.

Leaving the dining room, he stepped into a parlor that, from all appearances, was rarely used. Its furnishings included two wing chairs, a sofa, coffee table, and a Samsung QLED flat screen television mounted on the wall above a faux fireplace, electric, more for show than heating up the room. The seating didn't help determine how many persons had occupied the house at any given time, but Cody checked beneath the cushions anyway, leaving some loose change where it lay.

So far, he'd found no landline telephones, which meant no tracing any calls made to or from the house. Whoever had spent time there must use cell phones, likely burners meant to be disposable, long since dismantled and discarded.

Five rooms left: three bedrooms and two baths.

The first bedroom had been converted to an office, with a cheap desk shoved into one corner and a swivel chair on wheels tucked into the knee well. Again, no phone, no sign of a computer he'd been hoping to discover on the desktop.

Rifling through the desk's drawers, Jack came up with half a dozen pens, two pencils, paperclips, and a yellow notepad of the variety that lawyers often lugged around. He riffled through its blank pages, then used one of the pencils on its top sheet, hoping for impressions from a torn-off message.

Squat.

He checked the room's en suite: a shower, sink and toilet, all reasonably clean. The mirror opened to reveal a shallow medicine cabinet, nothing in there but a bottle of Bayer aspirin and a half-tube of Anusol cream.

Someone had piles, but if the tenant had a monkey on his back, he'd taken all the goodies with him when he left.

The two remaining bedrooms had been furnished to fulfill their normal purpose, any occupants required to share a bathroom down the hall. Jack checked the bathroom first, found a Gillette disposable razor beside the sink's hot-water handle and a bar of soap with two hairs clinging to it, in the tub. He thought about preserving them for DNA, then thought about the odds of an Islamic terrorist appearing in some database, and let it pass.

The medicine cabinet turned out to be another bust: a second razor, unused, and a Pepto-Bismol bottle that appeared as if it had come over on the *Mayflower*.

That left the bedrooms, one housing a double bed, a single in the other, both with smallish dressers from some big-box store where quality matched price. He took the larger bedroom first, scanned empty dresser drawers, an empty closet with a vacant shelf, then checked under the bed before he stripped its sheets and blanket, tipped the mattress off, and shucked the pillowcases.

All in vain.

Next-door, rinse and repeat. No landlines anywhere, and while Jack thought of fingerprints, he had no tools that might preserve them, and slim hope that any ones he found would turn out to be traceable.

It was a bust.

He was about to clear out, when he heard a key turn in the front door's lock.

"I still think this is all a waste of time," Rifa'a el-Haykal said.

"*Still* think it?" Lutfur Abu Uzza answered in a mocking tone. "I don't recall you saying that to Talal, when he gave the order."

Rifa'a made a sour face at that. Said, "I'm entitled to my own opinion."

"I agreed. In fact, why don't you call him now, and see if he will change his mind?"

"To what end, Lutfur? We're here, now."

"Exactly. Stop complaining, then, and let's get on with it."

All three of them—Uzza, el-Haykal, and Hussein bin Al Nahyan—carried pistols but did not expect to need them. They had been assigned to make a sweep of Abdul Qadir's now-empty house, searching for any small, incriminating clues against the time—perhaps soon, now—when lawmen in Nevada would see through his false Texas I.D. as "Habib ur Manaf".

With any luck, he'd left nothing behind. But as a last resort, if they had any doubts, Talal Ataullah had approved destruction of the house by fire. That call belonged to cleanup detail leader Lutfur Uzza, who had stopped en route to fill three plastic cans with gasoline, five gallons each.

Enough to raze this property and rob the filthy Christian landlord of his loot, *'ashad allah*.

Lutfur Uzza still had no details about how Qadir's Las Vegas cell had come to grief beyond the basics: sent to kill an *imam* thought to be informing for the FBI, successful on that count, then decimated by an unknown enemy who might be following their trail to Houston, seeking to disrupt the scheduled Day of Fire.

Which effort must be foiled at any cost.

Like every other Flame of Allah member, Uzza was prepared to die—would welcome it, in fact, believing that his sacrifice would be amply rewarded in the afterlife. Whenever he had any fleeting doubts, Uzza suppressed them with the thought that, if he'd been mistaken all these years, his life had been a bloody, tragic waste.

That prospect was unbearable, and therefore, obviously false.

If only Christian zealots could have seen the One Truth, as Uzza himself had done.

Sadly, they clung to false "truth" of their own, and therefore must be slaughtered.

"Be ready," Uzza warned his comrades, drawing his Beretta M9 pistol with his right hand, while his left applied the front door's key to both locks, knob first, then the dead bolt.

"If police were here, we'd see their cars," Hussein bin Al Nahyan said.

"Only if they desired you to," Uzza replied. "Did you not know Houston police were famous for their 'pop-up' squads, hiding in shops and wealthy homes to murder would-be burglars?"

"How do you know that?" Rifa'a el-Haykal challenged him.

"It is the sort of information hidden inside books," Uzza replied. "Try reading one, sometime."

"The only book I read is the *Quran*, Lutfur."

"Indeed? And what did Isa have to say about liars in the *Injīl*, Rifa'a?"

"He was against them, naturally."

"As I thought. You'll doubtless be promoted to the rank of Grand Mufti, after the Day of Flame."

El-Haykal muttered something underneath his breath that sounded very much like *al'ahmaq*—asshole, in Arabic.

"I missed that, Rifa'a." Uzza half turned, holding the Beretta. "Please repeat it, will you?"

"I said nothing," Rifa'a lied.

"So, then, may we proceed?"

"Just as you say."

Jack Cody switched his penlight off and stowed it in a pocket, raising his Glock with the Osprey sound suppressor in a firm, two-handed grip.

He didn't know who was arriving—maybe the police,

maybe some of the dead guy's cronies—and being in the rear bedroom, he'd missed a car when it pulled into the driveway. He couldn't check it now, but peering through the bedroom's doorway, saw no squad car flashers showing through the front room's distant windows.

Still could be official callers, following a lead from Vegas, but he dropped that thought when the latecomers switched on flashlight beams instead of going with the overheads.

Not cops, then, since they wouldn't try to hide their presence in a dead terrorist's home from nosy neighbors.

Someone else.

One of the prowlers spoke in Arabic, another answering in kind, both male, meaning a minimum of two.

One said, "We start in here. Be thorough. Overlook nothing."

"As if we would," the other answered, sounding peevish.

Dissidence among the goons was always good. It meant fault lines behind a unified façade.

A third man's voice chimed in. "Can we just concentrate and stop the bickering?"

The second voice, nearly a whine, replied, "I didn't start it."

Jack's options now: surprise them, double-tap each one as opportunity allowed, and search their bodies for whatever pockets or their car outside might yield; or try to cover them and make at least one of them spill his guts—the verbal way, not literally.

He could compromise between the two ideas, pop out and kill two of the three, but that risked being stuck with one who knew little or nothing about any plan the Flame of Allah might have in the works. Jack knew the outfit's top man, or his second-in-command, wouldn't have tagged along to carry out an errand better delegated to subordinates.

He flipped a mental coin, asking Fate for a hint as to which direction he should choose. It came up heads, which was his cue to talk first, then start killing.

Cody's language skills included fluent Arabic, acquired during his tours of duty in the sand, plus passable Russian and Spanish. He'd thought about going Rosetta Stone on some Chinese, but hadn't made his mind up so far, between Mandarin and Cantonese.

After tonight, that might be moot.

He watched the late-arriving trio start to search their dead pal's living room, hitting the same points Jack had, but also drawing knives and slashing open cushions on the furniture. One guy scooped up the coins Cody had left beneath the sofa cushions, stuffing them into a pocket of his blue jeans.

None had pistols in their hands when Cody spoke from darkness, using their own lights to mark his prey.

"'Ant matakhir," he cautioned them. "You're late."

Hussein bin Al Nahyan froze where he stood, his switchblade halfway through the act of disemboweling a wing chair's cushion. Neither he nor either of his two companions raised their flashlight beams to find the man who's spoken, but Nahyan's first thought was that someone from headquarters had hurried on ahead of them, to see how well they carried out their orders.

When he spoke, it was instinctive, a mistake he recognized almost before the single word escaped his lips.

"Talal?"

"Strike one," the phantom voice replied from darkness. "You boys just stand easy, now."

Time froze, five seconds seeming to drag out interminably. Off to Nahyan's right, Lutfur Uzza was bent over the other easy chair. Rifa'a el-Haykal, four or five yards to Nahyan's left, literally had his hand full with the sofa's mutilated cushions.

"Who is that?" Uzza asked the deep shadows of a hallway leading back into the house. He still spoke Arabic, as had the unseen interloper.

"I'm the guy who'd like to let you live," the disembodied voice replied, "if we can all just get along."

"*Eurif nafsak*," Uzza called out. "Explain yourself."

"Simple," the reply came back. "I need some information. Give it up, and you can walk away like nothing ever happened here. *La darar, wala darar.*"

"No harm, no foul?" Uzza translated, speaking English now. Nahyan knew their crew chief was stalling, trying to judge distance and direction in the dark.

"English suits me," the faceless stranger said, "as long as you're all hearing me the same."

"We speak it," Lutfur Uzza said.

"Great. Then you've heard my offer. What's your answer, fellas?"

"We must talk about it," Uzza answered.

"Fine. Out loud, so I don't miss a syllable. And make it

quick. My trigger finger starts to twitch after a little while."

Uzza straightened, as if stretching his back, and glanced toward where Hussein's and Rifa'a's flashlight beams still focused on the furniture they'd been examining. Their leader rolled his shoulders, then, without a hint of warning, hurled his Fairbairn–Sykes dagger into the darkness, toward what he presumed to be the voice's point of origin.

A muffled gunshot, like a leopard coughing, sounded with the fighting knife still airborne. Nahyan raised his flashlight beam in time to see a keyhole open in Uzza's forehead, releasing crimson spray as he fell over backwards, sprawling on the parlor carpeting.

And that left two.

Cody had rolled the dice and lost, but he'd still slashed the hostile odds by 33 percent. The two survivors, clearly not inclined to squeal, had dropped their blades and flashlights, digging under loose shirttails for sidearms as the living room went dark again.

Jack fired his second .40-caliber toward where he'd seen the nearest prowler last. A grunt rewarded him, as if he'd winged the guy but definitely hadn't ended him. With any luck—something in short supply right now—maybe the Arab's shooting arm was wounded, and he couldn't manage with the other one.

Dream on.

The third guy had his pistol clear, firing a wasted double-tap that sounded like 9mm Parabellum rounds. They smacked into a stucco wall, eight feet or so to Cody's right, the far side of the corridor where he was crouching now and triggering his third round toward the afterimage of his adversary's muzzle flash.

No joy, unless he'd drilled the guy and dropped him silently—about as likely in the present circumstances as a hole-in-one during the Scottish Open, the Old Course at Saint Andrews.

Cody ducked lower as two pistols fired back at him, blowing his hopeful theory of one gunman with a crippled arm. There was no question, now, of taking either one alive for grilling. The Osprey on Cody's Glock would likely mask his shots from any Reamer Street neighbors, but they could doubtless hear the other weapons loud and clear. That meant calls to the cop shop, frightened taxpayers demanding service right the hell now, some of them likely reminding the dispatcher that they personally paid his or her salary.

A neighborhood like this one, street patrols would be anxious to please, and maybe see some action that would normally elude them on the softer side of Houston.

Time to step up Cody's game.

Instead of ducking back deeper into the house, he wriggled toward his enemies, elbows and knees propelling him. He tried to do it without making any noise, assisted in that effort with more random hostile shots, until a harsh voice cut it short.

"*Waqf 'iitlaq alnaar!*" the man called out. In English: "Stop firing!"

Jack knew the guy wasn't addressing him, but he stopped crawling, waited out the momentary silence, picking up on shadows and involuntary shuffling sounds as his two would-be killers tried to shift positions, maybe working up their nerve to rush him in the corridor.

But Jack was wrong.

Instead of charging, the surviving prowlers tried to beat feet toward the front door and escape. Starting, they had a fifty-fifty chance of making it, until a car passed by outside, its headlights, briefly shining through the living room window's think drapes.

For just a second there, Cody had both of them in silhouette and didn't waste the opportunity.

Pop-pop! Two up, two down.

He rose and drew his penlight, closed the gap and kicked their guns beyond the reach of twitching hands. One more round each to settle them, first through the smaller man's left eye, then close behind the taller one's right ear, scrambling their brains.

He frisked them swiftly, ears perked for the cry of sirens homing in, and pocketed two wallets, their cell phones, plus a roll of greenbacks from a pocket of the last to die. Backtracking to the first man he'd put down Cody retrieved another billfold and cell phone. He could examine them at leisure, once he'd cleared the premises and didn't have to worry about cops.

Cody left the house the same way he'd gone in, retreating through the kitchen, out across the backyard with no watchdog, over the redwood fence and gone.

Back inside the Subaru, he popped open the console's lid, between the Legacy's front seats, and stashed his loot. Between wallets and cells, he hoped to get a look into the dead men's former lives, associations—and, of top importance, any indicators of their future plans.

He couldn't hope to find a helpful roster headed "Flame of Allah Plotters", but if there was something, anything, that he could work with or, in the alternative, pass on to Langley's techs, it couldn't hurt.

Conversely, failure could turn out to be extremely painful—no, make that deadly—for anybody on the damned jihadist target list. And with the Flame of Allah's record for preferring wholesale slaughter, wielding any tools of mass destruction they could purchase, steal, or fabricate from scratch, it was a safe bet that they wouldn't settle for a single mark.

So far, in its brief documented history, the group had never gone for penny-ante bets. Its leaders *always* raised, and ultimately went all-in.

What would it be this time? What would it mean to Houston, or wherever the fanatics might be headed next, if Texas was their staging area?

Cody still didn't have a clue, but he could count on two things.

It would be apocalyptic.

And no one who managed to survive it would ever forget the day they nearly died.

CHAPTER 6

Greater Eastwood district, Houston

Colonel Vadim Aleksándrovich Yezhóv loathed being summoned by anyone, much less a renegade terrorist asset, but certain times dictated that he swallow pride and keep the heathens pacified.

At least, until they had fulfilled his purposes.

The Greater Eastwood neighborhood lies in Houston's East End, between Interstate 45 and Harrisburg Boulevard, east of Velasco Street and west of Union Pacific railroad line. Yezhóv had initially believed that it was named for aging movie star Clint Eastwood, he of many Western and police thrillers, but later learned the naming was a simple matter of geography.

Ho-hum.

Yezhóv was an "illegal" in the sense of covert operations carried out on U.S. soil, not one of those border-hopping southern neighbors whom so many Anglo-Americans chose to call "wetbacks". He served the Russian Federation's Federal Security Service—FSB, for short—successor to the legendary KGB and its short-lived replacement, the Federal Counterintelligence Service, or FSK.

Name changes were a time-honored pursuit in Russia, the latest occasioned by communism's collapse in 1991, replaced by a new free-wheeling capitalist era ruled by oligarchs and gangsters, its politicians moving readily through both worlds, following the scent of wealth. Beyond the FSB's label, however, nothing much had changed. It still performed all its predecessors' same covert, illegal actions, even operating from the same HQ on Moscow's fabled Lubyanka Square—the site of countless midnight executions, disappearances, and nightmarish interrogations.

Some might say things were even worse today, under President Vladimir Putin, ex-KGB director and Russia's ruler since the final day of 1999, whose estimated personal net worth hovered north of $200 million. In fact, some *had* said it, but most of them were dead now.

Home sweet home.

Tonight, Colonel Yezhóv was answering a call for help from Abbas Abdul al-Rasheed Maarku, founder leader of the Flame of Allah. Yezhóv, as a connoisseur of names, knew that Maarku's mouthful translated as "stern, warlike, rightly-guided servant of God".

His victims would have understood the first two adjectives, but likely would have questioned whether he was rightly-guided and by whose bloodthirsty god.

The wouldn't know, as Yezhóv did, that Maarku was a backdoor relative of the Saudi royal family—born, as some quaintly put it, on the wrong side of the blanket, but still close enough to his half- and quarter-siblings, uncles, cousins, or whatever, to operate with their covert blessing abroad, financed from their bottomless oil wells.

In that respect, Maarku had much in common with the late Osama bin Laden...except for the "late" part, of course.

It still amazed Yezhóv that most Americans claimed not to know their Saudi "allies" ranked among the world's most prolific and virulent sponsors of terror, not only against Israelis, but against the very West that kept them fat and pampered. Fewer still admitted knowledge of the rogue nation's role in the 9/11 attacks. Fifteen of that day's nineteen "martyrs" were Saudis, and the raids—which launched America's seemingly endless Middle Eastern wars—were financed solely from Riyadh.

So, why did U.S. presidents still praise the Saudi monarchs, send them nonstop streams of cash and weapons, even pose for photos literally holding hands with King Abdullah, most recently helping whitewash the Saudi-sponsored murder of dissident expat journalist Jamal Khashoggi in Turkey.

Now, Abbas Maarku hoped to surpass all those "achievements", bringing down the Flame of Allah onto the United States and, not coincidentally, induce a crisis that would make the Great Depression seem like good old days, immeasurably benefiting Putin's Russia in the process.

All of which meant Yezhóv had to hold *this* Saudi's hand and coddle him along until Maarku achieved his goal—at which time, if he wasn't dead already, Yezhóv had orders to silence him for good.

Termination with extreme prejudice.

But not yet. Tonight called for more hand-holding and offers of support.

One of Maarku's pet monkeys greeted Colonel Yezhóv at the door of a house on Leland Street, purchased in the name of Chikatillo Ltd., a holding company with headquarters in Vladivostok and a private joke on the Americans, named for prolific Russian serial killer Andrei Chikatillo, the "Rostov Ripper".

Yezhóv brushed past the guard, with his shoulder-slung submachine gun, and waited impatiently while another frisked him for weapons. Midway through that process, Maarku himself appeared, barking at his men in Arabic and turning worried eyes upon the colonel's rugged face.

"Thank Allah, you have come!" he said.

"What troubles you, Abbas?" asked Yezhóv.

"We have enemies," Maarku replied, his voice dropped almost to a hiss.

"Of course. That's why—"

"No! I mean here and now, in Houston. We're under attack!"

Fondren Road, Houston

Cody was out of Braeburn, in the Sharpstown neighborhood, eating a hefty burger from a fast-food place that still had leggy carhops making their deliveries on roller skates, if you could picture that.

The latest triple killing hadn't fazed his appetite a bit.

Sharpstown was one of Southwest Houston's "master-planned" communities, built in the postwar era, later "gentrified" to add PlazAmericas mall, a golf course, and Sharpstown Country Club Estates. At this moment, it seemed a long way from mayhem, no patrons in the diner's other pricey cars aware that they were eating and conversing, with a stone-cold killer only yards away.

While working on his burger, fries and milkshake (chocolate), Jack pored over the pocket litter he'd retrieved from the three jihadists he'd left chilling out on Reamer Street. By now, he figured they were headed for the morgue, while CSIs checked out the former lodgings of "Habib ur Manaf", his birth name still unknown. All that remained of them to Cody was the small collection of wallets and cell phones piled up on the shotgun seat beside him.

From the wallets, he'd learned nothing. None contained I.D. of any kind, either legit or bogus, but he'd found a Trojan condom tucked away in one billfold, a wishful thinker's, resurrecting memories of high school and the guys who'd talked a great game, carrying preparatory gear around with them—even to school and church—without, in Cody's estimation, ever getting far beyond first base.

There was a dogeared business card in one wallet, Baitul Al-Sadiq mosque, with its address and phone number. Jack set that on the dashboard as he reached for one of the cell phones—and finally struck gold.

The phone's late owner, and the last guy Jack had put down in Braeburn, had received no less than seven calls over the past two days from—wait for it—the number on the Baitul Al-Sadiq mosque's calling card. He'd also placed two calls to that same number, on his own.

The other cells confirmed it. Each and every one of the extinct Three Stooges had received and/or placed more calls to the house of worship than they had to any other number. Otherwise, they'd mostly rung up restaurants—most of them tagged with Arab-sounding names—a movie theater (the automated line for screening times), and two gun shops.

Something was definitely cooking at the mosque.

Cody had been a bit surprised to learn that Houston harbored forty-one mosques and storefront Islamic religious centers, the first one built in 1928. Texas wasn't often viewed as Muslim-friendly, most particularly after 9/11, but overall, Lone Star State ranked third among fifty for thriving mosques—166 in all—behind New York's 257 and California's 246. H-Town alone also boasted fifty *halal*-certified restaurants, where "permitted" meat, as opposed to *haram* ("forbidden"), was butchered in compliance with the Koran's dietary laws.

That is to say having their throats cut by a butcher chanting *Basmala*, a short ritual prayer, before he drained each carcass of all blood.

As far as human victims of jihadists went, that was a "righteous" courtesy reserved for those beheaded on TV, for shock value and drumming up recruits.

Jack downed the last bite of his burger, giving little thought to where or how the steer had died, then used his phone to Google the Baitul Al-Sadiq mosque on Hillcroft Avenue, in the Mahatma Gandhi District, adjacent to Chinatown and Sharpstown in Houston's Southwest Management District. Befitting its nickname of "Little India", the district's populace was mainly Indian or Pakistani, but now Cody suspected that the Flame of Allah had planted its roots, as well.

He saved a web-shot of the mosque and memorized the names of other streets surrounding it: Freshmeadow Drive, Pagewood Lane, and Skyline Drive. All the potential routes of access and escape.

Jack had no clue what he'd be facing when he checked out Baitul Al-Sadiq. It might be vacant, locked up for the night, in which case he'd break in and do his best to silence the alarms before he had a nice, long look around, seeking inculpatory evidence. The flip side of that coin was that he might find it alive and crawling with rabid jihadists, placed on high alert after his hits in Las Vegas and Braeburn.

Either way, Cody would take no chances at the mosque. He'd go in hard, but silently if that were feasible, preferring not to wage another pitched battle in Houston before he could shake off jet lag from his recent trips crisscrossing the United

States. He'd been on longer flights before and hit the ground running, fighting, without a break, but Jack knew luck and stamina would only stretch so far.

And one day, he would have none left.

As for tonight, fueled by the diner's tasty offerings, he was raring to go.

Greater Eastwood district, Houston

Talal Wahid ibn Ataullah, as per usual, had been excluded from Abbas Maarku's urgent discussion with the Russian officer, conducted, as such meetings always were, behind closed doors.

When he was closeted inside that room with "special" visitors, Maarku turned on a TSJ Cell Phone Blocker Mini Model, smaller than most phones themselves, ostensibly designed to create "quiet zones" around theater patrons and restaurant diners, but useful to blocking any form of wireless communication within a twenty-yard radius. Sometimes, for sport, he also used it when they drove around Houston, laughing at the stupid drivers he left flustered when their cell phones died in mid-call or while texting.

Only when the Russian had departed, nodding curtly to Talal, was he—Ataullah—granted entry to Maarku's office and briefed on the results of their meeting. Abbas had called the colonel this night, after three adherents to the Flame of Allah had been massacred in Braeburn, on a run to cleanse the dwelling of Abdul Karim Qadir, slain with his soldiers in Las Vegas earlier today—or, now, yesterday evening.

"What news, sir," Talal asked before he sat down facing Maarku's desk.

"He will assist us," said Abbas. "It was embarrassing to ask, but I saw no other recourse."

"*Alhamd lilah.*"

Maarku nodded. "Praise God, indeed. Our friend is sending some of his assets to watch the mosque tonight. They will maintain security until the morning, when services shall resume as usual."

"And what word of the cargo?" Ataullah inquired.

"Still right on schedule," Maarku replied. "Two ships, with two containers, halve the risk of chance discovery."

Talal doubted whether chance or Fate would play a part, if their incoming cargo was detected by American authorities. It had already cleared Customs when leaving Russia—more specifically, departing Magadan Oblast in Russia's Far Eastern Federal District—in separate ships, starting their Pacific passage on successive days. From there, stops at Sapporo, Honolulu, Acapulco, passing through the Panama Canal and coming up on Houston from the south, through the Caribbean, and then across the Gulf of Mexico.

At each stop on their way, the ships dropped some containers and collected others, but the two loaded at Magadan continued on their journey undisturbed, their contents certified on bills of lading as mining equipment.

Which, of course, was not even remotely true.

Appearances were everything. Tack on some bribery was it might be required, and suddenly, officials paid to snoop and pry became disinterested, lackadaisical. Shell out enough, while taking adequate measures to ensure discretion, and there was no limit to the cargo moving round the world each day: narcotics, sex slaves, caged endangered species, weapons—or two objects that would set the Western Hemisphere aflame, spinning out of control.

The Russians had been useful, up to now, but Talal did not trust them, going forward. Be they communists, mobsters, or billionaire entrepreneurs, in Talal's personal experience, the former Reds *always* possessed ulterior motives. They shook hands but concealed daggers, hidden behind their backs, to lash out when it suited them.

"These Russian guards, sir. Do you trust them?"

Maarku made a sour face, mimed spitting on the carpet. "No," he said. "They're doubtless *aleisabat*, but the Russian gangsters know their business."

"Yes, sir," Talal replied. Thinking, *As long as they do not know ours.*

Mahatma Gandhi District, Houston

Entering the neighborhood reminded Cody of deplaning in New Delhi. Shops, groceries, and restaurants offered their wares in Hindi, Urdu, Pashto, Farsi, English—and in Spanish, if the owners felt like bothering. The theaters ran Bollywood productions, and houses of worship surrounded him: Sikh and Hindu temples, Muslim mosques and Christian churches, sometimes standing side by side.

At least within this enclave, maybe people could just get along?

The last census revealed that one in every four Houstonians was foreign-born, 40 percent conversing chiefly in some language other than English. An estimated 100,000 of those were Pakistanis, nearly all residing in this district, and Jack knew damned well that some of them were either assets of Islamabad's Inter-Services Intelligence agency, or else its tools, cooperating out of fear for relatives at risk back home.

Another 50,000 ethnic Iranians occupy Houston, controlling a twelve-block business district along Hillcroft Avenue that journalists had labeled "Little Persia". As with Pakistani immigrants and the ISI, some from Iran were doubtless agents or reluctant servants of that nation's Ministry of Intelligence, aka VAJA.

The problem: none of them were obvious about it, and U.S. relations with their homelands ruled out any background checks abroad. Only when individuals or sleeper cells were activated were they recognized.

And by then, it was far too late.

Cody drove past the Olympic Center, an Indian-Pakistani shopping mall, ironically constructed in the Spanish mission style common to Texas, and passed on, tracking his destination on the Subaru Legacy's GPS system. As he neared the Baitul Al-Sadiq mosque, he began exploring side streets, noting nearly all the businesses darkened and shuttered at that hour.

Bars were big in most of Houston, but in the Mahatma Gandhi District, not so much. Islam and Sikhism shunned all intoxicants, including tobacco for Sikhs, while diverse Hindu sects were all over the board, some banning alcohol entirely, others discouraging liquor but leaving it optional, still others touting wine as an aid to good health. Overall, the neighborhood's nightlife was nil.

Cody parked a block north of the mosque, switched off the Subaru's engine and headlights, lifting the FLIR Scout TK he normally packed in his carryon bag. The Scout is a pocket-sized thermal vision monocular. "FLIR" stands for forward-looking infrared, with a built-in video recorder, capable of spotting people, animals, and other objects from a hundred yards at night, or in other lowlight conditions. It measures 6×2×2 inches and weighs only six ounces. It is rated IP67 waterproof and submersible (in three feet of water, up to an hour), sold with a neck lanyard, USB cable, and lens cap.

Ideal for a man on the run, either from or toward danger.

Using the Scout, Jack scanned the mosque's façade on Hillcroft and the portion of its north side that was visible beyond a Persian dry cleaning shop. A Chevrolet Suburban full-size SUV was parked out front, black as the ace of spades and freshly waxed. It seated eight and featured fold-flat second- and third-row seats for hauling cargo at need, but all were in their usual upright positions now, so Jack would have to make a headcount or try guessing how many potential enemies might be waiting inside.

He spotted one a second later, on the mosque's flat roof, peering over its parapet into the street below, forgetting not to let his rifle show. Jack made it as some kind of Kalashnikov, although he couldn't peg the model number at that distance, in the dark. It had some kind of telescopic sight attached, likely the PSO-1 Optical Sniper Sight, manufactured by the NPZ Optics State Plant in Novosibirsk, with a reticle whose "floating" elements were used in range estimation, plus bullet drop and drift compensation.

Jack had killed with one of those before and didn't care to be on its receiving end.

As he lowered the Scout, another guy stepped from the alleyway between the mosque and dry cleaner's. He had a combat shotgun, muzzle pointed at the pavement, and Cody identified it as a Benelli M3 with extended magazine for seven twelve-gauge rounds, plus one in the chamber. The shooter had his choice of switching back and forth from semi-automatic to pump-action as he pleased.

Okay. Two men, well-armed, arriving in an SUV that could have seated six more just like them, with ease. If there were more around, they could be damned near anywhere.

And, if they matched the two he'd seen so far, they were not even vaguely Arab in appearance.

What in hell was up with that? Cody knew that there was only one way to find out.

And it was bound to mean more blood.

CHAPTER 7

Jack Cody killed the Subaru's dome light and pocketed its key before he exited the vehicle, watching the Baitul Al-Sadiq mosque's rooftop sniper all the while through his FLIR Scout.

He'd waited for a classic Ford LTD two-door hardtop to roll past him first, its windows down and blasting *filmi* songs in Hindi from its too-large speakers, drawing the sniper's full attention as it cruised along the block, sitars and high-pitched vocals echoing from shopfronts along Hillcroft Avenue.

The spotter never glanced Jack's way while he was scrambling from the Legacy and toward an alley running east-west, in between the dry cleaner and a pharmacy. Jack had the Steyr AUG slung over his left shoulder, muzzle pointing downward, one Glock on his hip, the other—fitted with the Osprey—ready in his fist.

From that point on, there was no turning back without admission of defeat.

Which damned sure wasn't happening.

The alley brought him to another, wider alley running parallel to Hillcroft, paved for garbage trucks that would come weekly, possibly more often, clearing out the bins and cans behind the thoroughfare's assorted stores and restaurants. Holding the Scout left-handed, Jack surveyed that passage, half expecting to find guards outside the mosque's backdoor, but none stood out amidst the shadows.

He'd spotted only two so far: one high up, and the other at street level, in the next alley before him. The Chevy SUV could handle eight in comfort, nine or ten if they were packed in like sardines. It made no sense to send a ride that size for just two men.

Where were the rest?

Smart money said another four or five, at least, would be inside the mosque, waiting to spring a trap.

Approaching cautiously, Jack wondered if the Baitul Al-Sadiq had normal worshipers, or if the place was just a front for radical Islamists hiding in plain sight. He knew how some *imams* and *mullahs* plucked Koranic verses out of context to inspire jihadists, the same way that certain "Christian pastors" focused on their Bible's exhortations to kill gays, "pro-lifers" terrorizing women's clinics without any thought to who their bombs and drive-by shots might harm.

That was a major reason why religion hadn't won Jack over, even as a kid. To him, no "truth" that offered something up for everyone—from selfless saints to rabid terrorists—was rational or trustworthy. If someone wanted to bestow wealth to a cause, why not support some kind of research to help the planet and mankind, instead of fattening a TV preacher's off-shore bank accounts?

But hey, to each his own.

Jack reached the alley where he'd seen the second lookout earlier and eased his head around the northeast corner of the dry cleaner's to take a peek. The shotgunner—some kind of skinhead-looking white guy, definitely not a Middle Eastern-er or South Asian. The FLIR Scout showed a tattoo peeking from beneath his shirt's collar, climbing the left side of his neck, but Cody couldn't see enough to work out what it was.

The guard was smoking, straight tobacco by the smell of it, leaning against the mosque's south wall, with ankles crossed and his Benelli M3 dangling. Cody heard the muffled strains of music, noting that the spotter wore headphones, their slender cord hooked to a belt-clipped MP4 player.

What Jack could hear of it the music sounded…was that Russian?

Yep. Something the Russkies called nu metal or aggro-metal, a mélange of styles performed by groups like Flymore, Slot, and Tracktor Bowling. Cody didn't care for it but kept on top of modern trends whenever possible.

The shotgunner was risking permanent ear damage, with his MP4 cranked up full blast.

Nothing he'd have to cope with as he aged.

The range was relatively short, no more than twenty feet. Jack raised his muffled Glock, sighted along its slide, and sent a crushing double-tap down range, into the sentry's left profile.

One down, a least one more to go.

And how many beyond the ones he'd seen?

Pyotr Annenkov thought his assignment, guarding the Baitul Al-Sadiq mosque, was a lot of bullshit, but he'd never questioned orders since serving a five-year sentence at White Swan penal colony in Solikamsk, Perm Krai, Russia.

It was there Annenkov had acquired his life story in tattoo ink and found a family for the first time, enlisting with the *vory v zakone*—"thieves-in-law"—that most police and journalists labeled the Russian Mafia.

The similarities were obvious: two secret, criminal societies, their members oath-bound to a rigid code of conduct that dictated the relationship between various members, with a rule of silence dubbed *tshina,* what Italian Mafiosi knew as *omertà.* The leader of Annenkov's *sem'ya* ("family) was *Krestniy Otets* ("boss of bosses") Stanislav Solonik, residing since 2003 in Brighton Beach, New York.

Solonik had imported Annenkov from Russia two years later, grooming him to serve the family as an *Avtoritet* ("authority"), in charge of a brigade (*bratva*), roughly equivalent to the Italian Mafia's *caporegime.* Assigned to Houston, Pyotr's *boyeviks* ("warriors") smuggled anything and everything of possible black-market value through the city's seaport, but tonight's errand was different.

Orders from Brighton Beach had placed Annenkov's crew on loan to Vadim Yezhóv, shady Russian expat businessman and the proprietor of Nochnyye Khody—Night Moves—a stylish Houston "gentleman's club" staffed by nude women, husky bouncers, and mostly-gay bartenders, chosen to keep them away from the strippers.

Pyotr's men ran drugs through Night Moves, paying off police to look the other way, but this night's job was unrelated to the boob bar. In addition to financial acumen, Vadim Ye-zhóv was understood to be "connected" in Moscow, a contract asset of the FSB, or possibly an agent working "black" in the United States. *Krestniy Otets* Solonik had been called upon to do a favor for the man of mystery, and it would surely be re-paid in Russia by the Putin government—a tidy quid pro quo.

To hear was to obey, but why a mosque, of all places? So far, Pyotr had seen nothing in the place that any self-respect-ing thief would deign to steal.

On top of that, the task was *yeblya* boring, nothing that Pyotr thought required his personal attention, plus five *boye-viks* armed to the teeth.

Annenkov leaned back in the *imam's* swivel chair, boots resting on the desktop, where his MP5K submachine gun lay, a quick-detachable suppressor mounted on its 5.8-inch, three-lugged barrel. Loaded with back-to-back thirty-round magazines of 9×19mm Parabellum ammo, the MP5K's fire mode selector included three settings: safe, semi-automatic, and full-auto, firing at a cyclic rate of nine hundred rounds per minute.

His backup weapon, holstered at the small of his back, was a Ukrainian Fort-12 pistol, loaded with thirteen 9×18mm

Makarov rounds, propelling six-gram FMJ bullets at a muzzle velocity of 1,050 feet per second, as rapidly as Annenkov could squeeze its double-action trigger.

Should those fail him, Pyotr's *boyeviks* carried a variety of assault weapons and pistols to defend him and the Muslim property they guarded. On the roof, Dmitriy Voloshina had the neighborhood under surveillance with his sniper's rifle. Josef Konev, in the alley south of where Pyotr sat, carried a shotgun. Killing time in other rooms, Boris Gakkel, Ivan Nartov, and Naum Zavoyko packed AK-104 carbines, chambered for the same 7.62×39mm rounds fired by their parent AK-47 and its other variants.

All that firepower going to waste in a church, for God's sake.

That stray thought made Annenkov laugh aloud. From an adjoining room, Zavoyko called, "Did you say something, boss?"

"*Nyet, nichego,*" Pyotr answered back, returning to his private thoughts and waiting for this night to end.

Cody found a rooftop access ladder mounted on the mosque's rear wall of cinder blocks, painted in stripes of four primary colors—white, black, green and red—that dominate the flags of eighteen Arab states spanning some 5.3 million square miles, from North Africa's Atlantic coast eastward to the Indian Ocean.

But don't let the "pan-Arab" colors fool you into thinking

Arab states all think alike. Wars sputtered across the region: Mauritania and Morocco fighting over disputed Western Sahara; in civil wars in Iraq, Somalia and South Yemen; minority Islamic rebellions and retaliatory mayhem in Iraq, Saudi Arabia and Syria; Iraq's invasion of Kuwait (launching U.S. "Operation Desert Storm"); fighting between Fatah and Hamas in the Gaza Strip; ethnic cleansing of Kurds in northern Iraq; random havoc wreaked by Sunni ISIL terrorists across the region and beyond.

Muslims killed each other in the streets, in homes and mosques, annihilating rural villages and turning larger cities, like Beirut, into grim mirror images of occupied Berlin in 1945. All in the name Allah, with the battles usually fought over the same Koran they all professed to follow, sometimes sparked by disparate interpretations of a single verse.

Slipping the Glock and Osprey underneath his belt, around in back, Cody began to scale the metal ladder. It was rusty, but securely bolted to the wall and made no sound as he ascended toward the rooftop. Near the top, Jack hunched his shoulders, ducked his head, and freed the pistol, pushing with his legs and pulling with his left hand until he could see over the parapet.

The sniper had his back turned, leaning slightly forward as he scanned the blocks of Hillcroft Avenue that he could see. His rifle—a semiauto VSK-94, Cody saw now, with a skeletonized polymer stock, 4x PSO-1 scope, and factory-standard suppressor, feeding 9×39mm ammo from a twenty-round detachable box magazine. Its maximum range was six hundred meters, "effective" range two hundred closer than that.

A shot across flat rooftop was nothing—if the shooter had his piece in hand.

Jack didn't want to shoot his present adversary in the back, risk spilling him into the street below and prematurely raising an alarm. Instead, he whistled softly, barely audible across the span of concrete, but the sniper heard him well enough, turning around and ducking to retrieve his weapon as he made the move.

Jack fired one .40-caliber into his groin, stripping the gunman's mind of conscious thought, then waited half a second, putting round two through his forehead as the he toppled forward, dead before he made an ugly face-plant on concrete.

Jack nimbly climbed onto the mosque's rooftop, crossed to the dead man—noticing an access hatch to the building's interior as he passed by it—then knelt down to roll the body over, face-up to the sky.

Swiftly, he rifled through the corpse's pockets, finding no I.D., then played a hunch and ripped his conquest's polo shirt wide-open down the front, pulling its halves aside. On the dead guy's right shoulder, an eight-pointed star had been tattooed, and that was all Cody needed to see: a mark applied to Russian mobsters who had proved themselves fit for a rank above the normal street or cellblock soldier. All the rest of it—skulls in a spider's web spanning the blood-flecked chest, against the background of a church with onion domes, flanked by two broken hearts—would have meant something special to the sniper when he was alive.

They didn't matter anymore.

Jack guessed that if he went back to the alleyway below and checked, he'd find a variation of the same art on the shotgunner he'd put to sleep. But why Russians? Why here and now?

Forget about it, he decided. *Deal with what's in front of you.*

Rising, he moved back toward the access hatch, no lock securing it, and raised its lid.

Pyotr Annenkov couldn't identify the sound at first. The mosque was unfamiliar turf, and while he had positioned his *boyeviks* at their posts upon arrival, there had been no opportunity to catalog Baitul Al-Sadiq's creaky floors, hinges in need of oil, and other trivia. He knew the bathroom tap dripped slowly, steadily, and that a minifridge in the small kitchen area vibrated slightly when its motor hummed to life, but otherwise, the mosque retained its petty mysteries.

Not that Pyotr gave a damn.

What was it the Americans once liked to say about *pediki* in their military ranks?

Oh, right. It came to him: "Don't ask, don't tell."

But this noise, small and distant as it was, had raised Annenkov's hackles all the same.

"Boris!" he called out to the next room on his left. "Did you hear that?"

"Hear what?" Gakkel replied.

"That noise, just now."

"What noise?"

"*Tupoy sukin syn!*" Annenkov muttered. Louder, he said,

"*Yob tvoyu mat!* Have you been asleep in there?"

"No, sir. I—"

From another room nearby, Ivan Nartov called out, "It sounded like the roof hatch, where Dmitriy is."

The roof hatch? Annenkov rose, scowling, from behind the *imam*'s inexpensive desk. If Voloshina was not at his post—

"Maybe he had to take a *ssat*," Zavoyko said.

"What's wrong with pissing on the roof?" Pyotr asked of no one in particular.

Nartov cackled at that. "Pissing on God? Lightning will strike him down!"

Snatching his MP5K off the desktop, Annenkov strode toward the short hallway between the *imam*'s office and large room set aside for prayers, divided into sections for the men to kneel in front, women in rows behind them, where their upturned buttocks wouldn't give randy parishioners any obscene ideas.

"Dmitriy!" Pyotr shouted as he walked. "If that's you slacking off—"

A voice Annenkov didn't recognize replied from somewhere down the corridor, saying, "Dmitriy isn't in right now."

And then: *Pop! Pop!*

Pyotr recognized the sound of a suppressed sidearm at once, although he couldn't guess the make or caliber. It hadn't been a lightweight .22, nor a .380. Something larger, then: 9mm, possibly a .45.

Pyotr shouted to his troops throughout the mosque. "Intruders! Sound off, *boyeviks*!"

Answers would mean his men were still alive. Whoever failed to speak was likely dead—except, perhaps, the two stationed outside. But if an enemy had entered through the roof's hatch, past Dmitriy Voloshina—

"Zavoyko here!" Naum called back to his brigadier.

"And Boris!"

Annenkov froze in his tracks, waiting for Ivan Nartov to respond. When he did not, Pyotr bellowed from the *imam's* office, "Ivan? Answer, *proklyat'ye!*"

Nothing at first, until a voice he didn't recognize replied, from somewhere out of sight, "Ivan's all done, comrade."

No accent to the voice. Call it "American" and let it go at that, for now.

"Who's that?" Zavoyko called into the silent void.

"Quiet!" Pyotr ordered. "Fall back now, to me!"

His men—the two survivors he was sure of—did not speak, but he could hear them scuttling from the rooms where they'd been stationed, rushing to obey as rapidly as caution and a nagging sense of fear allowed.

And as they came, the stranger's voice called out again, "Don't start without me, boys."

Such arrogance. It was infuriating. Annenkov wished he could rampage through the mosque, firing at every shadow, anything that moved, but surely that would only hasten death.

Returning to the desk, he crouched behind it, MP5K covering the open doorway, waiting for his men to join him—if they lived that long.

The trick, Jack knew, was getting his concealed opponents on the move, where he could pick them off. So far, it seemed his shout-out to the guy in charge had done the trick. People were on the move, and based on their commander's roll call, Jack had already reduced their team by half.

The third Russian he'd killed so far, called Ivan by his boss, had barely seen it coming. Cody thought that something must have tipped him—probably the muffled sounds Jack made descending from the roof above—but he'd been too slow off the mark, responding. Started turning in a big rattan chair, right-hand shoulder dipping as he tried to reach the AK-104 carbine lying beside him, on the carpet.

Never made it.

Looking at him now, one last, brief time—his left eye punched into his brain, a keyhole leaking blood above the right eyebrow—Cody confirmed that he had made a perfect double-tap. Now, with the stakeout team's survivors rushing toward reunion with their chief, he snugged the Osprey-snouted Glock into its shoulder rig and got his Steyr AUG ready to rock.

Jack only had to pivot in the doorway where he'd met and ended Ivan, to see the shooters bailing out of different rooms along the corridor, sprinting for one at the end of the hall, where a grim-looking, spiky-haired guy clutched an MP5K SMG against his barrel chest. The Russian's eyes met Cody's, and he might have fired on sight, except his soldiers were obeying their last order, galloping to join him, getting in his way.

No problem there, at least for Jack. He fired a short burst from the Steyer, toward the runner on his left, and stitched his spine with 5.56mm FMJ rounds, lifting him for a split-second, so that he seemed to be swimming through mid-air. His weapon clattered to the corridor's linoleum before he hit the floor facedown and slid another four or five feet, body-surfing on the blood that spurted from his mouth and ragged exit wounds in front.

The last runner was on the threshold—possibly an office doorway—when Jack fired again, cutting his legs from under him as if the Steyr's bullets were a sweeping scythe. Somehow. impact propelled the shattered limbs in front of him, so that he came down on his rump and cleared the doorway like a nervy third-base runner stealing home.

The team chief triggered off a quick 9mm burst, then slammed the door behind his crippled underling. Cody could hear the downed man sobbing, howling, from behind the door.

What would the man in charge do next?

Jack didn't have to ponder that. Within another couple seconds, Cody heard him talking on a phone, couldn't make out the muffled words despite his fluency in Russian, but he knew that only two options remained, now that the leader's team had been effectively wiped out.

One possible solution: call the cops. But that meant he would land in jail alongside Jack, if Cody didn't beat feet first and clear the scene.

The second option: call for reinforcements, stat.

Cody had no time to delay for either choice. With nimble

hands, he switched the AUG's gas valve to the "GR" position, mounted one of his rifle grenades on the Steyr's flash hider, and fired, ducking behind the doorjamb just behind him.

The grenade's explosion shook the mosque, must have been audible outside, if there was anyone around or passing by to hear it blow. The door blew off its hinges, flipping over once before it struck some heavy piece of furniture inside.

Jack followed in a rush, before the crew chief could recover from that shock, and caught his enemy trying to rise from all fours in the smoky office space. He twitched the Steyr's muzzle to his right and downward, drilled the crippled, sobbing Russian with a head shot, close to point-blank range, then swung around to cover the team's sole survivor.

Speaking Russian, Jack inquired, "Do you prefer to talk, or die?"

"Idi trakhni sebya, mudak!"

"Not my thing," Cody replied, and shot him through the heart, dropping the Russian where he stood.

No name or willing information, then, but Jack relieved both dead men of their wallets and cell phones, adding them to the stash he'd been collecting in the cargo pockets of his pants. Somewhere amongst the leftovers, he hoped to find another link, directions to someone who could fill in the missing information he required.

Why was a gang of Russian mobsters covering security for Muslim terrorists?

And what did Allah's Flame have planned for the United States this time?

CHAPTER 8

McKinney Street, Houston

Cody regarded it as logical that Houston's Chinatown would lie next-door to the Mahatma Gandhi District, in the city's larger Southwest Management District, with another ethnic Asian neighborhood, "Little Saigon", located to the west of Beltway 8.

In fact, Houston boasted *two* Chinatowns, the other—"Old Chinatown"—situated within the East Downtown district, but Jack didn't care. He wasn't looking for a bowl of hot and sour soup or heaping plate of yakisoba noodles at this hour.

He had Russian gangsters on his mind, and their connection to the Flame of Allah, still incomprehensible.

To solve that riddle, he would have to find the man who'd sent the stakeout team to guard the Baitul Al-Sadiq mosque overnight.

Checking the team commander's phone, Jack found one

number dialed repeatedly. He went online to check it, and discovered it was listed to a strip club called Nochnyye Khody, likely borrowed and translated from the old Bob Seger song. He was surprised to find it also stood on Hillcroft Avenue, but two miles farther south of Chinatown and the Mahatma Gandhi District.

Digging deeper on the Web, Cody identified the club's owner of record as one Vadim Yezhóv, a Russian expat. Tapping into the *Houston Chronicle*'s archives, Jack found a handful of articles on Yezhóv, mostly praising his philanthropy to worthy causes ranging from the March of Dimes to cancer, autism and Alzheimer's research. Not much in terms of background, but the published photos of him showed a smiling man of middle years, dressed to the nines, surrounded by Houston's social elite.

No *bratva* tattoos showing anywhere, of course, since Yezhóv didn't share the current Russian president's penchant for posing shirtless, on horseback.

Cody palmed his roam phone, keyed Sara Durell's number, and waited through three rings until she picked it up at Langley. "Go ahead," she ordered, in her best no-nonsense voice.

"Vadim Yezhóv," Cody replied.

"Russian," she said, not asking.

"Expat. Runs a strip club here, called Nochnyye Khody."

"Night Moves?" Sara was another fluent Russian-speaker, master of the same lingos as Jack, plus German, Cantonese *and* Mandarin. "Catchy, I guess, if you like being obvious."

"I visited the mosque tonight," Jack said. "It should be on

the wire by now. No Arabs, but I ran into some *russkaya mafi-ya* boys."

"It went your way, I take it."

"Not a problem. One of them, the crew chief, had been getting lots of calls from Yezhóv's dive."

"Connection to the other thing?" she asked.

"Unknown. Yezhóv hands money out to local charities like he was printing it himself, but otherwise, the local news outlets have squat. None of the raids, drug busts, or other hassles that you might expect. If somebody can look him up and hit me back within the next half hour, it could help when I drop in on him."

" 'Somebody,' meaning me."

"You must have staff on call, right?"

Sara countered that, saying, "You know distractions can be hazardous."

"The *bratva* crowd bought into my game, not the other way around," Jack said. "I need to know who staked them, and how Moscow may connect to *imam* Maarku and his peeps."

"Okay. I may need twenty minutes, give or take, depending on what's in our database."

"Sounds good. I'm on the move."

"You always are," she said, the bare suggestion of a smile behind her words, and cut the link.

No words wasted on Sara's side, one of the several things that Cody liked about her, even if she was a tough boss known for busting balls. Jack knew she'd taken heat from members of the Company's old-boys establishment for that—and in the military, prior to signing on with Langley—but she never seemed to let it get her down.

A strong man in her job would be admired across the board. A woman doing the exact same thing was often tagged a "bitch", but none dared say that to Sara's face.

At least, not twice.

Cody revved up the Subaru and started rolling south on Hillcroft, thinking blocks ahead, to how he would approach Night Moves and try to crack its secret before everything in Houston went to hell.

Nochnyye Khody, Hillcroft Avenue

Night Moves was jumping, its raucous display of downstairs hedonism framed on half a dozen flat screen CCTV monitors in Colonel Yezhóv's soundproofed office on the second floor. Nude women mingled with the club's overdressed patrons, serving alcohol to those already well beyond the legal bounds.

Yezhóv was seated at a massive desk, mahogany with polished granite topping, reviewing dual financial ledgers— one for Uncle Sam, the other for himself and *Krestniy Otets* Stanislav Solonik, back in Brighton Beach, eyes only—when his cell phone sounded the opening strains of *"Patrioticheskaya pesnya,"* Russia's national anthem.

His private line, and Yezhóv didn't need to guess who would be calling at this time of night. Pyotr Annenkov's grim face—a blood-red teardrop tattooed at the corner of his left eye—filled the phone's LED screen. The callback number printed underneath it made the photograph resemble a police mug shot.

Frowning at the distraction, Yezhóv grabbed the phone, keyed the "Accept" button, and ordered "Speak!"

"We're under fire!" Pyotr barked at him. "What is this *der'mo?*"

"I have no idea what shit you mean," Yezhóv snapped back at the mobster. "Remember that you're speaking on an open line!"

"My men are dying! *Blyad'* your open line, *mudak!*"

Before Yezhóv could chastise Annenkov for that insult, remind him who was boss, a thunderous explosion echoed from the cell's speaker, making Yezhóv jump and nearly drop his phone.

"Pyotr? Pyotr!"

A moment's ringing silence told him Annenkov most likely would not be answering, and Yezhóv switched the cell phone off, ensuring that whoever had just bombed the Baitul Al-Sadiq mosque would not catch him hanging on the line.

It took a full minute for Yezhóv to recover and begin sorting his options. As it happened, he could only think of one.

Like it or not, he must reach out and warn Abbas Abdul Maarku.

Yezhóv had struck a bargain with the founding chief of Allah's Flame. It served his purpose—and the Kremlin's—to support jihadist strikes on U.S. targets, both abroad and in America itself. The plan now underway, should it succeed, would be a game changer in the relationship between Moscow and Washington.

Already mired in debt to the Chinese—$1.17 trillion at the latest tabulation, or about 19 percent of the total $6.26 trillion in U.S. Treasury bills, notes, and bonds held by foreign countries—America could ill afford a financial catastrophe dwarfing the 1930s depression. When that happened, *if* it happened, Moscow could swoop in and save the day, strengthening bonds already forged between the White House and President Putin.

But if nothing happened...

There was no alternative recourse. Abbas Maarku must be advised immediately, thus forewarned.

Yezhóv had no doubt in his mind that he would take the blame for whatever had happened at the mosque—and worse, whatever flowed from that, upsetting Maarku's master plan. Yezhóv did not fear Maarku, even though he knew the Saudi madman specialized in nursing grudges and exacting vengeance from those he decided were his enemies.

Yezhóv absolutely *did* fear Alexander Bortnikov, director of the FSB since May 2008 and Putin's fierce right hand, already implicated in the assassination of FSB defector and *bratva* opponent Alexander Litvinenko, poisoned with radionuclide polonium-210 in London, a full year before Bortnikov assumed command of the Federal Security Service.

If Yezhóv's mission in America should fail, due to the interference of an adversary he could not identify, it was no great leap of the imagination to picture an FSB targeted killing expert approaching him casually, another bland face in the crowd, jabbing Yezhóv with the loaded tip of an umbrella or a walking stick, barely noticed, implanting a lethal pellet for which medicine had no cure.

Then would come lingering death: the loss of hair and teeth, wasting away, ending with organ failure on a massive scale, until his wasted frame resembled one of Dachau's walking skeletons.

And if that happened, Yezhóv knew that he would not be walking very far.

Resolved to face a tongue-lashing in Arabic, preferable to an agonizing death, Yezhóv gripped his cell phone and dialed his contact number for Abbas Abdul Maarku.

The strip club's parking lot was packed when Cody got there, mostly high-priced cars suggesting money was no issue for their owners, or the drivers lived above their means and didn't care. Rather than squeeze his Subaru into one of the farthest slots on Hillcroft, Jack circled the block and found curb space on a side street immediately to the south.

He'd thought about a means of entering Night Moves while driving over from his last engagement and decided trying to break in would be too risky this time. Rather than get caught picking a backdoor lock and fighting his way in from there, giving Yezhóv a golden opportunity to skip, he would be going in the front like other paying "gentlemen".

That meant a bit of dressing up and leaving certain weapons in the Legacy.

Jack had acquired a certain quick-change skill over the

course of time, and he applied it now, swapping a stylish suit and shoes for the night-prowling getup he had worn to raid the Baitul Al-Sadiq mosque earlier. He left the Steyr AUG and its grenades behind, but took along both holstered Glocks, after he had removed the Osprey sound suppressor from the one in the shoulder rigging on his left-hand side. The jacket's cut concealed them well enough to pass inspection by front-door security.

His phone blipped, just as Jack was squaring off his necktie's Windsor knot. Its LED screen warned him of an "UN-KNOWN NUMBER", but he answered anyway, hoping it would be Sara, trusting absolutely in the smart phone's twice-around-the-world security program.

"Go," he instructed.

Sara's voice informed him, "Vadim Aleksándrovich Ye-zhóv came over from the Russian Federation sixteen years ago, with a green card waiting for him and a ton of cash on tap. He's kept the card current since then and made all kinds of one-percenter friends in New York, Florida, and Texas."

A "green card", no longer its original primary color, signified legal permanent residency in America, if holders over age eighteen renewed it once per decade. Failure to perform that simple act carried a penalty of eighteen months in prison, followed by expulsion from the States.

"The millionaire's club?" Jack surmised.

"Bingo," Sara replied.

Members of the EB-5 "investor" class had to infuse America's economy in one way or another: pump $50,000 into rural projects, create at least ten paying jobs, or else invest at least $1 million in unspecified "other developments". Most EB-5s were Chinese nationals, roughly ten thousand of them, but the nationality was flexible, as long as money talked.

And some of that, Jack had no doubt, was passed under the table, greasing politicians with their hands perpetually out for ready cash.

"The kicker," Sara forged ahead. "We think he's with the FSB, reportedly a senior officer, but no specific rank on file."

In Russia, senior officers, field grade, included majors, lieutenant colonels, and full colonels, wearing one to three gold stars upon their epaulettes when they put on dress uniforms. An FSB agent in mufti, formally unrecognized as such, rated "illegal" status and—at least in theory—was liable to arrest regardless of his personal largesse.

Again, that was unless the right elected bigwigs got their sugar right on schedule and developed serious myopia.

"Connected to the *vory v zakone* that you know of?"

"Nothing so far, but I wouldn't put it past him."

"Home address, assuming I don't find him at the club?" Jack asked.

"According to his ICE file, he resides in River Oaks, one of the city's most expensive neighborhoods."

"Figures."

She gave him a Weslayan Street address and Cody memorized it. Heard her add, "It's a gated community. The first responders are their rent-a-cops, with Houston P.D. on speed dial."

"Got it."

"Action in River Oaks is top priority for the police and fire departments," Sara said. "Most of the residents are tight with pols from City Hall to Austin and D.C."

Jack had already figured that. He asked her, "So, okay to bag and tag him, then?"

"Your call," Sara replied. "It's one of those deals where I don't know, and I couldn't have stopped you."

"Roger that," he said, and severed the connection.

As Cody approached Night Moves, he heard the high-pitched strains of Jackyll belting "Down on Me" over a high-end sound system. Thankful he'd worn his unobtrusive earplugs, Cody let two husky bouncers look him over, then accept a twenty-dollar bill without offering him any change.

The posted cover charge was ten bucks, but Jack wouldn't miss it.

He was using cash skimmed from the *bratva* soldiers he'd already taken down this night, or maybe lifted from the late jihadists out in Vegas. Either way, their money spent the same.

To Jack, dead terrorists were an "investor" class unto themselves. Consider them EB-Expendables.

One of the skinhead sentries gave a half-inch nod, and Cody was inside.

Talal Wahid ibn Ataullah answered his boss's phone, presumably at Maarku's home on Leland Street, in Greater Eastwood. Yezhóv had no time to waste on seconds-in-command, saying, "I need to speak with him. Right now."

He could imagine the scowl on Ataullah's ferret face and didn't care. Ataullah passed the phone and Maarku's voice came on the line. "Yes?"

"Kiss the mosque good-bye," Yezhóv advised, no sugar coating it.

Anger was evident in Maarku's voice as he replied, "You could not stop our enemies?"

"I used professionals," Yezhóv replied, "but they weren't good enough."

"And so, I lose my *sakhif* base of operations? Through your *maleun* failure?"

Yezhóv let that pass. Answered, "It shouldn't matter. You're alive, and we expect your operation to proceed on schedule."

He didn't have to mention his Moscow superiors beyond the use of "we". Abbas Abdul Maarku was as susceptible to being poisoned as the next man, absolutely mortal, innate arrogance be damned.

"It *is* on schedule, yes?" Yezhóv demanded of his human tool.

On the defensive now, where Yezhóv wanted him, Maarku hastened to answer, "*Nem fielaan.* Certainly. Of course. We shall not fail."

"That's all I need to know. The consequence of failure at this point would be...severe."

"I serve Allah," Maarku replied. "Not Lubyanka Square."

"And you'd be nowhere, now, without our backing. I suggest you bear that fact in mind and keep your head down for the next few hours. Post however many guards you need to stay alive till then."

Rather than waste more time on fruitless back-and-forth, Yezhóv hung up and pocketed his cell phone. Turning from the open ledgers on his desk, he scanned the CCTV monitors and watched another scene from Sodom and Gomorrah playing out downstairs.

This time tomorrow, if the plans of Allah's Flame bore fruit, Night Moves and most of Houston would have been transformed into a charred, irradiated wasteland, while Vadim Yezhóv would be airborne, in transit to his homeland and the hero's welcome he deserved.

Cody stood just inside the strip club for a long moment, scanning the wall-to-wall festivities in progress. Jackyll had given way to AC/DC's "Back in Black", played at top volume over speakers mounted every thirty feet or so along the showroom's walls. Up on the long, circular stage, three topless dancers worked steel poles, three more crawling around on all fours, smiling as if each man they passed was Santa Claus and Brad Pitt, rolled up into one.

Six tiny thongs, now waiting for the tips offered by drunken fools at ringside, waving bills that ranged from five to twenty dollars each.

All longing for a G-string to be nudged aside—all accidentally, of course—trading a glimpse of shaved heaven for legal tender on the go.

The cover charge at Night Moves paid for entry and a

first drink, if the signs posted outside were accurate. They didn't say the liquor would be watered down, the price of beer tripled from what a six-pack would have cost in any local package store.

That was a given—and the only screwing patrons could expect tonight, unless they struck a bargain with the management for "special" treatment in a private suite upstairs.

What would it cost to touch the merchandise and be touched in return? Jack guessed the tab would start around a grand and escalate from there.

Cody proceeded to the bar, no easy task considering the crush of boozy, oversexed humanity around him, but still easier than seeking out an empty table. The showroom was dimly lit, helping conceal any specific dancer's imperfections that cosmetics or a touchup in an operating room couldn't disguise. Against that murky background, spotlights on the stage and random strobes added to visual confusion. Dancers in their downtime circulated through the crowd, pressing the flesh and hawking table dances for a ten-spot covering one song's duration.

Jack received his bottle of Corona, turned his back to the bartender, and surveyed the hectic showroom. Say three thousand square feet to be safe, but still conservative. He knew damned well the joint had passed its fire code safety limit, but again, "investment" by the owner would keep inspectors at a safe remove.

It took five minutes for him to pick out the first *bratva* gorillas circulating through the crowd, crew-cut and long on attitude, looking as if he'd love to start punching and kicking patrons for the hell of it.

On second thought, just as he spotted two more goons making the rounds, Jack recognized a singularity of purpose, understanding that they weren't simply pissed off at life in general or their assignment to a titty bar as watchdogs.

They were hunting.

Hunting who? And why?

He thought back to the mosque in the Mahatma Gandhi District, and the muffled sound of the *russkaya mafiya* team leader talking on his phone before Jack blew the office door in, stunning the troop's two survivors with concussive force.

Jack hadn't overheard that conversation, but he knew that it had lasted long enough to send a warning, possibly with a description of an enemy the *bratva* brigadier had glimpsed in passing.

Were the circulating soldiers tracking him?

It could, he knew, be someone else entirely: some fool who had tried to skip out on his tab and now was on the H-Town mob's "most wanted" list.

It *could* be, but he doubted that sincerely.

In other circumstances, Cody might have bailed and sought another angle of attack, but a sensation nagged at him now, telling Jack he had no time to waste.

If he was going to meet Vadim Yezhóv in the flesh, find out the Russian's link to Allah's Flame, it had to be tonight.

And if that meant some housecleaning beforehand, Jack was up for that.

CHAPTER 9

Over the pounding howl of amplified music, Leonid Koshkin heard the Big Man speaking to him through the Bluetooth wireless, hands-free headset plugged into his right ear. Cotton wadding in the left muffled the blasting strains of AC/DC just enough for him to understand the words spoken from Vadim Yezhóv's office on the nightclub's second floor.

"We have a possible intruder on the floor," Yezhóv advised, and followed up with a vague physical description: a white man, six feet tall, athletic build, dark hair.

Say 70 percent of all the patrons inside Night Moves.

"Nature of disturbance?" Koshkin asked the headset's reduction boom microphone that grazed his cheek, trusting Bluetooth's dynamic speaker to convey his voice upstairs while screening out most of the club's racket.

After a heartbeat, maybe two, Yezhóv replied, "If it's the man I think it is, he's killed six of your *tovarishchi* for a start, tonight."

Koshkin was too professional to ask which of his comrades were no longer living. Death was part and parcel of his life in the *russkaya mafiya*, even when he was out on loan to an effete club owner who despised getting his own hands dirty.

"Understood," he said, and spoke out to his fellow *boyeviks* scattered throughout the showroom's milling, noisy throng. He gave all six of them the message as he had received it, closing with, "*Voprosy?*"

No questions came back at him.

Koshkin was suddenly, intensely conscious of the Czech-made, double-action CZ 110 semiauto pistol snugged beneath his left arm in a fast-draw shoulder rig. Česká Zbrojovka's version of the fabled Glocks, its frame was from an impact-resistant polymer, the slide from steel. Its magazine held thirteen 9×19mm Parabellum rounds, plus one more in the pipe, perpetually ready to be fired except on rare occasions when Koshkin pressed the decocking lever.

He was not about to do that now.

His soldiers spread around the club were similarly armed with pistols of their own selection, save for hulking, bearded Yuri Losev, who preferred packing a Micro Uzi submachine gun, scaled down from its parent weapon's 18.5 inches to eleven inches with its stock folded, reducing the original's weight of nearly eight pounds to a mere 3.3. Both weapons fired the same 9mm rounds, but the Micro Uzi doubled its ancestor's cyclic rate of fire from 600 to 1,200 rounds per minute, burning through a 32-round magazine in 1.5 seconds.

The worst scenario that Koshkin could imagine was a

shootout in the club's jam-packed showroom. The first few shots might pass unnoticed, given the apocalyptic volume of the music, but as soon as patrons started dropping, dying, the mad rush for any nearby exit would begin, and what could halt the stampede of frightened, half-drunk humanity?

Nothing but death.

Still, thinking of his six dead comrades—without even knowing who they were, or if he'd liked them all that much—Koshkin decided that he didn't care. He'd been assigned a task: protect Night Moves' proprietor and his establishment, stressing that order of priority. So far, he'd never failed to carry out an order for the *bratva*, and he did not plan on letting down his side this time.

If he should die...so, what?

Leonid Koshkin's twenty-seven years had been replete with money, sex, drugs, violence, and all-around good times. The three years he had spent locked down, in his mind, had prepared him for the real world waiting for him outside prison walls. If life came down to this night, in the end, Koshkin believed that he was ready for it, savoring the final mystery, perhaps joining the seven men and one woman he'd slain with his own hands.

But first, he had to find out if there was an enemy somewhere inside Night Moves, or if Yezhóv had fallen prey to simple cowardice, seeing a threat where none existed.

If the Big Man was correct, *someone* had rubbed out six of Koshkin's fellow *vor v zakone* in Houston tonight, and that insult must be avenged at any cost. But if Yezhóv was fantasizing, letting his imagination get the better of him...

Brushing past the strip club's tables, moving toward the bar, Koshkin eyeballed each white man that he passed, scanning for solitary patrons with a shifty look about them, maybe armed and dangerous.

So far, all he could see were horny and inebriated fools, enraptured by the dancers who would only spare a smile if they were paid off for that privilege. How miserable and pathetic they all seemed to him, seen through a hunter's eyes.

Their money made the world go 'round, as Koshkin understood.

But it could just as easily be lifted from a corpse.

Jack Cody understood the whole strip club mentality, though it had never really been his scene. He knew some men came hoping to get laid, those without cash to burn inevitably leaving disappointed, with their wallets lightened. Some imagined that they were falling in love and chased that fantasy until a bouncer beat it out of them, or they faced stalking charges in a court of law.

The owner's end was easier to grasp. Dish up some flesh for fantasy, well lubed with alcohol, and fleece the suckers in the same way that casinos had been robbing them for centuries. One joker in a thousand, coming off the street, might buy a happy ending to his night, while the others went home disappointed, to cold showers or a well-worn copy of *Hustler*.

Sometimes there'd be a minor brawl, some handsy drunk

ejected to the hoots of fellow horn-dogs, but in general, the menu was established, scripted, and routine.

But not tonight.

There was a floor show in the making that the customers of Night Moves hadn't counted on, and they'd be joining in, not merely swilling booze and watching it, entranced.

Some of them might not make it home alive.

Jack always shied away from injuring bystanders, hating collateral damage. It was unprofessional and caused adverse publicity that made blasé police bestir themselves in search of answers, motives, viable suspects.

And none of that attention was appreciated by the Company.

Which didn't mean that it was necessarily avoidable.

Put hostile, well-armed killers in a room together, crowded with civilians, and there'd be no happy headlines in the morning, once the shit went down. That was a simple law of nature, as immutable as gravity.

The best-aimed bullet might punch through its primary intended target, do its wet work to perfection, and still mangle some sad sack who didn't realize his world had turned into a shooting gallery. Another round might miss its mark, through no fault of the shooter's, ricochet like mad, or fly straight for a hundred empty yards drop some hapless yokel in the middle of a crosswalk.

Fate.

It ultimately dealt with everyone. Jack Cody's job, tonight, was dropping it on target, each and every time, beginning pretty goddamned soon.

The nearest Russian mobster-looking type was drifting toward him, seemingly without direction as he navigated through the strip club's audience, but Cody watched the man's eyes flicking all around him, landing everywhere except upon the T and A displayed for all to see. He might have been a eunuch, wasting time in an establishment that held no interest for him, but smart money said that he was working.

Hunting, now.

Jack pegged the odds of his last victim at the mosque phoning a vague description of him on to someone else at sixty-forty, give or take. Without that tipoff, in the absence of remote surveillance cameras at the scene, Vadim Yezhóv could not possess the ghost of an idea who might be stalking him tonight. The shooter from Baitul Al-Sadiq might have been a man or woman, any color of the human rainbow, taking Yezhóv wholly unaware.

But the gorillas in the showroom clearly had a sense of purpose now, beyond mere crowd control. They weren't the nightclub's normal bouncers any more than cottonmouths were garter snakes dressed up for Halloween.

Jack guessed he'd find Yezhóv somewhere upstairs but getting there would be the trick. He'd have to thin the pack of hunters first, or preferably wipe them out entirely, causing enough chaos in the process, the police arriving on the scene would have their hands full with a wild stampede, instead of getting in Jack's way.

And so, he did the very last thing that the prowling *bratva* soldier might expect.

Instead of dodging through the crowd, hoping he wasn't spotted, Cody walked right up to the blond, lanky guy and asked, "Are you looking for me?"

The hardman's first reaction, as expected, was surprise. He blinked at Cody, then started to ask him, "Who the fu—?" before the tanto blade of Cody's lock-back Smith & Wesson M.A.G.I.C. automatic knife, purchased on special at Walmart once he'd cleared George Bush Intercontinental Airport, slipped under his sternum and he suddenly ran out of words.

The guy began to fold, wheezing, but Cody held him upright, dropping him into the nearest empty chair. The table's living occupant, a beefy businessman with thinning ginger hair, growled at him, "Hey, asshole! That seat's reserved!"

"So, take it up with him," Jack said, and let the half-drunk porker see his red-stained blade before he tucked it out of sight, leaving the guy to either leave or raise a hue and cry.

A retching noise behind Jack told him dude from middle management was throwing up, instead.

One shooter down. How many left standing between Jack and his target at Night Moves?

He started drifting toward the restrooms, situated at the northeast corner of the showroom, near an elevator that required a special key to operate. Noting that complication, Cody wished he'd given his first strip club kill a quick pat-down, but there was no way he could double back and check his pockets now, with Chubby Ginger spewing at the table and another likely gunman homing in to find out what the trouble was.

A few more seconds, and the new arrival would behold his leaking countryman. And after that, the feces would most definitely hit the fan.

Cody didn't know what kind of swift response the *bratva* had in place at Night Moves, whether some kind of an alarm would sound and interrupt the blaring music, but he clearly recognized that time was running down.

Tick-tock.

He had to get ahead of it and stay ahead, before it was too late.

Colonel Vadim Yezhóv watched on his central CCTV monitor as one of his *russkaya mafiya* assets was skewered like a fish and dumped into a seat downstairs, his startled tablemate at first protesting, then unloading supper and too many drinks onto the tablecloth and floor. The man who'd skewered Yezhóv's thug moved on, as if the killing meant no more to him than wiping mongrel *der'mo* from his shoe sole.

Not precisely casual, but certainly professional.

Oh, well. Yezhóv had done his best, warning their team leader downstairs, providing all descriptive details he possessed. It wasn't his fault if some third-rate bungler dropped his guard and suffered for it.

Yezhóv did not plan to wait around and see whatever happened next.

A fight was shaping up downstairs, moments away from an explosion now. It could go either way, he realized, but there was *no* way that he planned to wait around and deal with the police when they arrived.

No, Houston P.D.'s finest would find Yezhóv safe and sound at home, nursing a head cold, suitably surprised and horrified to learn that mayhem had descended upon Night Moves during his rare absence.

Bratva gangsters on the premises? How could he possibly be held responsible for that?

Of course, Yezhóv was Russian, as were they. What of it? Anyone was free to come and go at Night Moves if they paid the cover charge and passed inspection by front-door security. Discrimination on the basis of suspicion, much less any man's appearance or ethnicity, would be criminal under municipal statutes, as well as under state and federal laws. Unlike "driving while black", the simple fact of having Russian roots was not a crime. Yezhóv himself proved that each time he gave another briefcase full of cash to charity and earned public applause for his philanthropy.

How could he even know if certain patrons in his club were criminals, much less that they had smuggled arms into the showroom? Clearly, he would have to fire his bouncers and recruit wiser, more skilled replacements. But beyond that, what could Yezhóv do?

Job one: getting the hell out of Nochnyye Khody and proceeding home to his McMansion on Weslayan Street, in River Oaks.

And that meant getting out alive, unscathed.

First thing, he took a .45-caliber AMT Hardballer from

his desk, the upper right-hand drawer, and tucked it underneath his alligator belt, around in back. The pistol weighed two pounds four ounces, loaded with eight rounds. It had been purchased legally—no waiting period or registration mandated within the Lone Star State—and a Motorist Protection Act permitted all drivers to carry pistols in their vehicles, concealed. For traveling afoot, he had a concealed handgun license issued by the Harris County Sheriff's Office, recognized statewide.

Who would refuse the simple right of self-protection to an EB-5 investor who had paid a million dollars on arrival, to secure safe-haven in America and had been giving lavishly to his community from day one, onward?

Glory to the U.S. Constitution and its Bill of Rights, the bold Second Amendment in particular.

Within mere days of buying Night Moves, while transforming it into one of the city's foremost titty bars, Yezhóv had hired a separate, discreet contractor to provide him with a secret exit from his office on the second floor, which no examination of the blueprints would reveal. If questioned—which he never had been—Yezhóv would describe the hidden staircase leading to the joint's back alley as a fire escape, a sop to his woeful, even pathetic, arsonphobia.

In fact, he had no fear of fire, but why should he tell that to any nosy, prying *politsiya*?

No one who had ever seen *The Towering Inferno* liked the thought of being trapped upstairs, inside a building as it burned.

Before descending to the street, Yezhóv opened his briefcase, placed his "special" ledger into it, and left the other copy—suitable for viewing by the IRS or anybody else who might intrude—still lying open on his desk. That done, he pressed a hidden button on the north wall's cedar paneling, passed through the doorway hidden there, and flipped a switch to light the stairs below. He left the secret door ajar behind him, reckoning he might have finished with Night Moves, or it with him. It didn't matter if intruders found his hidden exit from the club, as long as he was gone when they came looking for him on the second floor.

Downstairs, a sleek Porsche 918 Spyder sports car sat waiting for him, candy-apple red, its 4.6-liter V6 engine finely tuned and lovingly maintained, as were the two electric motors on its front and rear axles. The sexy ride required no more than eighteen seconds to accelerate from zero, at a standing start, to 184 miles per hour—more speed than Yezhóv should ever need on Houston's streets.

Only when he was belted in behind the Spyder's steering wheel did he relax and start thinking ahead to his next move.

The next guy moving in on Cody was a giant, six foot five at least, built like his mercenary friend and sometime helping hand on special missions, Harley-riding weapons specialist Hog Wiley. In this case, the hulk had close-cropped hair, no beard beyond a couple days' deliberate stubble shading his craggy jaw.

In fact, he bore a vague resemblance to film actor Robert Z'Dar, except the guy closing on Cody now was obviously still alive.

But that could change.

The Bluetooth dangling from the hulk's right ear told Cody he was in communication with his fellow *bratva* goons, and likely also with Vadim Yezhóv. Befitting his dimensions, and the bulge beneath his jacket from some big-and-tall retailer, Cody judged his weapon to be something larger than your standard semi-auto handgun or large frame revolver.

What, exactly?

Cody didn't have to ponder that for long. Mouthing some comment to the Bluetooth's microphone, King Kong reached inside his unbuttoned coat and pulled a Micro Uzi, stock folded to its left side, the butt plate doubling as a foregrip if he chose to use it for enhanced control.

Rather than duck and run, risking the Uzi's epic rate of fire reducing him to steak tartare, Jack drew the Glock from his right hip and fired as soon as his arm reached its full extension. Hours of practice on the range, plus countless kill-or-be-killed confrontations, paid off for him now, his .40 S&W round striking Goliath's nose, inverting it, and passing on to shower anyone behind him with the contents of his skull.

That didn't stop a lifeless index finger clenching on the Micro Uzi's trigger, though, and when the whole 9mm mag burned down within a second and a half, the club's DJ suddenly realized that more was going on around him than some dancers gyrating onstage. Whatever Mr. Music did next, killed the blasting tunes and left the ringing silence after automatic gunfire filling up with frightened shouts from men, bare-naked ladies screeching as they ducked and dodged back toward their room where costume changes were performed.

And that was just exactly how a plan blew up and went to hell.

Two shooters down, and Cody saw four others homing in on him from different portions of the showroom, guns in hand now, shouting at the customers and waitresses who blocked them unintentionally, lashing out with steel or knuckles if the obstacles were slow to move aside. None of the other four were firing yet, but how long would they wait, now that they'd seen their massive point man hit the deck to rise no more?

Who knew?

The only answer that immediately came to Cody's mind was fighting fire with fire.

Leonid Koshkin cursed a blue streak in his native tongue while plowing through the crowd of patrons and employees anxious to escape the shooting gallery. Dancers and waitresses who didn't want to risk a dash backstage for clothes were running for the lighted exits, wearing only G-strings and high heels, a few with glitter added for effect. The "gentlemen" who'd paid to gawk at them ignored dictates of chivalry, adhering to the modern rule of fat old white guys first.

One of the good-time drinkers blundered into Koshkin's

path, collided with him, calling him a shithead as he flung a hand that grazed Leonid's crew-cut scalp. Koshkin repaid that insult with his CZ 110 semiauto, whipping it across the asshole's nose and loosing twin jets of crimson before the guy collapsed, wailing.

Leonid would have liked to stay and kick him for a while, but now he had a fix on Yuri Losev's slayer, sixty feet or more in front of him and moving toward the elevator that would only leave him frustrated and trapped, without the proper key in hand.

Koshkin risked a shot and missed, seeing his bullet wing a waitress on the fly and spin her toward a now-abandoned table that collapsed beneath her weight on impact. Rasping, "*Chertovski der'mo*," he ran after his retreating enemy, shouting into his Bluetooth's microphone, "Pavel! Konstantin! To me! I have him, moving toward the elevator. Capture him alive if possible."

"*Yebat' eto!*" Pavel Speransky answered back. "He's killed Yuri and Feliks!"

"Do as you are *pròklyatyy* told or get your *zhopa* out of here and don't come back!" Koshkin replied.

Silence from Pavel in answer to Leonid's order was the next best thing to a salute, right now.

Ahead of him and closing in, Koshkin saw his intended prey pause at the elevator's door and turn back toward the showroom, as he drew a second Glock from underneath his jacket.

For the first time, Koshkin wondered who had set the

trap, and who had stumbled into it.

Pavel and Konstantin had almost reached him when the stranger opened fire, both pistols simultaneously, almost seeming not to aim. But he was not just shooting randomly, erratically, to hear himself make noise.

His bullets zipped past Koshkin, to the Russian's left and right, passing within a range where Koshkin thought—imagined?—he could feel them passing by. To one side, he heard Pavel grunt and gasp, his gravel voice immediately recognizable, even as he was dying on his feet. When he collapsed onto the littered floor, the impact of his body sounded like a sack of laundry dropped from ten or fifteen feet.

Poor Konstantin, to Koshkin's left, did not go down as quietly. Instead, he made a high-pitched sound, somewhere between a scream and gargle, thick with liquid that could only be his life's blood pumping from a ruptured throat or jaw. Dying, he still got off one last shot from his Browning BDM pistol, and had the cursed luck to drill Leonid's shoulder from behind, causing Koshkin in turn to cry out from his pain and stumble, dropping to one knee before he caught himself.

Incredible! One of his own damned men had brought him down, his crippled right arm dangling from its socket, fingers barely clinging to his CZ 110 semi-automatic.

He was staring down the stranger's twin Glock muzzles, seeing death before him, part of his mind wondering how it had taken so long to come calling on him.

"All I need's the elevator key," his slayer said. "There's still no need for you to die."

They both knew he was lying. Leonid could read it plainly on the other's face.

In fact, there was no way Koshkin could live. Not now.

Snarling, he brought his left hand over, tried to raise the Czech pistol, but never got that chance. The Glocks winked at him, blasting him backwards and into darkness that he hoped would last forever, without dropping him into hellfire.

Cody was thankful that the Russian wore his keyring dangling from a belt loop of his slacks. He'd never cared for going through a dead man's pockets, sometimes getting bloody hands in the process, though he would do whatever his mission required.

Ripping the keyring free, scanning the nearly empty showroom now, Jack counted only three disoriented, injured stragglers remaining with the obviously dead. All three looked dazed, but two of them were fumbling with their cell phones, one trying to dial with his wrong hand, the right arm bloodied from a bullet's passage.

And the other one, still clearly drunk, was taking pictures of the carnage with his iPhone, if you could believe that ghoulish shit.

Cody crossed over to the wannabe photographer and snatched the phone out of his hand, dropped it onto a nearby tabletop, and blasted it to techno-purgatory with a .40 S&W round.

There'd be no candid snaps of him for the police, much

less posted around the world on social media. When the guy started cursing him, as if Cody had just run down his dog, Jack slugged him with a Glock and put him down, not feeling any pangs of guilt.

Screw all the online vultures, selfie addicts, and their brainless "followers". The world, in Cody's view, would have been better off without them, but that alas, wasn't his assignment.

With the key, he brought the elevator down, climbed in, and rode back up to reach the second floor. Jack was intensely conscious of his game clock winding down until Houston P.D.'s first cars arrived, and if he wasn't gone by then, things would get fugly in a rush.

The elevator car stopped with a subtle jerk, and Cody held one of his pistols ready to meet any opposition as the door opened in front of him.

Nothing.

Apparently, Yezhóv had either fled the club already, or was gone to start with, when the shit went down. Jack doubted that, remembering the Russian crew chief listening to someone on his earpiece, before giving orders to his team in the showroom.

The owner's office wasn't hard to find. The second floor had two doors showing. One was labeled PRIVATE, while the other had a cartoon toilet painted on it, the commode signage announcing its function. Unless there was a panic room Jack couldn't see from the hallway, his upstairs search should be abbreviated.

Bathroom first.

He kicked the door in, scanned the sink, wall-mounted urinal and empty toilet stall, then doubled back into the corridor.

The PRIVATE office door was locked. Nothing a .40-caliber couldn't defeat in record time, without more keyring fumbling around. He barged into the office, following twin pistols—but again, found no one waiting to confront him, maybe try to kill him, maybe pleading for a few more hours of life.

CCTV flat-screens had every angle of the Night Moves showroom covered, nothing on the move except the limping cell-phone caller, bleeding from a thigh wound underneath a short, short skirt. Jack guessed she'd caught a stray rough from the giant's Micro Uzi, through-and-through, certain the bullet wasn't one of his.

A lucky break, all things considered.

Cody eyed a ledger splayed on Yezhóv's desk but wasted no time on it once he'd seen the balanced columns of expenditures and income. Jack couldn't care less if Yezhóv screwed the Texas treasury or IRS on taxes. All he needed now was proof the Russian had been present, watching from his inner sanctum while the Grim Reaper was capering around downstairs.

He found it on the north wall, where a slab of paneling gaped open, showing him a lighted stairwell to ground level, at the strip club's rear. That told Jack all he had to know. He'd missed his man, now had to try again, elsewhere.

He cleared the stairwell visually, then descended, exiting into the night. Out front, the flashing lights of first respond-ers flickered almost gaily in the club's main parking lot. Jack holstered his twin Glocks and started jogging toward his borrowed Subaru.

Next up: a trip to River Oaks, to dump another steaming load of crap on Vadim Yezhóv's ruined night.

CHAPTER 10

The Houston guidebook in his head told Cody that the drive from Night Moves into River Oaks spanned seven miles, a northeasterly dogleg expected to take fifteen minutes at the legal posted speed.

That meant a run east on Willowbend Boulevard, intersecting I-610 northbound—alias South Post Oak Road—and following that through a curve to the east on I-69, aka the Southwest Freeway, till a hard right took him southward on Weslayan Street, toward River Oaks and its eponymous country club.

Folks lived high on the hog in that neighborhood, flaunting their wealth while they proved that cash couldn't buy class. Old money or new, those who had enough of it to preen in their own private spotlight, lording it over their servants and the "great unwashed" hoi polloi, they were still assholes in Cody's eyes. It didn't matter how you dressed them up, how thoroughly you covered them with spray tans or cologne, you really shouldn't take them anywhere except the bank, where they could drool over their safe deposit boxes.

Case in point: as he was pulling into River Oaks, eyes peeled to find the tree-lined side street he required, a canary-yellow Lexus LS 500h came blasting through the four-way stop from San Felipe Street, cutting corners on the screeching left-hand turn. The four-door ride sold for roughly $88,000 with all the bells and whistles, but it could have ended up this evening in a junkyard if it wasn't for the Subaru Legacy's EyeSight system and Pre-Collision Braking function.

As it was, the Subaru lurched to an idling halt and Cody watched the Lexus skim past, twenty-something wastoid driver laughing like a lunatic and shooting Jack the finger, while his collagen-disfigured squeeze was yanking down a tube top, baring high-priced silicone.

In other circumstances, given time to burn, Jack would have liked to chase the Lexus down and maybe force it off the road, into a tree or some estate's brick wall, then haul the driver from his heated body-memory seat to kick his ass.

Lucky for Richie Rich Junior that Jack was on the clock and it was ticking down.

River Oaks was stylish. Cody gave Vadim Yezhóv that much, though he ranked as nothing but a tenant passing through, no input to construction of his rented home, not much more interaction with the staff that kept it spic and span. Some of the cash undoubtedly derived from Night Moves, more from some shell company the FSB had set up in the Cayman Islands, the Bahamas, possibly in Switzerland.

An army of forensic bean counters could chase that paper trail around the world and never come within a thousand miles of Moscow's Lubyanka Square.

No problem.

Jack knew all he had to know about Yezhóv from Langley's files and Sara's dark suspicions. Cody had already proven links between the ED-5 investor with his green card and the Russian mob, as well as Allah's Flame. The only open question now was whether Jack could squeeze tidbits of useful information from the FSB black operator before snuffing him.

Sparing his life? As any Mafiosi you could mention might have said, fuggedaboudit.

Vadim Yezhóv had one foot in the grave and one on a banana peel. He simply didn't know it yet.

Cody looked forward to breaking that news in person, fairly soon.

Of course, he'd be expecting guards on site, whether Yezhóv had them on loan from the *russkaya mafiya*, from Allah's Flame, some half-assed outlaw biker gang, or wherever in hell an FSB illegal shopped these days for men who took life seriously. One thing that he absolutely, positively would not have was Spetsnaz triggermen or anybody else who might connect him to the Kremlin in these topsy-turvy times.

Jack could remember ancient U.S. propaganda posters from the 1950s, trumpeting the call of "Better Dead than Red". Today, beyond the wildest dream of Happy Days Republicans, their party's chosen color was the same crimson worn into battle by the Bloods street gang in skirmishes against the true-blue Crips, and the official government approach to Russia was a schizophrenic mix of rank hostility and snuggling up behind closed doors.

Real life, at least in Cody's world, was so much simpler. Get the I.D. on an enemy, acquire the target, and proceed to take him out—or *her*, or *them*. Whatever.

Smoking adversaries was the same as it had ever been, albeit with the modern benefits of virtual sci-fi technology, and Jack would use whatever tools he had on hand.

Until he cleared the board and it was time to find another game.

Questions plagued Vadim Yezhóv as he nosed the Porsche 918 Spyder into his driveway, rolling past two guards who manned his automatic gate and on from there into his rented home's three-car garage. The vehicles already waiting for him were a gray Mercedes-Benz E-Class W212 sedan and a safety-conscious Volvo XC90 SUV in white.

Yezhóv parked in between the other cars and left the Spyder's key in the ignition, nodding to his chief of staff, Ilya Vinogradov, a captain of the FSB and weapons specialist with anything from small arms to a range of toxins that produce slow, agonizing death immune to antidotes.

"All is in readiness, *Polkóvnik*," Ilya informed Yezhóv, using the Russian term for "colonel".

Yezhóv wasted no time complimenting Ilya for obeying orders he'd received by telephone while Yezhóv was returning from the Night Moves slaughter pen. Yezhóv expected competency from his various subordinates and never wasted praise on the accomplishment of routine tasks, in case it made them soft.

"We leave within the hour," he advised Captain Vinogradov. "The Lear is ready?"

"*Da, cer.* Fueled and waiting as per your command."

Under the present circumstances, Yezhóv would not risk flying from George Bush Intercontinental Airport. Instead, his Learjet 75—considered a light business jet with a maximum takeoff weight of 21,500 pounds, two crewmen, and seats for nine passengers—was housed at West Houston, fifteen miles west of downtown.

West Houston is a privately owned, public use airport built in 1962 on two hundred acres adjoining Addicks Resevoir, in Houston's Greater Katy suburb. Geography accounted for its startup name, Lakeside Airport, changed in the early 1980s. It featured one asphalt runway and charged no landing fees for fixed-wing aircraft, although airplane owners were charged a ten-dollar handling/security fee if incoming passengers failed to support the strip by making purchases inside its two-story facility.

"The flight plan?" Yezhóv asked, as Ilya followed him inside the house.

"Officially, we're going to Atlanta, Hartsfield–Jackson International. We shall report a deviation while en route."

Atlanta was within his reach from Houston—793 miles to the northeast, while the Learjet 75 had a range of 2,348 miles, cruising at 535 miles per hour—but Hartsfield–Jackson seemed too dangerous to Yezhóv, the world's busiest passenger airport since 2000, with state-of-the-art security measures in place, including facial recognition software and a glut of local, state, and federal law enforcement officers.

No good for a Russian spy on the run.

Instead, he planned on diverting to Alabama's city-owned Mobile Regional Airport, a shorter hop for the Lear at 468 miles, handling some 280,000 passengers yearly, compared to Atlanta's one million. Granted, it was home to the Mobile Coast Guard Aviation Training Center, but the coast guard's brief was catching smugglers and retrieving boaters in distress, not tracking foreign spies.

And in a few more hours, every airport in the country would be locked down, all flights grounded until further notice—that is, if Abbas Abdul Maarku and Allah's Flame pulled off their master plan.

If not...well, Yezhóv would rethink his options, choosing from a short list of tropical Third World nations, picking up the pieces of his life, eluding Moscow's manhunters as long as he could manage it.

An ultimately losing game, as he had every cause to know.

"Arrangements in Mobile?" he asked Ilya.

"Two cars on standby with the necessary gear, *Polkóvnik*."

That meant cash, weapons and ammunition, travel papers that would pass inspection nearly anywhere except for CIA or FBI headquarters. Yezhóv and his hand-picked entourage would travel overland from what most Alabamans called the

City of Six Flags, choosing from half a dozen methods of escape from the United States, depending on what seemed most practical.

But first, of course, they had to make it out of Houston, out of Texas, in one piece.

At least, *he* did. Confronted with a choice, Yezhóv would shed Captain Vinogradov and all the rest as if they were more than dirty, worn-out clothes.

Yezhóv did not concern himself as to whether one of his men might crack, betray him under questioning by *amerikanskiy* officers. All had been trained to withstand rigorous interrogation. And besides, if he was forced to ditch them on the run, he would leave none alive.

But first, before he gathered his essentials from the house that he would never see again, Yezhóv had a phone call to make. It could not wait a moment longer, even at a risk to his own life.

Abbas Maarku must be informed of what had happened at Night Moves, what he might have to cope with soon.

Above all else, the new day's main event could not be put on hold.

Jack Cody drove past Yezhóv's walled estate, noting the gate's two guards, its pair of CCTV cameras, and kept on rolling past. He saw the lookouts track his Subaru with wary eyes, no guns visible from the street, but doubtless somewhere close at hand.

Another angle of attack would be required.

Cody assumed that Yezhóv had arrived before him, gambling that he was still inside. A motivated fugitive, prepared for anything, might have abandoned rented hearth and home, but Jack hoped he'd surprised Yezhóv enough with the attack on Night Moves that the Russian wouldn't have a well-stocked go bag in his car, nor would he want to make a solo run for cover.

There might still be time to head off his escape, and failing that...

Then, what?

Aside from the Baitul Al-Sadiq mosque, already shot to hell and crawling with police, Cody had no idea where he could lay hands on the leadership of Allah's Flame. If Abbas Maarku—"stern, warlike, and rightly-guided servant" of his god—was still in Houston, that ramped up Jack's sense of urgency.

A smart man, which Maarku had proved himself to be over the long run, would have fled H-Town as soon as Cody killed his borrowed Russian watchdogs at the mosque. Remaining in or near the city after that told Jack that Allah's Flame had plans for Houston, rather than some other juicy target in the States.

What plans?

Again, Jack didn't have a clue.

That put him at a disadvantage, still behind the game, and in a perilous position once the fuse was lit.

Or was that fuse already burning down to Zero Hour even now?

Jack wiped that prospect from his mind, focusing on the here and now. He boxed the tree-lined block, cruising by homes with first-rate curb appeal, and rolled into an alley butting onto the rear wall of Yezhóv's acreage. Roving security might spot it, but he had to take that chance. At least, between the Baitul Al-Sadiq and Night Moves, plus its normal nightly rate of 911 calls, Houston P.D. should be distracted from his new target.

Until the action started, and rich neighbors started clamoring for help.

He suited up in darkness, literally dressed to kill, and eased up to the eight-foot wall of cinder blocks surrounding Yezhóv's property. Appearances meant everything in River Oaks, so Yezhóv hadn't added concertina wire on top, no spikes or shards of broken glass set in concrete. There *were* two CCTV cameras mounted at each end of the eastern wall's expanse, no way of knowing who—if anyone—had eyes on monitors inside the house.

Jack rolled the dice, jumped up and dangled by one hand below each camera in turn, applying black spray paint to their lenses, ditching the can while counting thirty seconds in his head.

If someone in the house noted a sudden blackout on two cameras, security would hasten to the scene and Jack would have to cope with that, losing his slim advantage of surprise. If not...

The thirty seconds passed by silently.

All good to go, then—or until he ran into the next hurdle.

Jack scaled the wall and sat astride it long enough to use a silent whistle, as a lure for any guard dogs lurking on the premises. When none responded, Cody felt relief. Capping a human adversary never seemed to bother him, but killing animals engaged in duties they'd been trained for always put him in a lousy mood.

When he was satisfied that no one had him spotted, Jack dropped to the grass inside Yezhóv's retreat. The Steyr AUG was slung across his back, Cody's right hand gripping the Glock with Osprey sound suppressor, moving toward the backside of the broad two-story house.

Next item on his worry list: a motion sensor that would activate the backyard's floodlights, also likely triggering alarms inside the house. That was a basic setup, normally a given for this kind or upscale neighborhood, but nothing happened as he neared a swimming pool equipped with slide and diving board, adjacent to a large brick barbecue.

Unusual, particularly for a man who ought to be preoccupied with personal security.

Or did Yezhóv put all his faith in men with guns, boots on the ground?

Jack got his answer seconds later, when a pair of sentries came around the southeast corner of the house, both with Kalashnikovs in hand.

Abbas Abdul Maarku released a snarl of rage and clutched his cell phone in a strangler's grip, tempted to fling it from him toward the fireplace of his home on Leland Street. With an extreme effort of will, he drew back from that petty, wasteful gesture, turning to face frowning Talal Ataullah.

"Al'akhbar alsayiyat ya sydy?" Talal inquired.

It was a foolish question on its face, considering Maarku's clear-cut reaction to the unexpected call, but he breathed deeply and restrained himself from screaming at his second-in-command.

"It seems bad news is all we ever get from our *alruwsia* so-called allies. Each time, in fact, the news gets worse."

"What's happened now?" Ataullah asked.

"Someone's attacked Yezhóv's decadent nightclub, killed more of his men. Yezhóv himself barely escaped, or so he claims. The *nadhil alqadhra* is running out on us, the way his country's soldiers fled Afghanistan when battle turned against them. He advises us to carry on alone."

Talal blinked twice at that, then squared his shoulders and declared, "We must. Is that now so, *alqayid*? Surely, we have come too far to turn back now."

"You're right, of course. We only needed Moscow to provide the necessary hardware, anyway. Nothing postpones the Day of Flame."

"Allahu Akbar!" Talal exclaimed.

Instead of mouthing the prescribed reply, Maarku asked his lieutenant, "Is the cargo still on schedule?"

"Yes, sir. One container, on the SS *Moucheron,* French registry, should dock at six o'clock this morning. The second, aboard the Greek freighter *Tryphon* arrives within the next half-hour. Payments have been delivered to secure swift unloading. If there is no difficulty from the CBP, one shall be set aside for subsequent collection by a rented truck. The other will proceed along the Houston Shipping Channel, inland."

Maarku translated Talal's "CBP" shorthand. It stood for U.S. Customs and Border Protection, one of several agencies that had been overhauled or built from scratch after the epic 9/11 skyjackings. Research informed him that the CBP, a branch of Homeland Security, employed some 45,600 sworn federal agents and officers, plus 16,580 support staff, directed from Washington's Ronald Reagan Building and International Trade Center on Pennsylvania Avenue.

The CBP duty assignments were diverse. Its force included a general Office of Field Operations, Agricultural Specialists, Import/Entry Specialists, Air and Marine Enforcement and Interdiction Agents, and the U.S. Border Patrol. All spent nineteen weeks at the Federal Law Enforcement Training Center in Glynco, Georgia, learning basic tactics and their respective specialties.

Not one would be prepared to face this morning's nightmare in Texas, with shockwaves spreading out around the globe.

"Security is paramount," Maarku told his subordinate, unnecessarily.

"I understand, sir."

"No man is to be excused from duty under any circumstances. I don't care if he has smallpox with a side order of leprosy. All hands on deck, as the *al'amrikiuwn* say."

"Yes, sir."

Americans. God, how Maarku despised them for their decades of imperialism and their squat-and-gobble pseudo-culture, fouling everything they touched, looting the world to feed their parasitic one percent. He saw no irony in that position and his own reliance on the House of Saud bankrolling Allah's Flame from its inception to the present day.

Over the past four hundred years, Americans had fattened from the labor of their slaves, stolen vast tracts of land at gunpoint from its native people and from other European settlers who preceded them, pursued a course of genocide against people of color from the Western Hemisphere across the vast Pacific, into Asia, and had raped the Middle East while branding those who would oppose them "terrorists".

Today, within a few short hours, Allah's Flame would strike a blow to change the course of history. All Maarku had to do—

"What's that?" he asked Talal, a sound from somewhere on the grounds outside cutting across his train of thought.

"Sir?"

"Listen! Was that noise—"

Before he could complete the question, automatic gunfire rattled in the night.

Cody brought down the strolling sentries with two rounds apiece, both solid double-taps to center mass, but he couldn't control the fact that one of them was careless, walking with his index finger looped inside the trigger guard of his AKS-74U, firing off a burst of 5.45×39mm rounds as he went down, chewing his own feet into deviled ham.

That tore it.

Anyone inside the house, awake or otherwise, couldn't miss the Kalashnikov's sound, nor could Yezhóv's neighbors to north or south. Cody holstered his muffled Glock—no point in subtlety from there on in—and gripped his AUG as he advanced on the nearest entry, through a broad sliding glass door that faced the poolside patio.

He couldn't see beyond the window's tinting, no lights burning in the room beyond, but that was no impediment. Jack crouched beside the redbrick barbecue, mounted a 22mm rifle grenade on the Steyr's flash hider, and switched its gas valve to the proper setting.

No aiming necessary at a range of thirty feet or less. He fired, then instantly ducked back behind the barbecue as glass imploded, tumbling like a jagged, frozen waterfall. That impact didn't trigger the grenade, but it went off a second later, having flown across the room within and struck its back wall before bursting into smoke and flame.

At that, Jack thumbed the Steyr's gas valve back to normal operation, rose, and charged the gaping maw where once a sliding door had kept the night at bay. No gunfire greeted him in transit, and he heard no sounds of movement from inside the smoky room as he entered, sweeping the space in search of targets.

It had been a rec room, but there'd be no recreation going

on in there until forensic cleaners did their thing. A vintage jukebox and pinball machine had suffered shrapnel damage from the blast, as had the walls and popcorn ceiling overhead. The sixty-five-inch Hisense Ultra HD flat-screen television dangleds from its cables, shot to hell.

No channels, nothing on.

Jack made a beeline toward a doorway to his left, with no idea where it might take him. Wishing that he'd asked Sara to hunt around for floor plans of the house—too late for that, by far—he forged ahead, determined to search every room on both floors if it came to that, until he found his man.

Or died in the attempt. And that was still an option anytime Cody was in the field.

Once in the corridor beyond the rec room, L-shaped, leading off to north and east, he could hear voices shouting back and forth in Russian. Some of it was comprehensible, the rest too far away and garbled by various intervening walls, for him to make it out. The usual response to a sudden assault: cursing, seeking directions, calling names, somebody endlessly repeating, "*Chto za khren*?"

A rough translation into English: "What the fuck?"

"Just me," Jack muttered in reply. "Keep talking, buddy. Lead me to you."

It was dicey, moving through the damaged house, not knowing hostile numbers or exactly where his adversaries were. Had Yezhóv even run straight home from Night Moves, looking for shelter here, or was Cody wasting his time?

The only way to know was moving through the house

and clearing it, room after room, cutting the dead wood as he went, until he knew for sure. A mental coin toss: if the Russian agent had come back, even if he intended to keep moving on from there, Jack had an opportunity to finish that phase of his mission.

If not...

Where would he look for Yezhóv next? How would he get the line, the intel that he needed to deploy his wrath against the terrorists of Allah's Flame?

The same way he did anything, of course.

One grim step at a time.

Vadim Yezhóv grappled with surging panic as he finished cleaning out his bedroom wall safe, hidden by a Van Gogh reproduction with a hinge concealed at one side of its frame. The lockbox was a Protex WES2113-DF, fire resistant, with a keypad lock whose combination was his service number with the FSB, impossible for anybody else to guess.

Sounds from downstairs, a smell of smoke, the AMT Hardballer wedged under his belt in back, assured Yezhóv that he was swiftly running out of time.

He grabbed the cash first, half a million U.S. dollars skimmed from Night Moves and his monthly stipend routed to a Texas bank from Lubyanka Square by way of Offshore Corporate Concerns, a Russian front in Bodden Town, Grand Cayman, specifically to meet his mission's needs.

Next came his travel papers: passports from Russia, Cuba,

mainland China and Morocco, duly issued under pseudonyms by countries lacking extradition treaties with America. Together with his U.S. passport and green card, they verified four alternate identities, each one expendable.

With time now running out, he didn't bother packing clothes, a task to which he had allotted thirty minutes if he was not actively pursued after the Night Club massacre. Now that the vision of a simple getaway was burning down around him, he could get by with the suit he'd donned at noon, acquiring other raiment in the course of his escape.

Hefting the black Adidas zipper bag, Yezhóv moved to his closet and retrieved a Beretta Mx4 Storm submachine gun, loaded with a thirty-round box magazine of 9×19mm Parabellum rounds, weighing the best part of six pounds.

Unlike its politics in general, gun laws in Texas were considered "liberal", meaning that nearly anyone could purchase any firearm in their price range, with a state-issued I.D. Machine guns were included, under terms of the 1934 National Firearms Act, requiring registration and a transfer tax each time a gun changed hands. Yezhóv's Mx4 Storm was duly registered in Washington, its bill of sale long since forgotten in a Lubbock gun shop.

Yezhóv, in his own strange way, had always been a stickler for legality.

Thusly armed and packed for travel, Vadim now needed to make his way downstairs, past sounds of battle, and slip into the garage, where all three of his vehicles sat waiting, their ignition keys in place. He planned to take the Volvo five-door SUV if he reached it alive, trusting its relatively bland appearance to help hide him on the road, until he reached West Houston Airport and his waiting Learjet.

Failing that, the Volvo got fifty-three miles to the gallon, drawing from a thirteen-gallon tank, which should convey him some 689 miles from his home in whatever direction he chose. Most major Texas cities lay within his reach before he stopped for gas, as did New Orleans and Biloxi, Oklahoma City, Little Rock, Memphis, Birmingham—or he could cross the border into Mexico at Brownsville, into Matamoros, and roll south from there.

The world awaited him, if he could manage to survive the next few minutes.

Unlike the Flame of Allah's coterie of psychotic zealots, Yezhóv had no yen for martyrdom. His parents had been ardent Communists, as he was a devoted servant of the Russian Federation now. He carried out the work assigned to him, but felt no personal investment in its outcome, other than advancement of his own ambition and survival. If to-day, mid-morning, brought the end of Planet Earth as he had known it up till now, he would adapt and carry on.

But Yezhóv could accomplish nothing from a grave.

Ilya Vinogradov almost collided with him as Yezhóv stepped from his bedroom. Usually cool and steady under pressure, Ilya's long face wore a grim expression of concern, not lapsing into outright worry yet, but likely on its way.

"Report!" Yezhóv ordered, before his minion had a chance to speak.

"At least one armed intruder is inside the house, *Polkóvnik*."

"And outside?"

"Unknown, sir."

"Have you seen the enemy yourself?"

"No, sir. He would be dead, in that case."

"Duty calls upon you to contain him, *Kapitan*. My orders require me to be elsewhere."

"Yes, sir! Understood." Was that a flicker of anxiety behind Vinogradov's gray eyes? "And when I have disposed of him?"

"You have my cell phone number."

"*Da, cer.*"

Yezhóv saw no point in telling Ilya that his cell was already switched off, or that its SIM card would be stripped, discarded once Yezhóv had put a mile or two behind him in the Volvo SUV. Vinogradov could call him until Hell froze over without getting through.

"You should make haste, sir," the captain advised.

"As soon as you return to lead your men and let me pass," Yezhóv replied.

"*Da, cer. Mne zhal'.*"

Yezhóv ignored Ilya's apology, half-heartedly returned the captain's brisk salute, and brushed on past him. Moving toward the stairs.

Battle was raging on the first floor of the house he'd never see again, but Yezhóv had to make it through all that somehow, reach the attached garage, and make good his escape.

Whatever happened next or in the hours ahead, he was determined to survive at any cost.

CHAPTER 11

Cody counted his adversaries as he took them down and out. It was a grueling business, fighting room to room, though maybe not as bad as battling house to house in little desert settlements across Afghanistan and in Iraq.

Close quarters killing, as he'd learned the hard way in his younger years, was all a matter of degree. Some enemies were harder to eradicate than others, more determined to survive, but when the smoke cleared, dead was still the same old dead.

After leaving the former rec room, where he'd slaughtered nothing but inanimate machines, Jack met his first human resistance in the mansion from a single Russian shooter on the stubby side, no more than five foot five, who had seen fit to have a spider's web tattooed across his throat, swathing his jaw from ear to ear. A fat arachnid perched atop his Adam's apple, that protrusion adding three dimensions to its glossy abdomen.

Not likely someone who the boss would send on jobs

where he'd be glimpsed by witnesses, unless the *boyevik* first donned a turtleneck and balaclava to conceal his warpaint. Otherwise, he'd be ID'd in seconds flat and wind up back in prison—where, in fact, he'd probably feel more at home than on the streets.

The tattooed goon was carrying an AK-107 rifle with its stock folded, made bulky by an AK-200-compatible casket magazine quad stacked with sixty 5.45×39mm rounds. Jack knew the weapon's specs—850 rounds per minute on full-auto—and he didn't plan to face that storm if he could head it off.

The trick to down-and-dirty, close-in fighting, is to get there first and make it count. Already tense and primed to let his Steyr AUG speak for him, Jack squeezed off a three-round burst that went in underneath the shooter's chin and changed the whole configuration of his ink.

No throat or jaw meant no tattoo, just bloody ruin where a craggy face had been before, the guy stone dead before his butt and shoulders hit the floor.

And with the backyard sentries, that made three so far. Still twenty-seven rounds in Cody's first Steyr magazine, another twenty-eight between his twin Glocks. Call it fifty-five before Jack had to think about reloading overall in a pinch.

Before leaving his latest kill, Cody improved his odds, slinging the Steyr AUG and scooping up the former tattooed man's assault rifle. He didn't bother looking for spare magazines. The AK-107's casket mag would empty out in just over four seconds, rocking on full-auto, but the weapon was selective fire, and Cody set its switch for three-round bursts to extend its usefulness.

Each boat-tail FMJ round he would fire weighed 3.43 grams and exited the AK-107's muzzle at a speed of 2,900 feet per second. Clad in copper alloy "gliding metal", each bullet contained a steel rod penetrator core, sheathed by a thin lead inlay that didn't fill bullet's pointed tip, allowing it to mushroom and project its nasty steel surprise when it struck home 979 foot-pounds of energy.

Prescription: instant death for damn near anything that lived on Planet Earth, including human beings clad in body armor lacking extra-thick metallic or ceramic plates.

The AK-107 wouldn't have been Cody's normal choice for an assault, but in the given circumstances, it was still a boost in firepower over the AUG and would extend his capability to fight without reloading under hostile fire.

The downside: with its fully-loaded casket magazine in place, the AK-107 weighed 10.5 pounds to his AUG's 7.9, but what was an extra 2.6 pounds in a crunch, getting lighter every time he stroked the trigger, if it helped keep Jack alive?

No sweat.

And as he moved deeper into the house, Cody knew he'd rather be lugging it than standing on the weapon's business end.

Captain Ilya Vinogradov believed in following *Polkóvnik* Yezhóv's orders to the letter, without question, as he'd done for every one of the superiors he'd served since he enlisted with the FSB. In this case, that meant letting Yezhóv watch his own back as he fled from River Oaks, while Ilya stayed behind to guard the house against their enemies.

That dedication might be tantamount to suicide, but even if he managed to survive, Vinogradov knew that his chances of escaping from the ritzy Houston neighborhood lay somewhere between slim and none. Police were almost certainly en route to Weslayan Street by now, responding to emergency alerts from wealthy neighbors roused from sleep, lovemaking, or a late-night round of drinks by gunfire and explosions on their block.

How many *ofitsery politsii*? It wouldn't matter if the home-invaders wiped out Ilya and his soldiers prior to squad cars and SWAT vans arriving at the scene, but if Vinogradov's soldiers could eliminate their enemies...

Then, what?

Ilya was briefed in on the plan devised by Allah's Flame, supported by the FSB on orders from the Kremlin. He had doubtless been denied access to some details, of course. The plan was strictly need-to-know, *Polkóvnik* Yezhóv sharing just enough for Ilya to perform his job effectively, withholding any crucial specs that might be tortured out of him U.S. agents trained in what their government labeled "enhanced interrogation".

For instance, Ilya didn't know—and therefore couldn't say, even if he was so inclined—precisely where the two in-bound cargo containers were to be deployed, or when they would be activated. He *did* know that it was critical for him to get away from Houston proper, well outside the calculated range of each device.

In fact, he knew the stats by heart.

Each payload packed approximately twenty kilotons, equivalent to the "Fat Man" A-bomb dropped on Nagasaki, back in August 1945. Unlike that bomb, however, Allah's Flame planned on two surface explosions, each with a fireball radius of 284 yards, an air blast radius of one-third mile, and a 500 rem radiation dosage radius of 1,531 yards.

Net result: catastrophic damage to all manmade structures within the air blast radius, with at least 160,000 persons killed outright and another 292,000 injured, the latter figure rising 917,000 within the first twenty-four hours.

All that, without trying to calculate long-term effects of fallout and radiation poisoning.

When Ukraine's Chernobyl Nuclear Power Plant melted down in April 1986, a year before Ilya was born, only thirty-one workers had died at the scene, but fallout was a gift that kept on giving. Today, the nearby city of Pripyat—former population 49,360—remained a deserted ghost town, while untold numbers of "survivors" fell to cancer or bore infants with grotesque deformities. Irradiated wildlife had been logged by fish and game authorities more than nine hundred miles away, in Germany.

Imagine Houston, then, with its population packed in at 3,900 persons per square mile, a total of 2.43 million at risk. And the financial havoc wreaked upon America's fourth-largest city: incalculable.

If the second device traveled any significant distance from Houston, either by land or water, the cataclysmic toll might double, even triple on all counts.

Now, the success or failure of that *konspiratsiya* resided in Captain Ilya Vinogradov's hands. Deserted by his colonel, left to hold the fort with *bratva* thugs in place of seasoned warriors, he could either save the day or watch it fall apart.

Success meant glory for his Russian motherland. Failure meant worse than death; his relegation to a laughable footnote in history.

Determined not to fail, Vinogradov clung tightly to his AKMS rifle, hoping it would keep his hands from trembling as he went to find his enemies somewhere inside the rambling house.

The next two Russians bent on killing Cody piled out of a doorway to his left and thirty-some feet farther down the corridor that he was pacing off, clearing each room in turn as he passed by, working his way toward stairs with access to the second floor.

They came out firing, one packing an Uzi submachine gun, while the other had an AKS-74U fully-automatic carbine. Both weapons had similar rates of fire—600 rounds per minute for the Uzi, 700 for the AKS—the major problem being that a shooter generally had to aim unless he had his target cornered in a phone booth or he simply didn't care who caught a dose of lead.

Did phone booths even still exist?

Instead of standing tall and waiting for his enemies to bring their fire under control, Jack hit the floor, milked two three-round bursts out of his captured AK-107. The same aiming rule applied to him as to his opposition, but he did a better job of firing hastily, cutting across their legs, dropping both *boyeviks* so that their final rounds ripped into walls and ceiling, spewing plaster dust and ruptured drywall on impact.

Before they could recover from their maiming wounds, Jack triggered two more busts—twelve rounds in all, with forty-eight still left inside the casket mag—and finished both of them for good. Rising, he double-checked to verify that both were dead, and found nothing worth stripping from their bloodied corpses, and moved on, alert to voices closing in on him from somewhere up ahead.

Two voices, minimum. There might be more, but in the given circumstances, Cody couldn't parse the vocal tones to make a better guess.

Whatever came at him from that point on, he meant to be prepared.

And if Houston P.D. arrived before he had located Vadim Yezhóv...then, what?

It might come down to a choice of fight or flight, and Cody didn't relish the idea of bugging out before he found his man. Ideally, he'd find Yezhóv, bag him, and convey him to a safer place where they could have a nice, uninterrupted heart-to-heart. The odds against Yezhóv revealing anything were slim, but Jack—although no sadist, far from it—could be very persuasive when he had to be.

And killing time in Houston had brought out the beast in him.

Jack reached a branching in the corridor and peeked around the corner to his left, in time to see a solitary gunman plodding toward him, carrying another of the private army's favored AKS-74U carbines roughly at port arms. The quick glance showed no *bratva*-style tattoos, but that just meant the solo shooter felt no need to mark his neck and face indelibly.

Regardless of his body art or lack thereof, the guy was going down.

Cody stepped out into the open, AK-107 leveled from the hip. He pegged the range at thirty feet or so, triggering two short bursts before astonishment could register on his intended target's face. A fraction of a second later, half a dozen 5.45×39mm shockers turned the Russian's crisp white shirt into a crimson scrap of tattered cloth, while he sprawled supine, twitching on the hallway's carpeting.

The guy hadn't entirely given up the ghost as Jack stood over him and asked, in fluent Russian, "Where can I find Yezhóv?"

Later, he was never sure if the near-dead man tried to answer, maybe cursing him, of if he simply exhaled raggedly, expelling bloody drool and bubbles while he faded out.

Jack told him, "*Spasibo za nichego.*"

Translation: Thanks for nothing.

Stepping wide around the leaky stiff, he suddenly picked up a high-pitched sound, repeated with the cadence of a shrill machine. At first, he thought it was a cruiser's siren, pulling up outside, but then it hit him.

Not a cop car's siren, but a car alarm.

Now, where in hell was the garage?

Vadim Yezhóv didn't believe in luck, per se, but he felt fortunate to reach his rented home's three-car garage without encountering armed adversaries on the way. Behind him, automatic weapons were still firing in the house, but all he cared about, standing before the lineup of his vehicles was rolling out and getting gone.

He still had hours yet, until the clock struck Zero Hour and unleashed pure hell on Earth. If he could reach West Houston Airport and his waiting Learjet, he'd be golden. Otherwise, it meant a wild dash down the nearest freeway leading west, north, east—whichever cardinal direction led to safety, but for south, which led directly to the Port of Huston and the Gulf of Mexico.

Or, as they would be henceforth known: Ground Zero for the blast of Allah's Flame.

Having decided in advance to take the Volvo SUV, he strode directly to it, dropped his go bag and his Mx4 Storm submachine gun on the shotgun seat, then jogged around to climb behind the steering wheel. The XC90's key was where it ought to be, in the ignition, and the B8444S engine came to life immediately, on demand. Yezhóv shifted the four-speed GM 4T65 transmission into "DRIVE", the SUV's nose pointed toward the driveway and the street down range, since it had been backed into the garage.

Smooth sailing now, except…

Yezhóv had no idea what caused the fender-bender. Possibly he'd jogged the wheel a bit in his excitement, while he reached up with his right hand for the push-button garage door opener clipped to the driver's sun visor. Maybe he'd parked the Porsche 918 Spyder too close to the SUV when he'd pulled into the garage and didn't notice, since the driver's door opened to Yezhóv's left, versus the Volvo standing to his right.

They hadn't scraped when he pulled into the garage, but now that he was in an even greater hurry to depart, the Volvo's right-rear fender, wheel well, whatever it was, collided with the Porsche right-hand side, scraping some of its paint down to bare metal, triggering the sportster's car alarm.

The raucous din made Yezhóv wince. He felt as if someone were jabbing at his eardrums with an icepick, probing deep, twisting the spike.

To shut it off, he'd have to leave the Volvo, run around the Spyder to its driver's side, climb in, and hit the kill switch on its dangling key fob. Failing that, it meant popping the hood and rummaging around beneath it, ripping free the wires transmitting power to the car alarm.

No time for either option now, when he had blasted out a signal through the house, informing anyone who cared to notice that a drive-away escape was in the works.

How long before his enemy—assuming there was only one

involved—responded to that summons? His soldiers might have stopped the man or men by now, since Yezhóv heard no further gunfire from inside the house, but he also considered the alternatives. The home-invader(s) might have finished off his *bratva* troops—or it was simply possible the blasting car alarm had deafened him, reverberating inside the garage and drowning out sounds from the rented home's interior.

"*Ladit' s ney!*" Yezhóv muttered in his mother tongue. *Get on with it.*

If he was leaving, it was time to go. The Porsche meant nothing, since he never would lay eyes on it again. As for the Volvo XC90, it had safety features up what some *amerikantsy* called the old wazoo, a folksy reference to one's *pryamaya kishka*. Already, impact to the Volvo's right-rear quarter panel had deployed a right-side air bag meant to shield the XC90's nonexistent backseat passengers from harm.

What else would happen when he powered forward, striving to break free?

Yezhóv knew there was only one way to find out.

Reaching across the center console, he retrieved the Mx4 Storm submachine gun, balancing it on his lap. No one had shown up yet to challenge him, but Yezhóv powered down the driver's window to be ready, just in case.

That done, he pressed down steadily on the Volvo's accelerator, listening to tortured metal scream as if in pain.

Cody ran into one more stumbling block while he was fol-

lowing the car alarm's clamor, to find Yezhóv's garage. The
noise alone proved nothing as to who was fleeing from the
mansion, but he'd laid out all the Russians standing in his way
so far, and Vadim Yezhóv wasn't one of them.

Well, make that all but one.

The guy who stood in Cody's way was even larger than
the Micro Uzi bearer he'd put down at Night Moves: six foot
eight, at least, well past 250 pounds, shoulders so broad he'd
likely have to turn sideways to clear a normal-sized doorway.
And where his slightly smaller *bratva* brother opted for a small
but lethal firearm, this one clearly thought size mattered in all
things.

His hands, nearly the size of catcher's mitts, cradled a Ban-
dayevsky RB-12 pump-action combat shotgun, thirty-two
and one-half inches long, feeding its twelve-gauge rounds
from a six-shot detachable box magazine. And if that weren't
enough, he wore a double shoulder holster, clearly visible
since he wasn't wearing a jacket, balanced by a matching pair
of Israeli-made Desert Eagle Mark XIX L5 semi-auto pistols
weighing close to five pounds each, their magazines loaded
with seven rounds apiece of .50-caliber Action Express
rounds.

"Overcompensating much?" Jack asked the Colossus of
Rostov in Russian: "*Sverkhkompensirovat' mnogo?*"

He got nothing back except a tic around one corner of the
bald behemoth's thin-lipped mouth. Instead of answering,
the gargantuan Gulag escapee raised his shotgun, squinting
down its twenty-inch barrel over the plain iron sights.

Cody didn't wait for him to line it up, squeezing his AK-107's trigger four times, rapidly, sending a dozen rounds down range, stitching the man mountain from groin to throat. Already dead or dying on his feet, the ogre still got off a shot as he was slowly toppling over backward, buckshot pellets ripping through the hallway's popcorn ceiling to release a rain of tattered insulation on his sprawling corpse.

That still left thirty rounds inside the AK-107's casket magazine, and Cody kept his finger on the weapon's trigger as he cautiously approached the biggest specimen he'd ever bagged. The Russian's chest heaved once and then again, almost receiving three more rounds to nail him down, before he sighed and farted simultaneously—mortal harmony—and finally went limp.

Jack edged around him carefully, pausing to pluck the shotgun from dead hands and fling it ten feet out of reach, before he picked up speed, now double-timing as he neared the source of the insistent car alarm.

Just give me one more minute, pled silently, to no god he could name. *That's all I need.*

Vadim Yezhóv had many skills, evasive driving well up on the list, but in some manner that he could not understand, he'd hooked the Volvo XC90's right-rear wheel well on the Porsche 918 Spyder's corresponding quarter panel, finding it impossible to extricate himself. He shouted Russian curses mixed hodgepodge with English epithets, and still found no relief.

Standing on the Volvo's accelerator did not help. In fact, it seemed to jam the SUV and sports car more tightly together, like a pair of frenzied robots having angry sex. When he reversed and tried to free himself that way, he only got more rasping, rending sounds but made no progress backward.

He was trapped and growing desperate, certain that he heard no more gunfire from within the mansion now. How many minutes still remained to him—or was it down to seconds now—before his enemies burst in upon him, blasting as they came.

Or, then again, perhaps they hoped to capture him alive, interrogate him, to discover what grim fate the sheikh of Allah's Flame might have in store for them? If so, Yezhóv would foil them, emptying the magazine on his Beretta SMG, then fighting with the AMT Hardballer if they let him live that long.

Surrender was unthinkable, the very notion of it sickening.

A fresh idea occurred to him, perhaps too late by now, but what did Yezhóv have to lose by trying it, if he was finished anyway.

He could not seem to separate the Volvo from the Porsche, but he still had another vehicle to try: the gray Mercedes-Benz E-Class sedan, waiting on the far side of the garage from where he sat, cursing, gnashing his teeth. Another key waited in its ignition, fuel tank full as he kept all of them, in case he needed to evacuate the property in River Oaks.

Like now.

Disgusted, sweating, Yezhóv killed the Volvo's engine, took his submachine gun and his loaded go bag with him as he bailed out of the SUV and ran beyond it, past the battered Spyder, glancing furtively outside through the garage door that stood open now.

At least he'd managed that much, wouldn't have to try again when he was settled in the Merc. Approaching the sedan, he spared time to examine both sides of the car and satisfy himself that neither would impact the Porsche or the garage's wall if he pulled straight ahead, and carefully, before he gunned it down the driveway leading to Weslayan Street.

All clear, which felt like something of a miracle after the weird snafu he'd just experienced. He slid behind the Benz's steering wheel, shifting his bag and SMG across it to the shotgun seat—and bumped the horn, eliciting a bleat that made him jump.

Snarling, "*Trakhni svoyu chertovu mat'*," he cleared his lap, twisted the ignition key, and gunned the V-6 engine to a throaty roar. Released the parking brake—always engaged when it was parked in the garage, although his driveway had no slope to speak of and the doors were normally kept shut— and started easing forward cautiously, more slowly than he would have liked, determined not to blow his last chance with some reckless action.

Almost clear.

He couldn't see the gate guards, but assumed they'd run back to the house when high explosives rent the night, with gunfire coming close along behind. He didn't need them now, in any case. Beside the black garage door opener clipped to the sun visor in front of him, another plastic box was keyed to start the wrought-iron gate rolling along its well-oiled tracks, granting him access to the street beyond.

Another thirty yards, and—

"*Iisus, blyad', Khristos!*"

Suddenly, as if from nowhere, an explosive hailstorm broke over the gray Mercedes-Benz sedan, smashing its tinted windows, hammering against the left side of its bodywork, punching through doors and fenders on the driver's side. The dashboard instruments exploded, sparking as they died. The leather cover on his steering wheel shredded, wilting like a snake's skin when it sheds. Both left-hand tires went flat as one, their rims crunching against concrete.

No hailstorm, that.

It only took a split-second for Yezhóv's mind to grasp the fact that he was under fire, slugs hammering along the Benz's port side, nose to tail, then sweeping back again.

He raised an arm to shield his face, while turning in his seat, groping half-blind to reach his submachine gun, then he felt the piercing agony of impact, bullets taking out his hip, perhaps the kidney on that side, punching him over with a stifled cry across the console, toward the shotgun seat.

Another minute, give or take, and Cody might have missed his man. The Merc sedan was pulling out with Vadim Yezhóv at the wheel, nobody else inside, when Jack barged into the attached three-car garage and saw the Russian on the verge of his escape.

No way to flag him down, as if he'd listen and meekly surrender anyway. Aiming around a Volvo SUV strangely entangled with a sporty Porsche, he braced his AK-107 and began unloading on the Benz, raking the driver's side and hoping that he didn't kill Yezhóv outright, before they had a chance to speak.

He saw windows implode, bright metal divots march across the Merc's gray paint from nose to trunk and back again, its left-hand tires collapsing with a double *pop* and hiss. Yezhóv slumped over to his right inside the car, wounded or reaching for a weapon—maybe both, why not?—and Cody rushed around the other cars to yank the driver's door open, then step back, covering the man huddled in front of him.

When Yezhóv moved, he tried to lift a submachine gun from the other seat in front. Jack fired a three-round burst into the Merc's ceiling, cowing the Russian long enough for Cody to reach in and snatch his weapon, flinging it across the width of the garage to land somewhere beyond the Volvo SUV. The next find was a semi-auto pistol sticking up from Yezhóv's belt in back, visible underneath his jacket. Cody took that, too, and lobbed it off to follow the Beretta SMG.

Disarmed and clearly wounded, bloody from at least one hit along his beltline on the left, Yezhóv barely resisted as Jack grabbed him by his jacket collar, dragged him from the driver's seat, and dumped him on the cleanest concrete floor Cody had ever seen in a garage.

"We need to talk," Jack said in Russian, guessing Yezhóv's mind would be muddled, abuzz with fear and pain, hoping to jump-start a coherent thought. "We're running out of time. *You're* running out of time, *tovarishch.*"

"Are we comrades now?" Yezhóv inquired. Then sneered, "*Idi trakhni sebya!*"

"That's a physical impossibility. And even if it wasn't, I don't have the time."

The Russian rasped a laugh of sorts at that. "In fact, you're already too late. Nothing that you do can change the future now."

"I'll be the judge of that," Jack said. "For now, while you're still breathing, tell me where to find Abbas Maarku and his jihadists."

"They are everywhere," Yezhóv replied.

"That's what you want to go out with? One last lie on your lips?"

The Russian forced a phlegmy laugh. "I have no fear of Hell, you fool."

"Neither do I," Cody replied. "Try fearing me."

He stepped a long pace backward, quickly aimed, and fired a single 5.45mm round into Yezhóv's right knee. Gristle and blood exploded from the shattered joint, as Yezhóv howled in agony.

Jack raised his voice to compensate, saying, "It only goes downhill from here. You want to play it strong and silent you can die piecemeal. If you won't help me, I've got nowhere else to be."

"*Politsiya...*"

"Can't help you now. You've got five seconds to decide." Jack paused a beat, then told the Russian, "Four. Three."

"*Trakhni proklyatykh arabov!*" the wounded Russian wheezed. "They've brought me down to this."

Jack didn't argue with him. Answered, "One. Time's up."

He raised his stolen weapon, sighted on the next-to-dead man's other knee, but Yezhóv stopped him at the final second.

"Wait! I have no loyalty to them, the *gryaznyye verblyudy*."

"Camels? Really?"

"I pity the camels." Yezhóv spent a moment heavy-breathing, then said, "Maarku has a place on Leland Street. You know it?"

"I can find it," Jack assured him.

"I can't say if he will be there now. This morning is supposed to be a busy day. A bad day for *Amerika*. Your worst day ever, I suspect."

"No longer your concern," Cody replied.

"Look to the sea, *mudak*," Yezhóv advised.

"*Tvoya mama*," Jack answered back, and shot him in the face.

CHAPTER 12

Look to the sea.

Jack Cody didn't need a psychic charging by the hour to interpret Vadim Yezhóv's dying words. He'd clearly been referring to the Gulf of Mexico, and more specifically the teeming Port of Houston, possibly including the Houston Shipping Channel.

Sadly, that didn't narrow down the target zone for Allah's Flame one bit. In fact, it just made matters worse.

Stealing a phrase from Creedence Clearwater Revival's 1969 hit song, Houston had been born on the bayou—or in this case, two of them, Buffalo and White Oak Bayous, their confluence once known as Allen's Landing, now a municipal park near the University of Houston's Downtown campus. The port's early terminals were all within city limits, but since 1836 it had expanded to include multiple satellite communities spanning a twenty-five-mile-wide complex of public and private facilities. The busiest site, called Barbour's

Cut Terminal, welcomed international shipping at Morgan's Point, located on Galveston Bay.

All told, the port generated some 800,000 jobs and handled 220 million tons of cargo yearly, including a total container volume of 1.8 million TEUs—*t*wenty-foot *e*quivalent *u*nit, the standard length of most intermodal shipping container units. Annual revenue: around $180 million, with net income for the port of about $50 million.

Oilfield's aside, it was the beating heart of Texas commerce. And if it was stilled...

The Houston Shipping Channel was a logical extension of the port, a natural watercourse widened and deepened by excavation to match the port's average depth of forty-five feet, lined with petrochemical refineries like ExxonMobil Baytown's installation on the east bank of the San Jacinto River, producing 584,000 barrels of oil per day on its own. Aside from petrochemicals, the channel moved Midwestern grain and any other cargo you could think of—legal and illicit, if the Customs men were on the take or simply napping—along its thirty-mile course from Buffalo Bayou to its upstream terminus at Turning Basin, in East Houston.

It was El Dorado on the Gulf, but as with everything in life, there was a down-side, too. Pollution was a major problem, ranging from general contamination over time to specific incidents like the shipping collision that spilled 170,000 gallons of extra-thick bunker fuel oil into the channel, hard by an imperiled bird sanctuary, forcing a four-day closure of the channel. A recent study by the University of Houston showed that children living within two miles of the channel suffered from leukemia at a rate 56 percent higher than the national average, sacrificed without apology or restitution on the altar of free enterprise.

None of Jack's business in the short term. None of his concern on this mission.

Anything that might retard the Port of Houston's commerce, much less shut it down completely, render it inoperable over any length of time, would spell disaster for the Lone Star State and for America at large. Begin with tumbling stock prices and from there, to factory and farm production slowed or terminated altogether in some places, mass job layoffs, and political shockwaves that would be felt around the globe.

How would a group of terrorists bring that about?

The channel's relatively narrow width—530 feet tops, compared to the Mississippi River's variable width of one to ten *miles*—required large vessels to pass each other by means of a maneuver called the "Texas chicken", both veering starboard on approach, allowing water displaced by their bows to move the ships away from one another and the channel's centerline. Passing complete, the suction of water displaced behind each ship drew both back toward the channel's center safely.

Any blockage caused by sabotage would swiftly replicate the collision disaster of 2014.

Or you could simply blow the port and shipping channel straight to hell, disabling all of it for untold days, weeks, months, or years.

To get the most bang for a lunatic jihadist's buck, that meant using a nuke—or more than one. And what was more appropriate than mushroom clouds and fallout, when it came to replicating Allah's Fire?

Jack dialed Sara Durell on his Iridium GO! roam phone, got her on the second ring routed around the planet by technology, and told her what he'd learned so far, spilling his darkest fears out for dessert.

"How sure are you about this, Jack?" she asked him.

"Sure? Not *sure* at all, but nothing else is making any sense to me right now."

"And confirmation?"

"Only comes if I lay hands on Abbas Maarku himself."

"Better get cracking, then, and hope you're wrong."

"I never had much luck with hoping, Sara."

"Right. So, while you're running down Maarku, I'll make a call to NEST."

The Nuclear Emergency Support Team, that would be, run by the U.S. Department of Energy in Washington, on Independence Avenue Southwest.

"Sounds right," Jack said, and broke the link.

Thinking the whole thing sounded absolutely, positively wrong.

Greater Eastwood district, Houston

In his rented house on Leland Street, Abbas Abdul Maarku

and his lieutenant, Talal Wahid ibn Ataullah, tracked progress of the freighters *Moucheron* and *Tryphon* as they reached the Port of Houston, one prepared for docking, while the other took its turn in line for entry into the Houston shipping channel.

Although the ships' captains were French and Greek, respectively, they spoke accented English to communicate with Houston's shipping directors. Maarku—or, rather, one of his tech-savvy aides—had also hacked into the massive port's computerized inventory control system, tracking individual shipping containers via their serial numbers.

Inside each twenty-foot-long box, a sweet surprise for the Great Satan, slumbering in apathy.

"Loose nukes", a term referring both to ready-built weapons and weapons-grade nuclear material, were readily available from various chaotic past and present states around the world. Included on that list were the former Soviet republics of Belarus, Kazakhstan and Ukraine, former storehouses of Moscow's excess warheads, plus Pakistan, its government effectively crippled by a long-running war between its beleaguered army and Taliban rebels. While no reports of lost or stolen warheads were officially confirmed, the Vienna-based International Atomic Energy Agency admitted "more than one hundred" certified nuclear smuggling incidents logged during the years since Soviet communism's collapse.

Make that more than a hundred that the IAEA knew about, the cases wherein they had interdicted trafficking. Meanwhile, media reports confirmed of twenty-five to fifty

cases yearly in which nuclear material was lost or stolen yearly, in varying amounts, from licensed civilian installations
in France, India, Mexico and South Africa. In the last year
with available statistics, the IAEA Secretariat's Incident and
Trafficking Database, established in 1995, listed 2,889 specific
incidents, including 762 reports of theft or loss, 454 involving
unauthorized possession and related criminal activities. In
the remaining seventy-one cases, information "was not suf-
ficient to determine the category of incident".

In short, nobody was truly on top of anything.

The two warheads acquired by Allah's Flame, purchased
with Saudi gold, had been obtained from Kazakhstan where
they were listed as deactivated and "destroyed" in Russian
Armed Forces records. They were 8F675 (Mod2) twen-
ty-megaton warheads intended for use on former Soviet
R-36M2 intercontinental ballistic missiles, designated as SS-
18 Satan by NATO. Each missile carried ten warheads, and in
the rush to purge back inventory after 1991, many had been
eliminated one way or another.

Among the "other" methods, army officers anticipating
layoff or retirement had dismantled some R-36M2s and sold
them off piecemeal—warheads, engines, their guidance sys-
tems, other software, take your pick—and in the process had
become rich overnight.

Abbas Maarku had no idea where most of the "deactivated" nukes had gone, but two of them were presently arriving
in the Port of Houston, soon to realize one virulent jihadist's
fondest dream of crippling an Evil Empire, killing several

hundred thousand smug, self-satisfied Americans.

The R-36M2 warheads initially were set to detonate as airbursts over preselected targets, but they had been overhauled by Russian experts hired to serve the House of Saud, thereby themselves becoming millionaires. Today, the bombs would detonate upon receiving signals on a certain frequency, transmitted via cell phones, pagers, and the like. To guarantee success, those signals would be sent by martyrs situated on shipboard, backed up by seconds no more than a half-mile from ground zero in each case if they should fail somehow, thereby winning salvation and admission to *Jannah*, with all its nubile, eager virgins, depending on faithful completion of the task at hand.

Self-sacrifice in an exalted cause.

Every member bound to Allah's Flame had volunteered. Maarku's task was selecting two, with alternates on standby, while deflecting disappointment from the warriors doomed to live a little longer on their earthly plain.

As for himself—the movement's founder, mastermind, and sole authority—he planned on being far away from Houston and environs on the stroke of Zero Hour, when the world caught fire.

He owed survival to the world and to his God, staying alive to carry on the fight until such time as every knee bowed to the One True Faith all false deities were purged by Allah's flames.

Not long to wait now, before Maarku triggered renovation of the world his Lord had made.

And did that not make Abbas Maarku a kind of minor god, at least, unto himself?

The house on Leland Street was nothing extraordinary. Terrorists enjoyed four walls around them and a roof over their heads, like anybody else, but even when bankrolled by OPEC overlords whose wealth was nearly inconceivable, jihadists had to mind their petty cash and give a strict accounting to their puppeteers.

If Riyadh's masters reckoned they were being cheated, they would cut off funds to Allah's Flame as readily as they severed the hands of thieves and skulls of blasphemers.

Abbas Maarku's Leland Street abode was less than half the size of Vadim Yezhóv's place in River Oaks, no walls around it, no sign of CCTV cameras or guards roaming around outside the house. To Cody that meant any one of three things: Allah's Flame had already departed from the premises; Maarku had stationed his guerillas at strategic points around Houston, in preparation for their Main Event; or they were all inside, ready to stage a last stand as the clock ran down on their conspiracy.

One chance in three that he had made a wasted cross-town drive. Conversely, once he breached the modest house, he might be facing only one or two armed men, up to a dozen or beyond.

So, it was time, once more, to roll the bones, find out if he could score a natural or if he crapped out of life's game.

One thing was certain: those who didn't take a chance could never win.

For the penetration, Jack was taking everything he had, from the AUG and Glocks down to the Smith & Wesson M.A.G.I.C. switchblade in his pocket, leaving out only the Steyr's rifle grenades. He didn't buy that Maarku's crew would have devoted time and resources to armoring the home's interior, much less specific inner doors.

Wherever Jack wanted to go inside, he'd find a way.

Unless somebody killed him first.

Parking the Subaru behind his chosen mark—another alley laid between two blocks of homes for the convenience of Houston's Solid Waste Management Department—and walked up to the backyard's six-foot redwood fence. Its gate was padlocked on the inside, just a hiccup, and he used the silent dog whistle again without any canine response.

Cody went up and over, landing in a crouch on too-long grass, ignored by the home's present renters, leveling his Steyr toward the backdoor that would likely open on a kitchen if he got that far. There was no swimming pool, no other trappings of conspicuous consumption, just a Weber propane barbecue on rollers for easy transportation, covered by a black faux-leather shroud.

When no one cut loose on him immediately, Cody double-timed to reach the backdoor, fired a three-round burst into its lock without trying the knob beforehand—no dead bolt in evidence—and followed with a kick that left the doorway gaping wide.

No kitchen occupants, same thing as back at Yezhóv's place, but this time he heard voices and the sounds of hurried scrambling from a nearby room. No closed doors in between him and the others, two men minimum, weren't cloistered in one of the home's two or three bedrooms.

Not yet.

Cody advanced, ready for anything.

Best case scenario, he'd caught the leadership of Allah's Flame by absolute surprise and had a chance to take them out after a heartfelt tête-à-tête with no illusions that their future could be anything but short and bloody.

The worst case: Maarku and company might find a way to turn the tables on him, maybe execute their plot before Cody could punch their tickets to *Jahannam*, also known to Muslims as The Blaze and The Abyss.

Just a few more moments, and with any luck, his adversaries would be leaving *Jannah*'s anteroom and plummeting downstairs.

Before the kitchen door had finished crashing open, powered by a solid blow and gunfire, Abbas Maarku leapt to his feet from the living room's sofa and lunged for his 5.56×45mm T86 assault rifle, produced by the 205th Armory of Taiwan's Combined Service Forces. He clutched the seven-pound weapon, thirty-one inches long with stock retracted, loaded with a thirty-round STANAG magazine.

Beside him, Talal Ataullah had retrieved a Czech Arms

Factory CZ 805 BREN, chambered for the same ammo as Maarku's weapon but heavier at nearly eight pounds and longer at thirty-four inches with its telescoping stock collapsed. Its magazines, while also holding thirty rounds, were not compatible with Maarku's T86.

In retrospect, poor planning, but Abbas didn't suppose the fight would last so long that either of them had to be concerned with trading magazines.

"Who is it, sir?" Talal hissed at him.

Stupid question. Maarku spat back, "How should I know? Who has hunted us and killed our men since yesterday?"

"I don't—"

"*Akhrus!* Shut up! Go after them!"

"Alone, sir?" There was sudden, unaccustomed fear in Talal's voice and in his eyes.

"Who else? Should we sit here, do nothing, while I call the others back! Move, damn you!"

Ataullah moved, albeit grudgingly, moving as if his CZ 805 BREN weighed a ton. Maarku, watching him go toward nearly certain death, eased down behind the couch and palmed the burner cell he'd purchased at a local electronics store, one of a dozen passed among his men for use only in dire emergencies.

Which clearly meant right now.

A glance over his shoulder, toward the open laptop on the room's low coffee table, showed him that the freighters still weren't in their proper places, likely half an hour yet to go before they were positioned in accordance with his master plan. But, then again, what was a plan, besides a wish list of proposed events that fell apart, as soon as Life stepped in and started toppling dominoes?

This was to be Maarku's great day, the crowning moment of his long crusade, and he was meant to see it through, survive to plot another, even more momentous strike against the West, should that be necessary.

Only idle daydreams? Wasted time and squandered money from his backdoor Riyadh relatives?

Not yet.

He could reach out and give the order now, though premature. His martyrs would be startled and confused, but they would follow his commands—or, if they failed, their alternates would step up, win eternity in Paradise by simply keying their cell phones to detonate the 8F675 (Mod2) warheads in their twin containers aboard ships whose captains had no clue what they were carrying on board.

Twin premature explosions weren't ideal, but they were better than nothing. The damage they inflicted might not be precisely as envisioned—slightly less widespread, to start, but in the crowded port, so close to Downtown Houston, they would still combine to leave a blackened and irradiated wasteland in their wake.

So be it.

And Maarku himself would be a martyr now, revered by the jihadists who inevitably followed in his footsteps to pursue the endless war against their damned Crusader enemies.

Grim-faced, dead-eyed, he turned the cell phone on.

A burner, fittingly. Now it would light a fire that burned

the city down.

Talal Wahid ibn Ataullah had joined Allah's Flame with eyes wide-open, knowing that he could expect to die by violence one day, a willing—even joyful—martyr to the Holy Cause he served. Until this moment, though, the bleak proximity of death had not been driven home for him, even when friends and comrades fell.

Now, in what he guessed would be the final seconds of his life, what did he honestly believe? What was he on the verge of dying for?

While listening to sermons on *Jannah*—the angels who would greet him, speaking words of peace, conveying him into a verdant garden and the arms of virgins who were beautiful beyond imagining, reclining between bouts of passion on a Throne of Dignity—the image had been easy to accept.

This morning, when his hands were trembling from a rifle's weight, echoes of gunfire stinging his eardrums, Talal was having second thoughts.

Too late.

There could be no reversal or reneging on his pledge to Allah or to Abbas Abdul al-Rasheed Maarku.

As if the enemy who'd tracked them here would listen to apologies in any case and choose to spare Ataullah's life.

Preposterous.

He reached the exit from the living room, turned toward the kitchen, where his enemies had made their unexpected and explosive entry to the house.

His first move, automatic and reflexive upon picking up the BREN, had been to switch its ambidextrous fire selector switch from safe to two-round bursts. Now, reconsidering, he shifted it again to fully automatic fire.

The rifle's cyclic rate of 760 rounds per minute, plus or minus one hundred, was erratic at best. Firing full auto, Talal would burn through thirty rounds in less than three seconds, the precise time unpredictable.

It struck Ataullah that he had no backup magazines, which nearly made him laugh aloud.

As if there'd be one chance in untold millions for him to reload.

His first attempt was all or nothing. He would either stop his enemies and leave them sprawled before him, lifeless, or his blood would paint the floor and walls.

A man Talal had never seen before stood waiting for him in the open doorway to the kitchen. He was white, dark-haired, unsmiling as befit the moment, leveling a weapon that Talal recognized as a Steyr AUG.

Only one man?

Perhaps Ataullah had a fighting chance, at that.

His index finger found the BREN's trigger, began to squeeze it, but too late. He saw the Steyr's flash hider and compensator winking at him, then its bullets ripped into Ataullah's chest and abdomen, slamming him over backward to the floor. His BREN hosed useless FMJ rounds toward the ceiling, its spent brass tumbling into Talal's face, adding pain that scarcely registered, immediately followed by cascades of shattered plaster.

Blinded by detritus, fading fast, Talal Ataullah felt as if the enemy was spading dirt into his shallow grave, entombing him alive.

But not for long.

Cody wasted no time in confirming what was obvious: the first jihadist who had come to meet him from the living room was either dead or on his way, an empty weapon at his side, spent brass strewn all around, one casing pinning down the lid of his left eye.

That had to sting—or would have, if the young man's body could still register a simple thing like pain.

The mag on Cody's AUG still held approximately half its starting load as he moved toward the living room. Before he reached its entryway, a male voice called, "Talal? Talal!" A split-second delay, and then a statement offered more sedately.

"So, you've killed him, then."

"Somebody had to," Jack responded. "He was overdue."

The raspy sound that followed might have been a forced laugh or a snarl of rage.

"Time's running out for all of us."

Cody said nothing, edging closer to the doorway.

"Are you there?" his enemy—Abbas Maarku or someone else—demanded.

Crouching, Cody took a chance. Responded, "Still alive

and kicking, pal."

A burst of automatic fire, eight or nine rounds, ripped through the wall above his head. Jack briefly wished he'd asked for frag grenades, then put that out of mind. It was too late for wishful thinking, and besides, he had to get a look inside the living room, find out who he was dealing with and pick up any clues he could concerning what came next.

"Damn, that was close," he jeered, and then, before his would-be slayer had another chance to do it right, Jack rolled out to his left, aiming his Steyr AUG by instinct, triggering two three-round bursts as if they were a six-round double-tap.

He glimpsed a human figure going down, veiled in a bloody mist, and scrambled to his feet, advancing in a rush to see if it was done.

It was.

Abbas Maarku lay on his back, wheezing from ruptured lungs, his left cheek opened by a round that struck him higher than the rest. A ruby-red bubble burst from his sinus on that side, drooling vermilion down his cheek, into his ear.

And still, against all odds, Maarku was smiling up at him. His lips moved, silently at first, but then he dredged up a remainder of his voice. "Too late, you are."

"Thanks, Yoda. I already got that from your Russian buddy."

"Who is...Yoda?"

Jack saw a laptop standing open on the coffee table, blood spots on its monitor. One look was all he needed to decide the Saudi's last words were superfluous.

"Don't sweat it," Cody said, and put a 5.56mm round through Maarku's left eye socket.

Knowing he was short on time to spare, Jack hunched before the laptop, scanning its display of real-time shipping movements in the Port of Houston. Two vessels—freighters according to the laptop's key, named *Moucheron* and *Tryphon*— were highlighted, blinking as they crept closer to docking.

No, scratch that. Only the *Moucheron* was easing toward a pier. The *Tryphon* was proceeding onward, toward the Houston Shipping Channel.

One in port, the other moving farther inland for a double strike.

With no time left to waste, Jack checked the laptop's charge—90 percent—and closed its lid, then snatched Maarku's cell phone from the sofa, where it had fallen as he tried to fight and failed. He had two ships identified, still no clear grasp of what the freighters might be carrying precisely, and he hoped the cell might help pinpoint accomplices stationed around the Port of Houston.

With some luck and high-technology, perhaps Sara Durell could even jam the other phones held by jihadists—hell, black out communications city-wide if that was what it took—and buy Cody some time to reach the port.

Sara.

Leaving the house of death behind, Jack left the way he'd entered, back across the yard, over the redwood fence, and loping toward his Subaru.

He had a call to make, and hoped it wasn't already too late.

With his roam phone's speaker on, Cody heard Sara's fingers rattling a computer keyboard somewhere in the bowels of Langley, fourteen hundred miles away. She had remotely accessed Abbas Maarku's laptop, sitting open on the Subaru's passenger seat, viewing the same display Jack saw, while she was busy working magic on another server simultaneously.

"Right," she said at last. The *Moucheron* is French. Its skipper is one Jeanne-Pierre Marceau, out of Lyons, employed the past nine years by Transport Global Ltd. No file with us, the National Police at home, or Interpol. That doesn't mean he's clean, of course, but no one seems to have a handle on him."

"Strike one," Jack replied.

"The *Tryphon*'s Greek, captained by Pavlos Astrinidis. Three years back, Customs detained him in New York after they found a hundred pounds of heroin aboard another ship, the *Adámastos*. It was shipped from Genoa, likely by someone from the 'Ndrangheta, but he got laid off from the Pankósmia Line regardless. Their headquarters suddenly decided they had one too many employees."

"A likely story," Cody said.

"Whatever. We can ask him all about it if we managed to lay hands on him."

"About jamming those cells…"

"I bucked it up to the Director, but he's turned thumbs down. Too much oil money and whatever riding on the line for us to black out Houston while we do our thing."

"She'd rather have H-Town blacked out for good?"

"We're dealing with 'conservatives', okay? They hear it loud and clear whenever money talks."

"What politician doesn't?"

"Agreed. But either way, my hands are tied. Yours aren't."

"What about NEST?"

"That's different. They're heading your way as we speak but going for a low profile."

"We need a full-court press," Jack said.

"Agreed. But we both know the guy who recommended paper towels for Puerto Rico after Hurricane Maria only goes for making waves on Twitter."

"You can see my problem, though." He didn't phrase it as a question.

"Absolutely. Two freighters and two containers, unknown contents, and there's only one of you."

"I don't mind being spread a little thin," Cody replied, "but I'm not blessed with DID."

Medical shorthand for dissociative identity disorder, formerly known as MPD—"M" for "multiple"—and before that, as "split personality". You've seen it staged by Hollywood in *Sybil* and *The Three Faces of Eve*, often precipitated by extreme childhood abuse, but Jack's fanciful version would have let him be in two or three places at once, when mopping up a mission absolutely could not be delayed.

A lot like now.

"All right," he said. "The *Moucheron* is docking now. You have its GPS coordinates and the container's number."

"Roger that."

"When can you have people on board?"

"They're rolling now," Sara replied. "Not NEST, yet, but some assets who can lock it down."

"That leaves the *Tryphon* headed inland."

"It's all yours."

"I love a challenge."

"Don't I know it. I'd say, 'Break a leg,' but you might take it literally."

"Not this time," Cody replied. "I'm going to need both of them."

He hung up, no goodbyes, and put the Subaru in motion

Jack supposed a game of Texas chicken was in order, but he had to wonder who would wind up getting fried.

CHAPTER 13

Driving east along U.S. Route 90 toward the Port of Houston, Cody trusted on the Subaru's anti-collision warning features while his eyes flicked back and forth between the highway and the laptop standing open on the passenger's seat to his right. At the same time, he was watching out for squad cars, trying for a steady seventy miles per hour despite morons texting and weaving in cars up ahead.

Sometimes he marveled at the fact that anyone showed up for work alive, as heedless as they seemed behind a steering wheel. In fact, he didn't care if all of them should crash and burn, except that it would slow him down right now.

In which case, Houston would be going up in flames, along with all those other people who the reckless drivers absolutely, positively couldn't leave in ten minutes for ten to twenty minutes on the road.

How long before covert alarms from Langley garnered any visible response? And was it already too late?

Jack couldn't let himself believe that, even as he tried to watch the twin blips of the *Moucheron* and *Tryphon* gliding toward their final destinations.

Stress that key word: final.

Cody wondered whether Allah's Flame had triggermen aboard the freighters or if they were hanging out somewhere in the nearby vicinity. If Maarku was as clever as he'd thought he was in life, Jack guessed the martyrs would be backstopped, with at least a second spotter standing by for each doomed ship, in case the onboard terrorists were interrupted or had second thoughts and fled without lighting the doomsday fuse.

Getting a terrorist aboard each ship wasn't the hardest part of pulling off the master plan. As pilots had been trained for 9/11 almost twenty years ago, recruits could easily be educated in performance of a merchant seaman's duties, duly licensed by Saudi Arabian authorities or any other Muslim nation with a working seaport to its name. Once they were safe on board, perhaps packing no weapon other than a cell phone or a cheap-assed pager, they were good to go.

The shipping companies that owned the *Moucheron* and *Tryphon* didn't need to be involved. In fact, Cody assumed they wouldn't be. The odds of a fanatical jihadist rising through the ranks of either corporation, French or Greek, were microscopic by comparison to placing starry-eyed martyrs aboard the two container ships.

But once they blew, if Cody and the Company's field troops let matters get that far, there would be blame enough to go around. Assuming that the government in Washing-

ton survived the strike—and face it, politicians rarely suffered personally from a terrorist attack in the "enlightened"
West—there'd be no end of hearings, top-level investigations,
finger-pointing, posturing for photo ops, and all that other
happy crap.

Too little and too late, as usual.

For now, Jack staked his meager hopes on NEST—and on
himself.

NEST had been organized in 1975 as the Nuclear Emergency Search Team, with "Search" changed to "Support" in 1994.
It was a team of scientists, technicians and engineers, whose
stated raison d'être required them to "respond immediately
to any type of radiological accident or incident anywhere in
the world".

Concern about a nuclear snafu, intentional or otherwise,
dated from the original Manhattan Project and the A-bombs
dropped upon Japan in 1945. Eleven years later, a prototype
fast breeder reactor at Michigan's Enrico Fermi Nuclear Generating Station had threatened to wipe out Detroit, the faulty
reactor dismantled and decommissioned in 1972.

Even that wasn't enough to put the feds in motion, though.
Late in 1974 a still-unknown extortionist had warned the
FBI that a dirty bomb was stashed somewhere in Boston and
would blow unless the government coughed up $200,000
ransom. That turned out to be a hoax, but the AEC's clumsy
response—fielding nuclear experts but sending their radiation detectors to the wrong airport, then renting a cool fleet
of surveillance vans but forgetting tools required for installa-

tion of same—played like a skit from *SNL* and fit the mocking line, "We're here to help."

NEST finally got off the ground a year after that fiasco, and rolled on its first deployment in November 1976, when an alleged group calling itself "Days of Omega" demanded half a million bucks to stop multiple nuclear blasts in Spokane. That proved to be another hoax, some psycho's notion of a "joke" but threats kept coming in with clockwork regularity. NEST headquarters admitted receiving 125 nuclear threats since the group went active, while deploying teams in only thirty of those cases, writing off the rest as scams demanding no response.

Until next time.

The team admitted possessing a small air fleet of three planes and four helicopters, all fitted with radiation detectors, and other unspecified gear on the ground. It claimed ability to field six hundred experts for a single incident, but rarely dispatched more than forty if a given incident impressed the folks in charge as threatening a clear and present risk.

When NEST took to the air, the FAA granted it top priority under the U.S. National Airspace System, designated by the call sign "FLYNET". If that meant grounding other air traffic, including *Air Force One,* well, that was too damned bad for travelers with meeting deadlines on the ground.

With Langley pushing it, Jack knew that NEST's response team should be airborne now. He didn't know where they'd be coming from—the outfit's experts scattered nationwide at major universities and military installations, but the nearest

U.S. Air Force base to Houston was Lackland, 197 miles to the southwest in San Antonio. Bush Intercontinental Airport was supposedly off-limits to military flights, but with FLYNET in effect, Cody supposed exceptions could be made.

As Cody closed in on the port, he saw a helicopter circling above one of the piers. A quick look through his Scout TK monocular identified it as a Harris County sheriff's chopper, which he guessed could be out on routine patrol—that it, until he focused on a ship directly underneath the whirlybird.

The SS *Moucheron.*

One down, presumably, or in the works, and left just one to go.

"Just" one. That almost made him laugh aloud.

As if one loose nuke in the heart of Houston wasn't plenty bad enough.

Hanan bin Al'aas might be deemed insane by Western standards—a jihadist loyal to Allah, even unto death—but he was no one's fool. And at the moment, he was having second thoughts about Abbas Maarku's grand plan for him to enter Paradise on bright wings of irradiated fire.

Al'aas had seen the sheriff's helicopter following the *Moucheron* as it pulled into port. Like any tried-and-true religiopolitical extremist, he was paranoid—which, as the modern joke of sorts admitted, did not mean no one was out to persecute him.

At this moment, Hanan bin Al'aas surmised, he might be

one of the most feared, most hunted enemies in all of U.S. history. Beside him, and the plot he was prepared to carry out, all others of his kind—Zacarias Moussaoui, Ramzi Yousef, Mohammed Salameh, whoever—must pale to insignificance by comparison.

But now, against all odds and his intensive training, he was having second thoughts.

Not about the plan itself, mind you, but his specific role in it.

Although he was *prepared* to die for Allah, Hanan bin Al'aas now questioned whether the idea was pleasing to him, or if death might be deferred while still rightfully claiming his place in modern history.

Aside from shipboard duties he performed by rote during the freighter's days at sea, Al'aas knew other things as well. His cell phone's range was one of them, assuring him that he could place the call required to trigger the *Moucheron*'s 8F675 warhead from miles outside the nuclear blast zone and possibly, just maybe, manage to escape from the United States alive.

What glory that would be, to live and fight again some other day, already lauded by his comrades in struggle for the single greatest strike America had suffered since the British redcoats torched most of Washington, D.C., in 1814.

So, the twenty-two-ear-old Yemeni had decided. He had waited for the *Moucheron* to drop anchor, its gangplank lowering onto the preselected pier, with Customs agents and Kenworth truck-mounted cranes approaching. Someone on deck called his name—or the name on his seaman's license, that is—but Al'aas ignored it, striding swiftly and with purpose down the pier, putting some fifty yards between himself and the moored freighter.

Still too close by far, but he wanted to see what happened next, before he cleared Ground Zero, hailed a taxi, and withdrew to a safe distance from the Port of Houston prior to triggering the warhead he'd been trained to arm and detonate.

Watching a sheriff's helicopter circle overhead, Al'aas wondered if something had gone wrong, if Allah's Flame had been betrayed somehow. At the same time, he thought about the backup martyr who Abbas Maarku had claimed would be in place, somewhere nearby, to execute the backup plan if Al'aas failed for any reason.

Had his fellow warrior in the cause observed him jumping ship? Would that prospective martyr even now be phoning Maarku to report Al'aas as a suspected traitor, blackening his name forever more?

A moment longer, he decided, just to watch and see what would transpire.

Disclosure of a nuclear threat was a federal matter, Al'aas understood. If the Crusaders were aware of Abbas Maarku's plan for Houston and the rest of their homeland, the circling helicopter should be FBI, or maybe one of those black aircraft from one of the several shadow agencies, devoid of traceable FAA serial numbers. Surely, Justice or Homeland Security would not rely on county deputies whom even state police officers labeled "local yokels".

Even so, still not abandoning his scheme to gain safe

distance from the harbor, Al'aas stood with his cell phone in hand, prepared to key the signal that would leap beyond him to the *Moucheron* and strike a deadly spark inside container number CSQU3054383. Al'aas did not pretend to understand the three-step calculation method for confirming ownership, contents and point of origin for various containers and he could not have cared less.

The only question now was whether he would view the doomsday blast while standing virtually at its heart, or if he would survive to watch its endless replays over global television networks.

Live or die? That was the question.

As he stood watching the *Moucheron* and the Harris County Sheriff's Airbus AS350 helicopter, Al'aas noticed a young man moving closer to him. Say late twenties, sandy-haired, clean shaven, relatively stylish in a blazer, matching tie, with slacks resembling skinny jeans above black wingtip shoes. For some reason Al'aas could not fathom, the stranger was smiling, and seemingly at him.

He could have blown the warhead then and turned them all into irradiated cinders, scattered by the warhead's blast wave, but he hesitated, eyeballing the new arrival without mimicking his grin.

Still thirty feet away, the white man said, "Excuse me, Mister? Can you tell me if I'm on the right pier for the SS *Totenkopf?*"

"No, sorry," Al'aas answered, keeping up polite appearances. "I don't know that one."

"Dammit! Are you sure? I'm running late and hate to miss it."

Al'aas had begun to nod his head when he felt something cold pressed to his nape, then he heard or felt a crackling in his head as voltage from a hand-held stun gun dropped him twitching to the dock. His final conscious vision framed the man who had accosted him, catching the cell phone that had tumbled from Al'aas' spastic fingers as he fell, before his world blacked out.

Cody was near the Houston Shipping Channel's mouth, on Independence Parkway 5, when he spotted the *Tryphon* through his Scout TK monocular and noted two immediate problems.

First up, the Greek ship wasn't stopping at the watery turnout christened Houston-Jacintoport, but rather gliding on past Boggy Bayou Basin, entering the fifty-three-mile east-west passageway of Buffalo Bayou.

His second problem: there was neither hide nor hair of law enforcement to be seen tracking the freighter as it made its way inland.

Cody reviewed his options in a flash. He couldn't wait for NEST to turn up, if and when it ever did, nor could he hope for any sweet *deus ex machina*, no timely intervention from above.

Granted, a General Atomics MQ-1 Predator drone cruising at ten thousand feet, piloted remotely from an air base situated who knew where, could strike the freighter with an

AGM-114 Hellfire air-to-surface missile and be gone before the semi-active laser homing rocket slammed into its target, but at what cost to the Port of Houston and America at large?

Would the Hellfire's high-explosive anti-tank warhead set off the weapon Cody needed to deactivate, or simply sink it in the shipping channel, so that salvage divers had to deal with it while radiation leaked into the water all around?

No matter how you looked at them, even with one eye closed, the other narrowed to a slit, both options stank.

His sole remaining choice was finding some way he could board the *Tryphon*, take out any terrorists who might be lingering aboard the ship, and then deal with the weapon on his own. Jack didn't know what kind of nuke was presently aboard the freighter, thus had no idea whether he could deactivate it on his own, without special equipment he didn't possess.

Was it a military surplus warhead, or some kind of homemade IED, which could make all the difference, and how would it be triggered?

Cody ruled out timers as too unreliable. A bomb could certainly be set to blow at sea, if that was what the terrorists desired, but having it explode at any preselected point once it reached port was problematic. Damn near anything could stall a freighter docking at a given pier on time, or even slow arrival into port. A slow cruise through a commonly congested shipping channel just made matters worse, precision likely going out the window.

Did that even matter with a nuke?

Maybe, or maybe not.

It all depended on the terrorists behind the plot and what they wanted to achieve, if anything, beyond random destruction.

So, he'd have to board the ship—which naturally wouldn't stop until it reached its final destination somewhere along Buffalo Bayou, from Burnet Bay to Downtown Houston. That meant dealing with however many terrorists might be aboard, as passengers or crew members, before Jack even had a chance to neutralize the weapon.

And he had to start right now.

A tugboat caught his eye as he passed by the Battleship Texas State Historic Site, on Independence Parkway in LaPorte. The name stenciled across its stern read Nellie Bly, presumably referring to the journalist who'd beat Jules Verne's fictional record by circling the globe in less than eighty days and later infiltrated Blackwell's Island to blow the whistle on Gotham's horrendous mental asylum.

The only guy Jack saw on board the *Nellie Bly* was in his mid-fifties and heavyset, with skin like tanned leather from long exposure to the Texas sun. He wore a jaunty cap that didn't seem to fit his round head properly and kept a stogie in his mouth although it seemed to be unlit.

Jack parked the Subaru and left his slung Steyr AUG over one shoulder, watching out for witnesses as he jogged down a flight of concrete steps to reach the pier and tugboat tethered to it by a bow line. He cast the bow line off before he went aboard the tug, greeting her pilot with the rifle's muzzle when he turned at the suggestion of an unfamiliar sound.

STEPHEN MERTZ

"The feckin' hell is dis?" the skipper asked, in a surprising Irish brogue.

"We're going for a little ride," Jack said.

"Is dat a fact?"

"Well, I am, anyway. You're coming with me is completely optional."

"Let you handle the *Nellie*? Not a chance in Hell, boy-o."

"Is that a 'yes'?" Jack asked. "Because I can't leave you running around to call the cops right now."

"I thought as much. A goddamn hijacking."

"Think of it as a loan. You might even be reimbursed."

"And where will we be going, if it's not some kind a hush-hush deal?"

Jack nodded toward the *Tryphon*, now pulling away from them. "You see that freighter?"

"Pretty hard to miss her."

"Get me close enough to board it, then go anywhere you like and talk to anyone you want."

The Irishman surprised Jack with a smile. "Follow dat freighter, eh? Just like a feckin' movie."

"That's as good a way to think of it as any," Jack replied.

Wondering whether it would have a happy ending, or if it would morph into a 3-D disaster flick.

Rifa'a Abdul Alim Zaghloul suffered none of the private doubts endured by Hanan bin Al'aas aboard the *Moucheron*. Assigned to serve the *Tryphon*'s crew and see its Russian warhead to the target site where he would detonate it and proceed immediately to *Jannah*, he had no latent fear of death, no last-minute suspicion that the Prophet and his holy scripture had misunderstood the spoken words of Allah.

So it was that in the final hours of his earthly life, Zaghloul was not on deck, but rather in the small cabin he shared with an oversized Turk who usually reeked of alcohol and spoke of little else but sex. Zaghloul would happily have killed his oafish bunkmate on the long, so very slow journey to Houston, but he knew that no one on the freighter, or for miles around, had more than thirty minutes to survive.

Aside from martyrdom and its rewards in Paradise, Zaghloul treasured the thought of all those heretic Crusaders— tens of thousands, at the very least—snatched from their daily grind and dumped into the fires of *Jahannam* without so much as a last farewell from anyone they'd known in life.

Eventually, all of them would writhe in fire together for their sins, while only true believers in Islam were favored with an afterlife of bliss.

All students of the great *Quran* knew only Muslim true believers would see Paradise.

Job one for Zaghloul now was checking that his cell phone was switched off, untraceable by enemies until he needed it to detonate the warhead, and that it was fully charged. No frail human technology or act of carelessness on Zaghloul's part must be allowed to interfere with Allah's great design.

Next, he began to double-check his personal weapons, concealed beneath his bottom-level bunk in a padlocked sea bag. His cabinmate—the gross, malodorous Ekrem Üngör—was busy at his chores on deck, and if he prematurely happened to return, he would become the day's first sacrifice to Allah's wrath.

From the sea bag, Zaghloul first lifted out a Swiss Brügger & Thomet MP9 submachine gun, chosen for its compact size—11.8 inches long—and weight of only 2.86 pounds without its thirty-round transparent polymer detachable box magazines. His weapon had its folding stock removed but compensated with a molded plastic foregrip for better control. Aside from that, the MP9 vaguely resembled the American MAC-10 and fired the same 9×19mm Parabellum rounds, while offering a choice of semi-auto or full automatic fire, the latter rated at eleven hundred rounds per minute.

Just in case the well-maintained Brügger & Thomet failed him, Rifa'a Zaghloul also had a Spanish Astra A-100 pistol chambered for the same rounds as his SMG. The sidearm weighed a smidge over two pounds, loaded with seventeen rounds in its detachable box magazine plus one more in the chamber.

Guns aside, in case he met real opposition prior to triggering the Russian warhead hidden in container No. UUVX0016949, Zaghloul had packed four Russian F1 fragmentation hand grenades, nicknamed "lemons" due to their shape and yellow-green color. Each tipped the scales at 1.3 pounds, including sixty grams of TNT, with a shrapnel dispersal deemed lethal inside a thirty-meter kill zone.

Prepared for anything but failure at the most important

mission of his life, Zaghloul felt almost traitorous for wishing that he might encounter opposition at the final moment, but his zeal was only natural.

It would be sweet, he thought, to spill Crusader blood with his own hands before he turned their oil-based city to a wasteland of irradiated ash.

The tugboat *Nellie Bly* was making five knots—just under six miles per hour—with skipper Mike MacAuley in its wheelhouse, jabbering nonstop to Jack Cody as they pursued the freighter *Tryphon* through the Houston Shipping Channel. At sea, the *Tryphon* might have managed twenty-five to thirty knots, some forty-five to fifty-five mph, but the shipping channel's relatively narrow confines held it down to twelve, maybe fifteen at the outside.

Which meant the *Nellie Bly* was slowly, *very* slowly catching up.

"Some kind of secret agent, are ye?" asked MacAuley.

"If I answered that…"

"Ye'd have to kill me. Sure, I've heard that lots a times before."

I'll bet you have, Jack thought. *Too bad it doesn't shut you up.*

"Thing is," the Irishman pressed on, peering at Jack over his shoulder while he steered the tug, "I got this this natural born curiosity, ye know? I try to learn me somethin' new and interestin' every day."

"And how's that working out for you?"

"I'd say so far, so good."

Jack estimated that the *Nellie Bly* measured some sixteen feet in length—not much by shipping standards, formally labeled a "boat", mostly confined to inland waters and protected coastal areas—while "ships" were ocean-going vessels, vastly larger, some the literal equivalent of towns adrift, their passengers and crew numbered in hundreds, even thousands.

"Thing is," MacAuley said, "I figger if you ain't some kind a secret whatzit, then you can't be nothin' but a gangster, am I right? And you don't feel like that to me."

"In spite of hijacking your tug?"

"I wouldn't call that friendly, mind you, but the truth be told, it ain't my boat. It might as well be, all the time I've spent aboard, but she's the property of Holt and Seinfeld Limited."

"To what?" Jack asked.

"How's that?"

"Your Holt and Seinfeld. Limited to what?"

MacAuley thought about that for a moment, then burst into laughter. "I'll be goddamned if I know. That's somethin' else I need ta learn."

"Sounds like you have your plate full without thinking about me."

"O' course, I wouldn't *be* thinkin' about you, if you weren't hijackin' me boat."

"Fair point."

The *Nellie Bly* was typical of other tugboats Jack had seen, although he'd never been aboard one in his life, till now, much less commandeering one at gunpoint. The tug had used tires hung over its bow and sides as fenders, plus a winch behind the wheelhouse and a mainmast sprouting from its roof, along with a Morse lamp, siren, radio antenna, and red blinking masthead light. The bridge was totally enclosed, accessed by ladders situated forward and on the port side.

"What's so all-fired important on this Greek tramp anyhow?" Mick asked.

"You seriously wouldn't want to know," Jack said.

"Oh, but I would, boy-o. Is there a Commie spy aboard her?"

"Grab a *Time* or *Newsweek* sometime," Cody answered back. "We don't have Commies nowadays."

"Oh, no? What do ye call that Putin fella, then?"

"An asshole, thief and a murderer," Jack said. "He *used* to be a Commie, granted, but their party bit the dust back in the early Nineties. If you want to find one now, try Vietnam or China."

MacAuley brayed another laugh at that. "You learn that shite in college, boy?"

"Something like that."

The school of hard knocks with post-graduate training in *harder* knocks.

"Ha!" Mick appeared to think he'd scored a winning goal. "Professors with their PhDs.. Ye know what that stands for, don't ye?" And before Jack could respond, MacAuley answered his own question. "Pile higher and deeper, boy-o. Like the shite piled on a honey wagon back in County Cork."

"About this freighter, now," Jack interrupted him.

"How's that?"

"Assuming we can overtake it—"

"Ach! You know the definition of 'assumin',' don't ye?"

This time Cody beat him to it. "Sure. Making an ass of you and me."

MacAuley laughed some more, as if he'd served the punch line up himself. "Damn straight!"

"So, if we catch the *Tryphon*—"

"Ain't no *if* about it, boy-o. Next time she meets somethin' comin' down the channel and she has to slow, we've got her."

"With the difference in size between the vessels, how would you suggest I get on board?"

"The easy way would be one of their port side ladders," Mick replied. "O' course, for that you'd need a grapplin' hook and rope. I didn't notice if you brought them things on board, bein' distracted by your guns and all."

"Shit," Cody muttered to himself. A grappling hook and rope had never crossed his mind. Why should they have?

"Caught short, are ye?" MacAuley teased him. "Never mind. I got equipment ye can use."

"Lucky for me," said Cody.

"Maybe not. The heat you're packin' tells me you're expectin' opposition from the Greeks or whoever's in charge aboard the tramper. Maybe you'd be luckier if we just turned around and wrote the whole thing off."

CHAPTER 14

The huge Turk, Ekrem Üngör, startled Rifa'a Abdul Zaghloul by barging in as Zaghloul finished checking out his weapons, seated on his bunk. Üngör blinked like a drunk trying to focus bleary eyes and blurted out, "*Bu da neyin nesi?*"

Zaghloul was clueless as to what that meant and didn't care. As Üngör turned to flee their shared cabin, Zaghloul snatched up his Astra A-100 pistol, squeezed its double-action trigger, aiming from a range of six or seven feet at Üngör's back. His goal was severing the giant's spine and crippling him, but Zaghloul was a fraction off the mark. Still, impact dropped his man and gave him time to rise, stand over Üngör, and dispatch the next 9mm round into the gasping seaman's skull.

That done, ears ringing from the gunshots, Zaghloul stepped into the cramped passageway outside their cabin, glancing left and right, checking to see if anyone responded to the noise. He counted off a full minute, deciding that the

Tryphon's engine sounds and racket on the deck above had served him as an unintended silencer.

Next came the hard part, after Zaghloul tucked the warm Astra under his belt. He had to grip Üngör's stout ankles through his unwashed crew socks, straining as he dragged the leaking corpse clear of the passageway and back inside their shared cabin. It seemed to take forever, and his back ached by the time he finished shifting some 250 pounds of lifeless Turk, enabling him to shut the cabin's door.

And then, another problem: Üngör's bulk took up most of the meager floor space, as if someone had deposited an out-sized mannequin beside the double-decker bunks. Zaghloul was forced to step on him, feeling his flab and muscle shift beneath his cheap deck shoes, as if he trod upon a lumpy and foul-smelling beanbag chair.

Cursing in Arabic, Zaghloul finished his preparations, picking up his submachine gun, slung his sea bag filled with hand grenades and extra magazines over his shoulder, nearly stumbling over Ekrem Üngör's dead hulk as he reached the cabin's door.

There was a sticky pool of blood in the ship's passageway, where Zaghloul's second shot had penetrated Üngör's head and slammed his flat, misshapen face into the slip-proof steel decking. Zaghloul made no attempt to hide it, no longer concerned about his other shipmates, what they saw, or how they might react.

Soon, they would all cease to exist, consumed and turned to vapor by the heat of Allah's cleansing fire.

He hurried toward the steep metal companionway, ascending toward the *Tryphon*'s main deck and the open air. When he was halfway there, another pair of seamen—Portuguese, jabbering in their native tongue—met him and stopped dead in their tracks, seeing the stubby MP9 Zaghloul held in his hands.

"O que é isso então?" asked the taller of the pair, surprised into forgetting English was the universal language used aboard the freighter.

Zaghloul let his submachine gun answer for him, firing two short bursts that brought the crewmen tumbling down on top of him, blood spurting from their lethal wounds. He was forced to grab the polished banister as first one, then the other falling body caromed into him and nearly made him drop his load of weapons. As it was, Zaghloul fell to his knees and cried out from the sudden pain of impact.

"Alqarf!" he cursed, and struggled to his feet again, regained his balance and a firm grip on his SMG.

There was no time to think about the corpses sprawled below him now, blood mingling as they lay together in a spreading pool of viscous crimson. Someone might have heard the automatic fire and already be coming to investigate.

If so, he would kill them as well.

Zaghloul glanced as his MP9's transparent magazine without extracting it, guessing that he had fired roughly one-third of its thirty 9mm Parabellum rounds. He thought about reloading but decided not to bother.

There were other, more important things for him to do

just now.

The upper deck awaited, and above it, towering over the *Tryphon*'s crowded cargo deck, the freighter's bridge.

Before he keyed the doomsday button on his cell phone, Rifa'a Zaghloul had another stop to make.

Jack Cody's military training had included boarding ships and boats of varied sizes—cabin cruisers, yachts, and larger vessels—under various conditions, moored in port, sailing on rivers, and on open seas. He'd learned to board from speed-boats, zodiac inflatables, and rising from beneath his chosen mark with scuba gear, ready to deal with hostile members of the crew at any moment.

Still, transferring from a tugboat like the *Nellie Bly* onto a freighter in the middle of the Houston Shipping Channel was a challenging, unique experience.

He couldn't fault the gear that Mick MacAuley had pro-vided him: a four-clawed grappling hook, three pounds or so of blackened stainless steel, attached to thirty feet of nylon cord intended to support three hundred pounds. The trick, he realized, would be making his toss connect without repeated tries and needless racket to the *Tryphon*'s port-side ladder, then ascending to the freighter's rail unnoticed till he reached the cargo deck.

Jack doubted that the *Tryphon* was controlled by terror-ists. More likely, Allah's Flame had one or two jihadists on shipboard, retained as members of the crew, prepared to strike by prearrangement when they reached a certain target, somewhere along Buffalo Bayou. They might arrive within the next few minutes, or it could take half an hour.

All Jack knew for sure was that his time was running out.

The *Nellie Bly* was gaining on the *Tryphon,* pulling up beside it as the larger vessel throttled back. Jack stood against the tugboat's starboard railing, watching as MacAuley closed the gap between his boat and the Greek ship's accommodation ladder, bolted to the *Tryphon*'s rusty hull.

Cody and Mick had gone over what was supposed to happen next. Whether Jack made it to the freighter's deck alive or not, MacAuley had a phone number to call that would connect him to a Langley operator. He would use the passwords "stratagem emergency" and hold the line until a woman answered, then give her his name and GPS location in the shipping channel, with a short, succinct description of what Cody had achieved—or failed to do—so far.

And that done, Mick had strict orders to turn the tug around and get the hell away.

Not that he had a chance of clearing the blast zone, should Cody's adversaries carry out their mission in a timely manner.

Jack had kept that tidbit from the skipper, understanding there was nothing to be gained—and everything to lose—by sending his pilot into a panic.

Cody needed Mick alive and at the tugboat's helm until Jack cleared the smaller boat and made his scramble for the *Tryphon*'s rail. Beyond that point...well, it was each man for himself.

Jack had no time to spare on feeling guilty now and wasn't even sure he still remembered how.

This mission could be what he'd sought in vain from the moment his wife and kids were massacred by terrorists: an exit from the world where he had spent his life fighting in foreign lands, neglecting treasures that were far from safe and sound at home.

Maybe this time…

And if not—try, try again.

The *Tryphon*'s ladder was within range now. Jack gauged the distance, swung the grappling hook and tossed it over-hand, snagging one of the ladder's lower rungs on his first try. He kicked off from the tugboat's rail and swung between the vessels, legs outstretched to brace him as he struck the freighter's hull six feet or so above the waterline.

Cody ignored the *Nellie Bly* as she lost speed, fell back, and started huffing through a U-turn in the middle of the shipping channel. Captain Mick was on his own now, free to dial the number Jack had given him or opt for 911 instead. If he decided on the Port Authority Police Department, it would mean a waste of precious time and likely guarantee MacAu-ley's death while some dispatcher questioned him or made him wait on hold.

And if he reached the CIA instead, then what?

There wouldn't be much difference. Sara Durell already knew where Cody was—if not precisely at that moment, then at least approximately, from the GPS on his abandoned Suba-ru. She had the *Tryphon*'s fix and should have backup teams en route, although Jack couldn't guess their ETA and didn't plan on waiting for them to arrive.

Houston was swiftly running out of time, while most of its inhabitants were happily oblivious.

Rifa'a Zaghloul paused as he reached the *Tryphon*'s upper deck crowded from rail to rail with code-numbered portable shipping containers. Only one of them concerned him, hidden in the second row from starboard, sixty feet or so back from the freighter's bow. As for the rest, he didn't care what they contained: machine parts, clothing, huddled slaves, cocaine, or Nazi gold accumulated from the Holocaust.

Before much longer, they would all cease to exist.

The bomb dropped over Hiroshima, more or less identical in megatonnage to the 8F675 (Mod2) Russian warhead tucked inside container No. UUVX0016949, had produced a surface temperature of 10,830 degrees Fahrenheit, vaporizing thousands or persons, searing their shadows onto concrete like graffiti from the afterlife. Blazes lit by fireball heat throughout the blast-damaged area had merged into a firestorm twenty minutes later, drawing surface air from all directions to feed an inferno that devoured anything flammable.

Of some 350,000 Hiroshima inhabitants, around 90,000—say 26 percent—were killed outright, another 69,000 injured to varying degrees, 30 percent of those suffering radiation burns or poisoning.

Comparing that to Houston's demographics, with a

population of 2.3 million, the initial death toll could exceed 600,000—more, if Zaghloul added in commuters from the city's suburbs and a portion of its average 17 million tourists per year. In round numbers, he hoped to offer up the best part of one million sacrifices to Allah.

The four coordinated strikes on 9/11, by contrast, had only claimed 2,996 lives, with double that number injured.

This would indeed be a day to remember for all time in prayer and in song.

Watching for crewmen as he went, Zaghloul walked briskly to the nearest of two companionways granting access to the *Tryphon*'s bridge, where Captain Pavlos Astrinidis supervised a handful of subordinates: an officer of the watch, an able seaman at the wheel, and a communications officer.

Four men, unarmed, although a weapons locker stood nearby, stocked with an AK-47 rifle, two pump-action shotguns, and four pistols.

None of which would help the *Tryphon*'s officers today.

Since no alarms had sounded yet, after the shooting below decks, Zaghloul reckoned that he could reach the freighter's wheelhouse unopposed, and once inside, the ship would be at his command. If Captain Astrinidis would not follow orders, Zaghloul planned to execute his lowest-ranking officer first thing, then move on up the ladder of command one victim at a time until the skipper bowed to his command.

And failing that, he'd kill the captain, too. Zaghloul had learned enough about handling a ship to take control himself and do what must be done—a simple grounding of the

Tryphon on the shipping channel's southern shore, before he placed one last call to the warhead slumbering on deck.

One simple call, and he would be remembered for a thousand years.

There was no need for him to speak. Just dial the number on his cell, hit "SEND", and close his eyes on Earth, to open them next time in Paradise.

Rifa'a Zaghloul wondered if he would feel it when the warhead detonated, searing heat, or if there'd only be a flash so bright that he could see it through his lowered eyelids, merging into the eternal sunshine of *Jannah*, where vestal virgins waited to conduct him on a tour of the garden where Adam and Hawwa dwelt at the beginning of all things.

If there *was* any pain involved in crossing over, Zaghloul knew that it would barely last a micro-second before he was vaporized, his martyr's atoms scattered to the super-heated winds.

A first mate who he recognized was just emerging from the bridge as Zaghloul reached it, starting to descend. He gaped as Zaghloul aimed the MP9 at him and ordered, speaking English, "Turn around. Go back inside. Say nothing, or you're dead."

The first mate nodded, turned, and did as he was told, the idiot believing that obedience would save his worthless life.

Jack Cody scrambled up the *Tryphon*'s port-side access ladder to the rail. There was a gate up there, latched now, and he made no attempt to open it. Instead, he scanned the deck for witnesses, saw none, and double-checked his personal exposure to the wheelhouse windows situated twenty-odd feet overhead.

The freighter's officers had a 360-degree view of the *Tryphon* its surrounding waters from their high perch, save where the stacks thrust up behind them, trailing smoke despite whatever laws allegedly existed to control pollution on the open sea or inland waterways. Sun glaring off the bridge's windows meant Jack couldn't tell if anyone up there had spotted him, but he would find out soon enough.

And he had no more time to waste.

Clutching the rail, a standard chin-up grip, he vaulted over fluid movement, foot-assisted at the crest, and dropped crouching onto the *Tryphon's* deck. He was surprised and instantly disgruntled by the ranks of lookalike containers, lined up on the deck, and realized there must be more below him, in the freighter's hold.

Even if he'd been privy to the one code number he required, among those hundreds, Jack had no idea if it was up on deck, or maybe on the lower level, where more hundreds lay in wait, all jammed together so he couldn't reach—much less open—their padlocked doors.

How long would searching for the one he needed take?

Much, much too long.

Which meant Jack had to hope there was a terrorist on board, instead of following the *Tryphon* in a vehicle, cruising beside the shipping lane, or sipping one last soft drink in some joint where he could dial a given number on his cell phone and dispatch a silent signal to unleash the fires of Hell on Earth.

But not only a terrorist aboard, mind you. It had to be one Jack could overpower without killing him, then squeeze the necessary information out of him despite the bastard's training at resistance to interrogation he'd sworn commitment to a "holy" cause that would determine where he spent eternity: in the blissful garden of *Jannah* or in the furnace of *Jahannam*.

The odds of pulling off that coup were minimal at best, and that was looking on the rosy side.

No warning voice rang out to Cody from the speakers mounted overhead, at all four corners of the bridge. No clamoring alarm sounded to rally crewmen in pursuit of an unauthorized, armed boarder. Cody took what he could get— small favors—as he slipped the Steyr off its shoulder sling and started for the nearest set of metal stairs providing access to the freighter's wheelhouse.

Where else could he start, aboard a ship the *Tryphon*'s size, when any member of the crew might prove to be a lurking enemy?

Braced for a challenge with each step he took, Jack homed in on the bridge.

Captain Michael Ferriday MacAuley—"Mick" to anyone who knew him since he'd been in grade school, dialed the number he'd been given by his unnamed passenger and heard the call picked up before it finished ringing twice.

A man with no discernible accent, presumably checking Mick's cell phone number on some version of Caller ID, said simply, "Please authenticate."

MacAuley knew what that meant and replied with the two words his hijacker had left him: "Stratagem emergency."

"Wait one," the bland voice said, and left Mick with the lilting strains of elevator music, an instrumental cover of the Beatles' "Eleanor Rigby". Before it finished one refrain, a woman's voice came on the line.

"Mister MacAuley?"

Startled, Mick replied, "Yes, ma'am. I'm skipper of the tugboat—"

"*Nellie Bly*. I see all that. What information do you have for me?"

"Um, well...I'm here in—"

"Houston, right. Can we cut to the chase?"

"Okay." Feeling a little miffed, MacAuley forged ahead. "Some guy I never saw before hijacked my tug at gunpoint and we chased this tramper down. It's Greek, the—"

"We already have that information. Can you give me a description of your visitor and anything he said?"

Mick did his best describing Mr. X, trying to keep it simple and straightforward. "I was focused mostly on his gun."

"That's understandable. What did he say?"

"'Follow that freighter,' basically. Like in the movies, yeah? But not a taxi."

"And?"

"So we caught up to her, and then he asked me for a grapplin' hook and line, to get himself aboard her. Gave me your number—well, *some* number—and off he went. Last thing, told me to turn my tug around and make this call."

"He's on the *Tryphon* now, then?"

Hearing the tramp's name from her lips no longer came as a surprise. He answered, "That's affirmative," trying to sound a little military, not sure if he'd pulled it off or not. Adding, "Now what, ma'am?"

"Now, sir, go on about your business and accept my thanks for touching base. It's obvious you won't forget this, but I'll caution you that it would be unwise to share it with your friends."

The way she said "unwise" with just a heartbeat's hesitation spent choosing the proper word, told Mick that he'd been threatened with a thin façade of courtesy. It rankled, but if there was one guy wandering around the Port of Houston with an automatic rifle, who could say there wouldn't be another, maybe several?

"I get it, ma'am. Glad I could—"

Click. The line went dead before he got to "help."

"Go on about me feckin' business, is it?" he inquired of no one. "Well, maybe I will—and then again, maybe I won't."

But that was bluster, and he knew it. Mick wasn't a big-time reader, but he kept up with the supermarket tabloids, plus the discount paperbacks that taught him all about a world fraught with conspiracies. He knew about the Men in Black, Majestic 12, the Bilderbergers and Trilateral Commission, pick your poison. Mick wasn't a joiner—never had been, Seafarers International Union—but if anyone had bothered asking over drinks, he would've said he knew the down-and-dirty score.

And what MacAuley's common sense was telling him, right now, was that he ought to get the hell away from Houston for a while, as far and fast as he could move.

"What is the meaning of this outrage?" Captain Pavlos Astrinidis asked the gunman now confronting him, using his best authoritative tone. "Must I remind you of the penalty for mutiny or barratry?" Before the Arab-looking seaman could reply, the skipper said, "It's death, for both."

The armed wheelhouse intruder barked a laugh devoid of humor. Said, "So death it is, then. Who goes first, Captain?"

The man's insane, thought Astrinidis, but that didn't help him, staring down the muzzle of a gun. He didn't know the crewman's name, imagined he had glimpsed him on the *Tryphon*'s deck or moving through some passageway, but at this moment Pavlos didn't care. He recognized a submachine gun when he saw one, conscious of the havoc it could wreak within close quarters.

"So," he asked, "what is it that you want?"

"Not much," the gunman answered. "Just a minor change in course."

"A change in—"

"*Minor* change," the madman said again, correcting Captain Astrinidis. "Just a small degree or two, and I leave the direction up to you. Am I not generous?"

The skipper flicked a glance toward Buffalo Bayou, stretching away before his loaded cargo ship. No calculations were required to judge the obvious result of such a deviation.

"But that means—"

"Grounding the ship," his adversary finished for him. "Bravo, Captain. Choose port or starboard, as you please, and do it now."

The skipper tried to reason with his enemy. "But you must understand, the damage we would suffer—"

"As you wish," the gunman said, and fired a short burst from his weapon, virtually disemboweling First Mate Yiannis Lazaridis. Yiannis crumpled almost silently, but for a strangled cry of agony and thrashing sounds he made after he hit the deck, twitching in his own blood and other bodily fluids.

"*Allah kahretsin!*" Captain Astrinidis swore. "Stop this at once!?

"Then do as you are told," the murderer replied. "Starboard or port, but do it now, *'ayuha alwaghd!*"

"For this," Astrinidis said, "I take the wheel myself."

The killer jerked his head. "Get on with it," he snapped, waggling his weapon's smoking muzzle between Pavlos and the wheel where Theo Daskaloudi stood, trembling in fear.

Clutching the *Tryphon*'s wheel, Pavlos allowed himself another millisecond's hesitation, then decided, steering her to starboard.

It was painfully slow going, or at least it felt that way to Captain Astrinidis, then a jolt of impact rippled through the freighter's hull from bow to stern. Its spinning screws propelled the *Tryphon* forward against stiff resistance, its bulb gouging deep into the shipping channel's elevated bank before the great ship shuddered to a halt.

Cody had just begun to climb the stairs—or "ladder," using shipboard lingo—when a burst of automatic weapon's fire rattled the freighter's wheelhouse. Freezing for a moment, scanning all around in search of gunmen other than the one engaged above him, Cody felt the tramper veering off to starboard, plowing toward the shipping channel's northern bank.

Collision's impact rocked the ship, regardless of its bulk and tonnage. Cody clutched the left-hand banister to keep himself from tumbling back and downward to the cargo deck.

The shooting and its aftermath answered the foremost question on Jack's mind—namely, whether or not the late Abbas Maarku had any jihadists aboard the *Tryphon,* as opposed to standing by with cell phones at a safer distance from the floating bomb. At least one of them had engaged the freighter's crew and forced the ship to run aground, positioned so that it would block the channel while the rest of Maarku's plan played itself out.

How many seamen dead aboard the ship already? Cody wouldn't know until he reached the bridge and checked it out himself. As for the enemy…

He started up the ladder once again, moving with greater haste now, even though it amplified his risk. What other choice remained?

Why else did Jack even exist?

He had covered half of the remaining distance to the bridge when an interior explosion shattered all the wheelhouse windows, spewing a cascade of fractured glass, smoke swirling from open window frames, a vague banana smell of TNT that could induce headaches.

In fact, Jack knew, people exposed to trinitrotoluene over long periods of time suffered anemia, abnormal liver functions, spleen enlargement and, damage to their natural immune system and male fertility. Some published studies even fingered TNT as a possible human carcinogen.

But mostly, it just blew your ass to smithereens.

Bleeding from half a dozen minor cuts, Cody finished his brisk climb to the bridge and stepped into a scene of carnage, five officers down, some dead already, the remainder on their way. At the same time, he glimpsed their killer exiting the far side of the wheelhouse, disappearing down a parallel companionway to reach the cargo deck.

First aid was obviously out. Jack didn't have the necessary gear, medical expertise, or time to waste on dying men. Likewise, while he was up to date on handling the controls of most ships, ranging from tugboats to giant ocean liners, trying to reverse the *Tryphon* from the shore where it was grounded simply meant letting the terrorist he'd briefly seen escape with time to carry out his doomsday scheme.

Pursuing that son of a bitch was paramount, still had to take a stab at catching him alive.

Dead men can't answer questions, after all.

Skirting as much blood as he could, Jack crossed the bridge and went after his quarry, mindful of the fact that seeing one man didn't mean he was alone on board. Cody was quick enough to spot the fleeing gunman as he hit the deck running and risked a hasty shot that plucked one of the killer's denim sleeves but didn't slow him down at all.

Spinning around in mid-stride with an athlete's grace, the Arab fired a quick 9mm burst at Cody, forced him backward to the wheelhouse doorway, long enough to let the runner vanish down one of the narrow walking lanes between cargo containers lined up end to end along the deck.

"Out-freaking-standing," Cody muttered to himself, and started down the starboard-side companionway.

CHAPTER 15

Rifa'a Abdul Zaghloul had no idea who was aboard the *Tryphon* now, pursuing him, nor did he care. A quick glimpse of the enemy had shown him it was no one he had seen before, his ironclad memory for faces, even at a distance and in frantic haste, his proof of that.

No matter.

If the gunman had not been the other crewmen from the time they'd sailed, it only meant that he had come aboard today. And that, in turn, meant Zaghloul's vital mission was at risk.

His life was insignificant. Indeed, it had been sacrificed in principle the moment Zaghloul had joined Allah's Flame and started training for the journey that had brought him to this moment of the here and now. He'd volunteered to die, had come aboard the *Tryphon* for no other reason, but oblivion must come on his terms, or his whole life would have been a waste.

During their first encounter, he had failed to drop the enemy with submachine gun fire but spoiled the other's aim so that the rifle shot he'd managed only cut through Rifa'a's sleeve and stung his arm, no worse than a mosquito bite. Zaghloul had then eluded him, if only for the moment.

But with any luck, a few moments were all that he required.

Of course, he could have pulled the cell phone from his pocket and dispatched the detonation signal now, moving along the narrow aisle between cargo containers, but the mental image of that action did not satisfy him. And in Zaghloul's mind, he did not believe that it would satisfy Allah.

The *Quran* breaks "sin" into five categories, with the worst being *dhunub*, a class of heinous sins against Allah that would be punished for eternity in *Jahannam's* blazing fire. Some of the worst included robbery, idolatry, adultery and fleeing from jihad.

But there was also pride, a moral crime so universal it was, even Christians ranked it first among their seven deadly sins.

Was Zaghloul being prideful when he planned the final seconds of his life, standing atop cargo container No. UUVX0016949, raising his burner cell—what irony that was—above his head and shouting Allah's holy name when he incinerated Houston with the simple pressure of his thumb?

In his mind, he was not.

A truly prideful man would bellow out his own name or voice some trite expression of self-satisfaction at the end. James Cagney dying on the silver screen, perhaps, ringed by flames in the final frames of *White Heat,* shouting, "Made it,

Ma! Top of the world!"

Rifa'a Abdul Zaghloul was not that man. His sacrifice would be for Allah's gain, and nothing else.

Besides, if he wanted to glorify himself, he would have posted commentary onto Facebook, Twitter, maybe Instagram, instead of casting his last words into a fiery void, where no one would survive to hear, much less repeat them.

When you thought of it that way, Zaghloul was being absolutely *selfless,* exercising the direct antithesis of pride. His final actions, thoughts and words served only Allah the Almighty.

But in order to do that, he must survive a little longer, reach his goal on deck and carry out his plan before the damned Crusader cut him down.

First thing, jogging along the claustrophobic corridor between metal containers, Zaghloul checked his submachine gun's magazine. The Brügger & Thomet MP9 had burned through all but seven of its thirty Parabellum rounds, a fact he ascertained by quickly glancing at its transparent polymer magazine. No guesswork was required: those last rounds would be spent in half a second flat of automatic fire.

As a precaution, Zaghloul pressed the weapon's magazine release catch, dropped the almost-empty mag, and slid another into place. A live round in the chamber meant he didn't need to cock the weapon. It was "good to go" as the Americans would say, requiring only pressure from his index finger on the trigger safety to unleash another spray of sudden death.

A bit more time was all that he required, nothing to speak

of by comparison to Allah's glorious eternity.

But if Zaghloul could first eliminate the *maleun* Crusader who was stalking him, would that not be another parting gift to God?

"*'awlawiat*," the warrior muttered to himself.

Priorities.

He must not lose his focus on what truly mattered—detonation of the warhead packed inside container No. UUVX0016949—and fall short of his goal by trifling with the man some agency in Washington had sent to stop him. If Zaghloul did that, he would be playing into hostile hands, his mission cast aside to satisfy a private craving for revenge.

And that *would* be a mortal sin.

But since his enemy clearly was not about to stop pursuing him, by not take a word of advice from the Crusaders he despised and kill two birds with but a single stone.

Or, in this case, with automatic fire from his MP9 SMG.

Pausing, Zaghloul shouted down the aisle between containers and across the *Tryphon*'s cargo deck, "Where are you? Come and get me, *mawzir*, while you can!"

And hearing no answer come back to him, moved on.

Jack Cody heard the Arab's taunting call but didn't answer back. Simple psychology told him that it was better for the jihadist to wonder where he—Cody—was, rather than giving him a fix that he might use to lay a deadly trap.

And while the terrorist kept moving forward, drawing

closer to whatever goal he had in mind, he would be leading Cody there as well.

What was the bastard thinking? Was it possible the bomb on board the freighter could be detonated by hands-on involvement, maybe flicking up a toggle switch or pressing down a button? While that seemed improbable to Cody, every second that passed by without a white-hot blinding, world-igniting flash brought Jack a few steps closer to his prey.

And if the enemy was stalling, that meant there was time to bring him down.

Maybe.

Cody had checked his Steyer AUG's translucent, double-column box magazine and counted twenty-three rounds remaining, plus one up the spout. More than enough, if he could line up one clean shot, but he was packing spares in any case, with his twinned Glocks for backup in a pinch.

Enough to take down a small army in the field, but on this day or days, only a single adversary mattered.

And if Cody couldn't stop that one, the other blood he'd spilled to reach this point would all have been in vain. He might achieve his own death—what Shakespeare had Prince Hamlet call, in his renowned soliloquy, "a consummation devoutly to be wished"—but at what cost?

A million other lives wiped out by Allah's mushroom cloud?

"Screw that," Jack muttered to himself, then wondered what the odds were of him forcing Abbas Abdul Maarku's psychopathic brainstorm off the rails and driving it into a ditch.

How many lives had been snuffed out already, in pursuit of that nightmare?

How many of those deaths had been in vain?

None yet, he thought. At least, not necessarily. But if he let the jihad nightmare run its course…

"*Allaenat ealayk, al'ahmaq!*" the terrorist shouted, cursing Jack bitterly in Arabic. "You know what that means, eh? How about *adhhab wayumaris aljins mae walidatik*, you stupid *shadh jinsiaan*? I'm about to set your world on fire!"

To Jack, that sounded more like desperation than contempt—and he could use that, if his adversary kept it up.

"I hear you, scumbag," Cody said, under his breath. "Just keep it up until I've got you in my sights."

And then, as if he'd heard Jack whispering, the enemy shut off his flow of angry words, damming them as effectively as beavers blocking off a mountain stream.

Maybe he wasn't quite as rattled—or as pissed off—as he'd seemed a moment earlier. Maybe he'd realized that shouting taunts and insults was the surest way to help Jack run him down. In any case, as Cody cleared the starboard-side companionway descending from the freighter's bridge and headed for the aisle between containers where he'd seen his quarry disappear, he guessed the hunt would be protracted for at least a short while longer.

One way or another, though, it had to end in someone's death.

Jack peered around the corner of a red storage container, down the access lane, and glimpsed the man he hunted duck-

ing to his right or starboard, down an intersecting aisle. Cody
was just about to follow, when a voice behind him shouted,
"*Hvem i helvete er du?*"

Jack didn't speak Norwegian, but he recognized the language when he heard it, and the speaker's tone assured him
that he was a country mile past angry, verging on the homi-
cidal. Turning, Cody saw a burly, bearded six-footer advancing on him, brandishing a crowbar while he mouthed more
furious questions.

"Back off!" Jack tried in English, tacking on, "I'm here to
help," and almost laughed despite the situation, when he heard
how lame that sounded.

"Help this!" growled the Norseman, rushing forward with
his hooked weapon held high, preparing for a caveman swing.

Jack slammed a 5.56mm FMJ round into Olaf's left leg, just
above the knee, and left him writhing on the deck as Cody
turned away from him.

"Next time, mind your own business," he advised the fallen
seaman. "You might live longer that way."

Or maybe not, if Ali Baba Bombardier managed to trigger
an apocalyptic blast within the next few moments, before Jack
could take him down and out.

Sara Durell was in a sweat, but no one else inside the situation room at Langley, two floors underground, could have
determined that by looking at her, or eavesdropping as she
spoke to Denham Boyd in Washington, nine miles away and

standing in another basement room almost identical, down to the president's wall-mounted portrait gazing down at those who served him.

"How much longer until NEST is on the scene?" Sara asked Boyd.

"They should be airborne at the Port of Houston as we speak," came his reply.

Should be, thought Sara. Those were weasel words aimed at creating an impression of assurance that the speaker didn't feel, in fact, offloading the responsibility for failure—or, in this case, for the damned Apocalypse itself—on someone else.

"Specifics, if you don't mind," Sara prodded Boyd.

"They're on our screens here," Denham said. "Should be on yours, too."

Sara flicked a glance at her computer jockey and the guy gave her a thumbs-up in response. She took a quick sidestep and peered over his shoulder, watching as three bogeys—Bell UH-1 "Huey" helicopters in this case, each with a crew of two to four, machine-gunners included, and seating for fourteen passengers—each bird's Lycoming T53-L-11 turboshaft engine propelling it toward the Port of Houston at an average 125 miles per hour.

Some of those on board the choppers would be eggheads from the AEC, experts in finding, readily identifying, and defusing nuclear explosive devices. The others airborne with the techs would be warriors from Delta Force, armed to the teeth, and the Hueys—designed as general-purpose utility choppers since 1956—could also serve as gunships at need.

Basic Huey armament included swivel-mounted M60 machine guns in one or both sliding side doors, often backed up by six-barrel rotary M134 Miniguns firing the same 7.62×51mm NATO rounds as the M60s, but at 6,000 rounds per minute versus 650 rpm. If that wasn't enough, add six-barrel pods loaded with 70mm "Mighty Mouse" Mk 4 Folding-Fin Aerial Rocket, used both as air-to-air and air-to-surface weapons packing a variety of high explosive warheads.

The Hueys were lethal and then some, but their heavy-hitting weapons were largely superfluous for jobs like finding and safely defusing nukes.

Conversely, if the lunatics from Allah's Flame were out in force this morning, it could be a chance to put them in the ground before they set Houston on fire and made its land untenable for years to come.

"We've got them spotted," Sara told her White House liaison. "Let's hope they're not too late."

"So, where's your boy?" asked Boyd.

He's only my *boy, now,* she thought, frowning. *unless he pulls your fat out of the fire.*

Instead of jumping on that, she replied, "He's gone aboard the *Tryphon* but we're not in touch by now."

"And what about the *Moucheron?*"

"Their trigger dropped the ball and went ashore. Who knows what he was thinking? Anyway, our people tasered him and he's out of action, waiting for interrogation."

"Will he spill, you think?"

"I gave up telling fortunes," Sara said.

"Uh-huh. And no sign of the package from the *Moucheron,* so far?"

"Waiting in NEST," she said, telling Boyd what he must have known already.

"Right. Their team should be on board before much longer."

If we have that kind of time, she thought, but didn't voice that either. Settled for, "They'd better hurry up."

"They're likely waiting on the *Tryphon* to be cleared."

"All of them? Seriously?"

"Well…"

"Well, nothing. They're inside the blast zone now, unless they're using false transponders just to throw us off."

"You know better than that."

"I hope so. But there's no point waiting on one bomb until we have the other one secured, is there? I mean, if that's the way they roll, why didn't they hang back in Austin or in Dallas? Hell, why not in freaking Omaha?"

"From what I've heard they're moving with dispatch."

More weasel words, like when the nation's highest court ordered fourteen Jim Crow states to integrate their public schools "with all deliberate speed". The states came back with varied plans that would accomplish that, all right, and only take four centuries or so to get it done.

Small wonder that some folks cracked up from time to time and ran amok.

"Maybe I'd better talk to them, myself."

"Sara—"

"Just making sure we're all on the same page, before the

book goes up in smoke."

"I'll get them on the horn as soon as we hang up, okay with you?"

"Depends on the result," she said.

"I'll tell them to fish or cut bait," he replied. "Get the lead out, whatever. All right?"

"Mention loss of their jobs if you think they've been dicking around, playing safe."

"Got it. I'm going now."

"Later," she said and cut the link, telling her coms guy, "I want ears aboard those Hueys, stat, so I can listen in on what he's telling them."

"Yes, ma'am," the techie said, and fingers started dancing on his keyboard.

While Sara thought about the company's motto: *The truth shall set you free.*

And thought about its flip-side: Or might get you killed.

Jack was closer to his adversary now. Too damned close, maybe, once the guy had spotted him and fired another submachine gun burst that nearly parted Cody's hair. A blue cargo container took the brunt of it, a couple rounds zipping on past to punch holes in another twenty-foot container, that one painted black.

Funny if someone had his favorite Rolls-Royce in there, Jack thought, then fired a three-round burst back at his enemy, shooting left-handed and not bothering to aim through its

Swarovski scope. His target cursed in Arabic again, immediately followed by the sound of running feet.

Jack let a fraction of a second pass, then trailed him, keeping track of noises the jihadist made now that he'd dropped from sight again. Turned out the rows of cargo carriers lining the *Tryphon*'s deck two-deep, weren't only separated by a few aisles running stem-to-stern, but formed a maze of sorts when viewed from overhead, cross-hatched with other passages laid out from port to starboard. All for the convenience of unloading, he supposed.

Which told him overhead was where he ought to be.

Ignoring their various colors and coded I.D. numbers, the containers were basically identical: most twenty feet long, but some forty, each eight feet tall and eight feet wide, for interior capacities of 1,280 or 2,560 cubic feet depending on length. Two sides and one end of each box were corrugated vertically, the end you opened sporting double doors secured by padlocks and four upright stainless-steel bars with their own set of locks.

Jack's goal now: to climb up atop the nearest double row and start his search anew from overhead, hopefully taking his opponent by surprise.

And failing that, if he was shot down from the second-level roof, a drop of sixteen feet onto the freighter's deck would be the least of his worries.

It was a truism that dead men tell no tales, although continuing advances in forensic science had invalidated that.

But one thing still held true: a dead man felt no pain.

He made it to the top and knelt there for a moment, scanning row on row of more containers stretching out from port to starboard on the freighter's cargo deck. He knew approximately where the terrorist was going—thought he did, at least—but couldn't see him yet.

Rising, Cody moved along the length of the container that supported him, leaped to the next in line, and soon came to another narrow aisle running across the deck, instead of bow to stern. Some fifty, sixty feet away a scuttling movement caught his eye, and Jack identified his target, scrambling up as he had done, to gain the surface of two stacked containers sitting one atop the other.

"That's it," he whispered to his quarry. "Just a few more feet."

Rifa'a Zaghloul gasped from exertion as he pulled himself atop container No. UUVX0016949 and paused to catch his breath. It must be the excitement, he supposed, that made him feel so enervated suddenly, as if he might collapse.

But he had made it and was still alive so far. Nothing else mattered in the world.

That was the moment when a bullet grazed his shoulder, staggered him, and he dropped down to one knee, conscious of the pain and scanning for a clear glimpse of the man who'd tried again to kill him. When the echo of the shot came, it was like a crack of thunder peeling miles away, perhaps out in the Gulf of Mexico.

He'd spotted the crusader now, same white man who had fired upon him earlier, and raised his MP9, his left arm throbbing as he clutched the weapon's foregrip, focusing down range over its tritium-illuminated sights. He stroked the submachine gun's trigger, firing half a dozen Parabellum rounds and seeing that, in haste, he'd missed his mark.

Even in pain, ears ringing from the gunfire, Zaghloul heard another sound intruding on his jumbled thoughts, coming from somewhere overhead and all around him.

"*Sakhif alqarf!*" he swore, then turned the curse into an urgent prayer. "Allah, for your sake, give me strength!"

Clutching the MP9 in his right hand, he thrust his left into a pocket of his cargo pants and found the cell phone hidden there, extracting it, using his thumb to turn it on. With all the strength he still possessed, Rifa'a Zaghloul rose to his feet, holding the cell at arm's length overhead, and shouted at the world he was about to end, "*Allahu Akbar!* Praise your holy name!"

Jack Cody saw his shot and took it, triggering a three-round burst of 5.56mm rounds. He saw at least two of the FMJ slugs strike on target, shattering his target's skull and dropping him, a rag-doll figure slumping as if boneless, wreathed in bloody mist.

The dead guy's SMG and cell phone dropped beside him at the same instant his corpse touched down, a trick of physics that confounded Cody every time he witnessed it. Some teacher's question from a grade school science class came back to him: Class, which weighs more, a pound of feathers or a pound of lead?

The right answer: No difference. All falling objects plummeted at terminal velocity.

Two Huey helicopters reached the grounded *Tryphon* then, an amplified voice from the sky demanding that Cody drop his Steyr AUG and raise his hands. He followed orders for the most part, stooped to set the rifle down gently, then straightened with his hands raised, empty, so the nearer Huey's doorway gunner wouldn't get a nervous twitch and chop him into stew meat where he stood.

The same deep, disembodied voice demanded of him, "Where's the package?"

Shifting cautiously, Jack lowered one arm, pointing toward the nearly-headless guy who lay supine within a spreading pool of blood, some fifty feet away. One of the Huey's crewmen must have tipped their backup, as a second UH-1 closed in and claimed a hovering position over the last man Cody had shot.

Last man today, that was—so far, at least.

Two soldiers dressed in camouflage fatigues descended first, rappelling from the chopper, covering the corpse with automatic weapons until they were standing on the lid of his cargo container, one giving a thumbs-down to its pilot. Cody couldn't hear the order issued next, but two men and a woman, all in black, were next to exit from the whirlybird and make their way down to the soldiers like three spiders dangling from the silken product of their spinnerets.

The woman held what Cody took to be a Geiger counter, crackling audible to him from where he stood. A hit, that was. Her two companions lugged a toolbox and what seemed to be a compact cutting torch.

Acetylene or butane? Something else that didn't come to mind. Whatever that might be, Jack hoped the NEST team members knew what they were doing, slicing into the container that presumably contained a doomsday bomb.

And what about the other one? Was it already neutralized aboard the *Moucheron*?

Jack wished that he were miles away right now, then caught himself and heaved a sigh of resignation. If the NEST group—either one of them—screwed up and triggered something, rather than defusing it...so, what?

He'd made it through another day of so-called living, left another trail of bodies in his wake, and wound up watching as the final act played out so close to him that if it all went wrong, he doubted there'd be time to register the nuclear fireball, much less to feel its heat before his atoms were disintegrated.

As he knew first-hand, there were a thousand worse ways to give up the ghost. A thousand, and then some.

Relaxed at last—or, anyway, as close as he could come to it these days—Jack settled down to wait and watch the other pros at work.

EPILOGUE

"Close one this time," Sara Durell observed and sipped her whiskey sour.

"As per usual," Jack said.

"You pulled it off, though."

"Once again…"

"As usual. I know."

"What did they have?" he asked.

She named the Russian warheads for him, an impressive double-whammy if they'd detonated, just more scrap metal and toxic waste now, on their way to some desert locale where they would be disposed of in a safe way, to avoid polluting anything.

And if you bought that story, Jack would gladly sell you his rights to a certain bridge in Brooklyn at a bargain-basement rate.

His next question, after a taste of rum and Coke: "What's left of Allah's Flame?"

"Not much, but you know how that goes. Like Al-Qaeda, ISIL, take your pick. The leaders fall and someone else pops up to take their place. Pick any Arab country you can name. They've got new martyrs lining up in droves, and more not even born yet. Look on the bright side, though."

"What's that?" he asked.

"If there was ever peace on Earth, like in the Christmas carols, we'd be out of work."

Jack almost smiled at that. "Retirement, eh? I'd settle for a week off, with no phones or Internet access."

"We can't escape the world, Jack. *It* finds *us.*"

"How 'bout I put a sign on my front door. 'No peddlers or solicitors'?"

"You have a front door now?"

Jack shrugged. Replied, "Who knows? I can't remember."

"Well, if you're caught short without a place to stay..."

"Sounds good."

"And what now? I mean, till the next time?"

"Someplace tropical and reasonably private, I suppose."

"Want any company?"

He arched a brow at that. "You get time off? Is that a thing, now?"

"Rarely, but it happens," Sara said. "I even keep a swimsuit tucked away for an emergency."

"The beach I have in mind," Jack told her, smiling now, "you may as well leave that at home."

Her turn to smile, as she replied, "Cody, I like the way you think."

A LOOK AT: DAY OF RECKONING (CODY'S WAR FOUR)

FROM THE MODERN MASTER OF THE ACTION AD-VENTURE M.I.A. HUNTER SERIES COMES CODY'S WAR!

This time it's personal!

Sara Durell is missing. Sara was the best friend of Car-ol, Jack Cody's late wife who died with their children at the hands of Islamic terrorists. Cody now shares a deep platonic bond with Sara, whose compassion and counsel has contrib-uted to his emotional recovery in the wake of that traumatic loss. Jack owes Sara . . . and Sara has gone missing on a deep cover mission in Afghanistan.

When a SEAL team rescue operation goes terribly wrong, Sara and Cody have no one but themselves to rely on as they forge their way across a harsh desert frontier in a desperate trek for survival against the elements and a relentless Taliban hit team hot on their trail.

"One of the best adventure writers of our time!" - James M. Reasoner, NYT Bestselling author

AVAILABLE DECEMBER 2019

ABOUT THE AUTHOR

Stephen Mertz is an American fiction author who is best known for his mainstream thrillers and novels of suspense. His work covers a wide variety of styles from paranormal dark suspense (Night Wind and Devil Creek) to historical speculative thrillers (Blood Red Sun) and hardboiled noir (Fade to Tomorrow). Mertz is also a popular lecturer on the craft of writing and has appeared as a guest speaker before writer's groups and at universities.

Steve's writing output increased dramatically when he emerged as one of the country's most in-demand writers of adventure paperback novels, averaging four books per year for ten years. His work on Don Pendleton's Mack Bolan series is regarded by fans as some of the best in that series. He also created the Mark Stone: MIA Hunter and Cody's Army series, written under the pseudonyms Jack Buchanan and Jim Case respectively.

Stephen Mertz lives in the American Southwest, and he is always at work on a new book.

Find Stephen online: www.stephenmertz.com